A CALDER
AT HEART

JANET DAILEY

NEW YORK TIMES **BESTSELLING AUTHOR**

A CALDER AT HEART

KENSINGTON
PUBLISHING CORP.

www.kensingtonbooks.com

KENSINGTON BOOKS are published by

Kensington Publishing Corp.
119 West 40th Street
New York, NY 10018

Library of Congress Card Catalogue Number: 2022947426

ISBN: 978-1-4967-2746-6
First Kensington Hardcover Edition: March 2023

ISBN: 978-1-4967-2749-7 (trade)

ISBN: 978-1-4967-2752-7 (ebook)

10 9 8 7 6 5 4 3 2 1

Printed in the United States of America

This book is dedicated to Elizabeth Lane.

CHAPTER ONE

Blue Moon, Montana
Spring 1919

*T*HE PRAIRIE GRASS HAD LONG SINCE SPREAD OVER THE LONELY HILL-top grave. Even the headstone, fashioned from a slab of oak, was so weathered that the name and dates were barely readable. But Dr. Kristin Dollarhide had no trouble finding the spot her sister-in-law had described.

Dismounting from the dun mare that had carried her here, Kristin dropped the reins and looped the riding crop around her wrist. The long grass swished against her boots as she walked toward the grave of the boy who'd been her first love. Her lips whispered his name.

"Alvar."

The wildflowers she'd stopped to pick along the way were wilting in her hand. But they were all she had. Kneeling, she laid the sad little bouquet at the foot of the headstone. Alvar Anderson had been shot in a senseless fight between ranchers and immigrant farmers two days before Kristin had been due to leave Blue Moon for travel and school. They'd said goodbye the night of his death. But she'd been unable to stay for his funeral.

In the ten years that had passed, there'd been other men in Kristin's life, most of them killed in the Great War. But Alvar would always own a piece of her heart—his memory the last remaining part of her that was pure and good.

Maybe here, on the Montana land where she'd grown up, that memory would help her find peace.

Her gaze took in the broad sweep of the prairie, rising to wooded foothills and then to peaks that towered above the tree line. The wheat fields she remembered were gone, the immigrant homesteaders driven away by drought, locusts, harsh winter blizzards, and finally the Great War in Europe that had taken so many of their young men.

One of those young men had been Axel Anderson, Alvar's younger brother, who would never come home again.

In the near distance, she could see the remains of the Anderson homestead—the foundation of the pillaged house, a few fence posts, the toppled privy. Everything else had been stripped for building materials made scarce by the war.

A white butterfly settled on Alvar's headstone, rested a moment, then fluttered away. Kristin's gaze followed it as it dipped and danced over the tiny yellow flowers that dotted the grassland.

They had been so young, she and Alvar. Her one regret was that they hadn't made love. Instead, her first time had been a groping encounter with a fellow medical student she barely knew, in the rumble seat of his Model T.

But why think of that now?

She was about to get up and leave when a shadow fell over her, like a cloud passing across the morning sun. Turning, she gave a startled gasp. Silhouetted against the glare, a tall, rough-looking man in trail-worn clothes stood a few paces behind her. He had come up so silently that she'd been completely unaware of him.

The rifle she'd brought along for safety was on the horse. All she had was her riding crop. If the big man wanted to overcome her, the flexible leather rod with its flat tip wouldn't be much help. Worse, she could see that he was armed. But he made no move to draw the pistol that rested in a holster on his hip.

Scrambling to her feet, she faced him, the sun in her eyes and the crop in her hand. "Not a step closer, mister," she said. "Not unless you want a whipping."

"Take it easy, miss." He tipped his weathered hat. His speech—easy-paced, with a hint of a drawl—was pure Texan. "I didn't mean to scare you. I was about to speak when you turned around."

"A likely story." Kristin kept her grip on the riding crop. "Why didn't you say something sooner? Why did you sneak up behind me like that?"

"I wasn't sneaking, miss. But I was at a loss for words. I didn't expect to see a woman out here alone. I was as surprised as you were." He moved to one side, changing the angle of the sunlight. She could see his face now—features that could have been chiseled from granite. His short beard, peppered with gray like his hair, failed to hide the jagged scar that ran from his left temple to the corner of his mouth. His dark eyes had a haunted look—the kind of look Kristin had seen on far too many veterans who'd survived the war—as this man likely had.

But that didn't mean he wasn't dangerous. The horrors of combat had a way of twisting men's minds. Some, even those who'd come safely home, still saw the enemy everywhere. Driven by fear and delusion, this powerful stranger could hurt her, even kill her.

Kristin looked past him to the rangy buckskin horse that he'd left near her mare. She knew horses. That one showed quality breeding. Her danger senses prickled. Where would the stranger, who had the look of a vagabond, get a horse like that unless he'd stolen it—maybe even killed for it?

Fear crawled up her spine like a snake's cold belly. But she knew better than to let him see how nervous she was.

"This is private property. What are you doing here?" she demanded.

"I might ask you the same question."

"But I asked first. What's your business on this land?"

His mouth tightened. He nodded and spoke. "Actually, I was looking for a family. I have a map, showing the way to their place, but I must've read it wrong because there's nothing out here. I was about to ask you for help when you saw me and got the wrong impression—not that I blame you."

She exhaled, less afraid now but still keeping her guard up.

"Most of the people who used to live out here have moved away. What was the family's name?"

"Anderson. I'm looking for the Lars Anderson homestead."

"You've found it." Kristin lowered the riding crop, relieved in spite of herself. "Their house stood right over there. You can see the foundation."

"So you know the family?"

"The eldest Anderson daughter married my brother."

"Then you must know where they've gone. I need to find them. It's important."

"They live in town now. Mr. Anderson homesteaded this land and farmed it for years. He wanted to leave it to his two sons. But he lost heart after both of them died—one of them years ago. He's buried right there." She nodded toward the grave. "The other one died in the war. He's buried in France."

"That would be Corporal Axel Anderson, right? He's the reason I'm here." Reaching into an inner pocket of his vest, he drew out a creased, stained envelope. "My name is Logan Hunter— Major Logan Hunter, not that it makes much difference these days. I was Corporal Anderson's commanding officer. He wrote this letter before he died in the Argonne Forest. I promised to get it to his family. See—he didn't have an address, so he drew this map on the back."

The man's story rang true, especially with the letter as evidence. As Kristin's gaze took in the sealed envelope, something tugged at her emotions. The young boy she remembered had been so bright and full of promise. Axel's death must have broken his father's heart.

"I apologize for threatening to whip you, Major," she said. "I'm Dr. Kristin Dollarhide. I was stationed in France and posted to a stateside veterans' hospital after the war. I've just come home myself. If you want, I could give that letter to my sister-in-law for her family. It would save you the trouble of finding Axel's parents."

He slipped the letter back into his vest. "That's a mighty kind offer, but I'd rather deliver it in person. Corporal Anderson was a brave young man who died a hero's death. I'd like his folks to hear that from me."

"I understand. Lars Anderson works as a carpenter these days. Blue Moon is a small town. Anyone who lives there can tell you where to find him."

"Thank you, miss—or should I say Doctor?"

"Doctor will do. I've certainly earned the title."

"Then please allow a gentleman to see you back to your horse. No woman, not even a doctor, should be alone out here. It isn't safe."

"This *woman* killed two German soldiers who were trying to rape one of her nurses. I have a rifle on my horse. If trouble comes along, I know how to use it."

"And I've no doubt you're deadly with that riding crop, as well." His mouth twitched in the barest hint of a smile. "But if you'll allow me the pleasure . . ." He offered his arm. With a sigh of resignation, she accepted. Laying a light hand on his sleeve, she felt rock-hard muscle through the thin fabric.

"Will you be setting up a practice here?" He walked with a limp, favoring his right leg. The horses weren't far off, but he took his time.

"I hope so," she said. "The town needs a doctor, and I need to support myself. I've no intention of living off my brother."

"Well, then, maybe our paths will cross again." He stood by while she mounted the mare, then swung onto the tall buckskin, mounting easily despite his impaired leg.

Only then did Kristin notice something that jerked her back to full alert. The buckskin horse was wearing a distinctive brand— the well-known Triple C, for Calder Cattle Company, the biggest ranch in the state of Montana.

Acting on reflex, she whipped the rifle out of its scabbard, slid back the bolt, and aimed the muzzle at his chest. "Hands up high, mister!" she snapped. "Reach for that pistol and you're a dead man. We don't take kindly to horse thieves around here."

He raised hands. His face wore a thunderous scowl. "I don't know what you're thinking, *Doctor*, but nobody calls me a horse thief and gets away with it."

Kristin steadied her grip on the rifle. "Now throw down your weapon and ease out of that saddle. While you're doing it, you can explain why you're riding a horse with the Calder brand on it."

He made no move to drop the pistol or to dismount. "My mother was Benteen Calder's cousin. With my family dead of the Spanish flu back in Texas, Webb Calder is the only blood kin I have left. I wrote him, and he invited me to come here and settle. Webb lent me this horse, so you can put that damned rifle away. I don't like guns pointing at me. They make me nervous."

Kristin held the weapon steady. "Your being a Calder doesn't count for much with me or my family. And what about that letter you showed me? It strikes me as almost too much of a coincidence, your showing up here to deliver it when you're in league with the greediest land-grabbers in Montana. What's your real game, Major Hunter, or whoever you are?"

His expression darkened. "Only a woman could get away with calling me a liar," he growled. "A man would've been dragged off his horse and beaten to a bloody pulp. Now put that rifle away before I decide to take it from you. Every word I've spoken is God's truth, and that's all I'm going to say about it."

Wheeling his mount, he rode away at an easy trot, as if daring her to shoot him in the back. She wouldn't do it, of course. That would be murder.

Shoving the gun back in its scabbard, Kristin watched his tall figure vanish in the direction of town. Had she unmasked a criminal or insulted an honorable man? Either way, Kristin sensed that she'd made an enemy—maybe a dangerous one.

The Great War had ended with an armistice last November. But after talking to Blake, her brother, Kristin already understood that she'd come home to a different kind of war—a war between families—the Dollarhides and the Calders.

CHAPTER TWO

IN THE WHITE-PILLARED CALDER MANSION KNOWN AS THE HOME-stead, the dining room table was big enough for a banquet. But tonight, there were just three places set at the end nearest the kitchen. Webb Calder, a vigorous man in his forties, sat at the head of the table. Chase, his eleven-year-old son, sat on his right. Logan Hunter, freshly bathed and shaved, sat on his left.

For distant relatives whose common bloodline had thinned over generations, the two men looked remarkably alike. They had the same broad-shouldered build, similar rugged facial features, thick brows, and dark hair. Webb's hair was more silver than black. Logan, a decade younger, was just beginning to gray. Apart from their eye color—Webb's blue, Logan's brown—and the scar that slashed the side of the latter's face like a lightning bolt, the resemblance was striking.

Young Chase, a miniature version of his father, was dipping chunks of bread in his beef stew, ignoring the conversation that passed between the two men.

Logan knew that the boy had lost his mother shortly after he was born. She'd been shot in one of the senseless range wars that flamed like tinder on the Montana prairie. Now, according to Webb, yet another war appeared to be smoldering.

Logan, who'd seen far too much violence, wanted no part of it. But now it appeared that he might not have a choice.

"So, were you able to find the Andersons and give them the letter?" Webb buttered a second slice of bread.

"I did," Logan said. "I've lost track of how many such letters I've delivered in the past few months, some of them on my way here. This was the last one."

"And you delivered them all in person?"

"As many as I could. For the ones that had to be mailed, I wrote my own accompanying letters. It was the least I could do."

"But the Andersons—what did you think of them?"

"Good people. Strong. But there were tears when I gave them their son's letter. Why do you ask?"

"Because most of the drylanders who quit farming, even the few who stayed around Blue Moon, have sold their land for pennies on the dollar. I've bought almost every parcel that butted onto my own property. But the Andersons are holding out. I just wondered if they'd shown any signs of wanting to sell—like maybe needing money."

"We didn't talk about that. But why would you want their land? You've already got the biggest spread in Montana."

Webb sighed. "Cousin, you've got a lot to learn. Land isn't just a place to plant crops or run cows. It's water rights, access rights, maybe even mineral rights—you should know about that part. You got a bundle of cash for the mineral rights on that old family ranch of yours when drillers found oil under the property. Hell, you could've stayed and become one of those Texas millionaires."

"Not me," Logan said. "I've seen what oil drilling does to the land. It turns dirty and ugly, with no life on it—reminds me too much of the battlefields I left behind in France. With my family gone, I figured I might as well take the money and clear out. But we were talking about the Anderson parcel and why you want it."

"Dad, can I be excused?" Chase had waited for a pause in the conversation. "Buck and me are going down to the cattle tank to hunt frogs."

"All right. Just be back before your bedtime. Don't make me come out looking for you."

The boy hurried away, leaving his father to continue where he'd left off. "Yes, the land. As I said, for the past couple of years I've been buying up everything that borders the Triple C. It's not for cattle—those damned wheat farmers plowed up all the good grass. It's mostly for protection, to put a safe distance between this ranch and anybody who fancies our being neighbors. That means, among other things, protecting our water and our fences." Webb dabbed his mouth with a napkin. "But I have another reason for wanting the Anderson parcel. I can show you better than tell you. Come on into the study."

Getting up from the table, Logan followed his host down the hall. The Calder study was the heart of the Triple C Ranch, and it was suitably impressive—from the ornate walnut desk and leather seating to the fireplace, which was crowned by a mounted pair of massive horns from Captain, the longhorn steer that had led herds of Calder cattle along the trail from Texas to Montana.

Above the mantel a giant, framed map displayed the full expanse of the ranch. The acreage was even more vast than Logan had imagined. "Pretty impressive," he said.

Webb picked up a billiard cue that served as a pointer. "Let me show you why I'm so keen on buying the Anderson property."

He ran the tip of the cue along a dark line that defined the eastern border of the Triple C. "I've bought almost all the properties along here for cents on the dollar—but I haven't bothered with this ranch in the foothills." He tapped a section at the top of the map. "It's owned by a scum of the earth Irishman named Angus O'Rourke. He lives up there in a shack with a wife and two scraggly kids. I don't trust the bounder, but as long as he doesn't steal from me, I leave him alone.

"Now here—" Webb tapped the cue point lower on the map. "This is the Lars Anderson property. The original homestead didn't touch my ranch. But when Anderson's neighbor to the west moved away, Lars bought it to expand his own acreage. Now that big stubborn Swede is my next-door neighbor. And even if he needed to sell, he'd starve before he'd do business with a Calder."

"I suppose I should ask why," Logan said.

"It's because his daughter's married to that hell-damned water-stealing Blake Dollarhide."

The connection clicked in Logan's mind. He remembered the

beautiful, dark-haired woman who'd claimed to have no use for the Calders. Kristin Dollarhide. *Doctor* Kristin Dollarhide.

"I met one of the Dollarhides this morning," Logan said. "Prickly as a blackberry bush. She pulled a gun and accused me of stealing your horse. When I mentioned that I was related to the Calders, I could feel the chill from ten feet away. She must've been Blake Dollarhide's sister."

Webb frowned. "That's all we need around here, one more Dollarhide. I heard that she was back, and that she's a doctor now. If I get sick, remind me not to go to her. She'd be liable to slice open a vein and let me bleed out."

"So tell me more about the Anderson property." Logan steered the subject back on track. "Why are you so interested in it?"

"It comes down to one thing—water," Webb said. "When the drylanders, including the Andersons, settled here, they dug wells. But the water was too alkaline to be of any use. They ended up having to haul water from town for drinking and washing. The farmer who owned the parcel behind the Andersons' was a late-comer. He didn't bother with a well because he'd seen that it would be a waste of time. Now here's where the story gets inter-esting."

Again Webb pointed to the map. "Last year, I needed a well dug near the eastern boundary of my ranch, so I called in a team of experts. They put down a borehole and brought up good, clean water. While they were here, I asked them to do an analysis of the land around the new well. They dug more boreholes and tested rock samples. It turned out there's an aquifer—that's a layer of water-bearing rock—that lies under my land and extends partway into that second Anderson parcel. If anybody had bothered to dig a well close to the property line, they'd have found usable water."

"I see," Logan said. "So if you owned that land, would you dig more wells?"

"No. But a well on that property could pull water from the one on my land. What I want is to keep any more wells from being dug. I need all the water from that aquifer on my ranch."

"Does Lars Anderson know about the aquifer?"

"No. But he could sell the land to somebody smart enough to figure out that it's there—somebody like his son-in-law, Blake Dollarhide, who'd put down a well and maybe poison it just to spite me."

"I get the picture." Logan did, and he didn't much like it. "But while we're on the subject of land, I'd like to know more about that ranch property you picked for me to buy."

"That can wait till tomorrow. When it's light, we can ride out and see the place. You'll like it, I promise. If not, you can choose something else. But for now, I'd like you to think about a favor you could do for me."

"Name it," Logan said. "I certainly owe you a favor for your help and hospitality."

"Just this. Lars Anderson would never sell that parcel to me. But as a man he trusts—his son's commander who was kind enough to bring him the boy's last letter—I'll bet you could sweet-talk Lars into selling the land to *you*."

After dinner was over and the children were getting ready for bed, Kristin walked out onto the broad covered porch of the Dollarhide family home. With her hand on the log railing, she watched the risen moon cast cloud shadows over the landscape below. The fields and pastures were dark, but here and there, dots of light glimmered like distant stars. To the north, the town of Blue Moon glowed like a faint beacon in the night.

Joe Dollarhide, her father, had built this sprawling log house on the crest of a high bluff to command a view of the prairie with its meadows, pastures, and farms. Kristin had always loved this place. But some things had changed in her absence. Joe was gone now, and his wife, Sarah, with him. Both had been lost in the past year to the ravages of Spanish flu, which Sarah had brought home after going out to deliver a baby.

Kristin mourned her parents, whose deaths had left a hole in her heart. But at least her brother and his young family had been spared. Blake, his wife, Hanna, and their three children were all in good health. And Blake now helmed a family empire that included land, horses, cattle, and a lumber mill.

As if summoned by her thoughts, Blake came out to stand beside her. "Are you cold?" he asked. "I can bring you a shawl."

"I'm fine," she said. "It's good to be home. But I'd forgotten how quiet it is here. After the war and the chaos of the hospital, the stillness seems almost unreal."

"You'll get used to it. Maybe the peace and quiet will help you forget what you've seen and heard for the past two years."

The words were well meant. But Kristin would never forget the horror and the misery, shells exploding in the trenches, shattered limbs that had to be sawed off, men dying in her arms. And the gas attacks—men screaming when they couldn't get their masks on or hadn't been issued any.

"Was it hard being a woman doctor among all those men?"

"I was a doctor. Under those conditions, my being a woman didn't matter. And there were nurses with me—the bravest young women I ever knew. They had no protection. When the shells hit a hospital tent or an ambulance, they died along with the men."

Blake took a long, deep breath. He stood silent for a moment, as if trying to imagine the unimaginable. "Will you be all right?" he asked.

"In time. I'll have to be, won't I?" She forced a smile, then leaned forward, resting her forearms on the rail. "I rode into town today and checked on possible places to set up my practice. I'll make a final choice in the next few days. Then, as soon as that crate of supplies I ordered arrives in Miles City on the train, I'll be open for business."

"So soon? Are you sure you're ready?"

"To treat fevers and sprains and deliver babies? I'm more than ready." She sighed, inhaling the fresh, clean mountain air and the smell of awakening grass. "I rode out to the old Anderson place to visit Alvar's grave. The family was gone, of course—Hanna told me they'd moved into town. But a man showed up while I was there. A stranger. He struck me as someone you'll want to watch."

She told him about meeting Logan Hunter at Alvar's grave, the letter and his story of being Axel Anderson's commanding officer, and the revelation that he was a blood relative of Webb Calder.

"Did you believe him?" Blake asked.

"I saw no reason not to. He looks enough like Webb to be related. And he got angry when I implied that he might be lying.
He said he was looking to buy some property and even joked that
we might become neighbors. I hope that doesn't mean trouble."

"What it means, I think, is that Webb Calder has brought in re-
inforcements. With most of the drylanders gone and so many
people lost in the war and to the flu, there'll be plenty of land to
choose from. If I know Webb, he'll encourage this relative of his
to settle someplace that will give him an advantage over me."
Blake fell silent, as if he might know more than he was telling her.

"When do you plan to start up the lumber mill again?" she
asked.

"As soon as my order for the first wagonload of logs comes in.
With veterans returning home, starting new families, there'll be a
need for new homes and businesses. And I shouldn't have any
trouble hiring a crew. Robertson, my best sawyer, said he'd welcome the work. He can train the rest."

The lumber mill had been idle for two years, with no logs available because the lumberjacks in the Northwest were off fighting.
Now everything was about to change. During the war, the chief
source of income for the Dollarhides had been selling horses and
beef cattle to the army. Now, with the lumber mill starting up
again, they were poised to take advantage of the building boom
that was bound to come. Blake had planned well. The Dollarhide
fortune was in capable hands.

"You have a beautiful family," Kristin said, changing the subject. "Your little girls are as pretty as their mother, and so smart.
And Joseph—he's getting tall. I have to remind myself not to call
him Little Joe anymore."

Blake chuckled. "He put a stop to that when he started school.
He's in sixth grade now. He saddles his own horse every school-
day morning and rides it to town. You'll remember Hanna's sister
Britta. She's his teacher now. She says he's the brightest student
she's ever taught."

"That doesn't surprise me." Kristin's gaze followed the flight of
a nightjar, the moonlight glinting on its white-barred wings as it

swooped after insects. She took a deep breath. "I don't suppose you've heard from Mason, have you?"

She sensed a sudden rise in tension. Mason Dollarhide, their half-brother by Joe Dollarhide's first wife, had left Blue Moon twelve years ago in the dead of a winter night. The reason why was known only to the families involved—but surmised, perhaps, by longtime residents of the town.

"I haven't heard from Mason since he disappeared," Blake said. "I don't even know whether he's alive. His mother is still running the Hollister Ranch. She could be in touch with him. But that's all I know—or care to know."

"What about Joseph? People talk. Sooner or later the boy's bound to learn the truth. Have you told him anything at all?"

"You mean have I told him that Mason seduced an innocent girl and got her pregnant—and that I married her at my father's insistence, to save her honor and keep her child in the family? *Have I told him that Mason is his father?*"

Blake kept his voice low, but the words rasped with emotion. "How do I dump all that on a boy who's just beginning to find his way in the world?"

"You tell him the rest of the story," Kristin said. "After you married Hanna, you fell in love with her. You learned to love her baby, and you became his father in every way but one. People have survived far worse beginnings than that."

"You've never been a parent, Kristin. You can't imagine what it's like, having to hurt a child you love—especially if it means telling them they've been lied to all their lives."

"I'm aware of that. And no matter what I might think you should do, he's your son. I promise not to meddle in this—it's your decision."

"I'll hold you to that." Blake turned away from the rail as Hanna stepped out through the double glass-paned doors, which had been left partway open.

"I'm sorry to interrupt." Her smile was genuine. "Elsa says she won't say her prayers and go to sleep until her daddy comes to tuck her in. I'm afraid we've spoiled her."

"It's fine," Blake said. "We were about to go inside anyway, weren't we, Kristin?"

"Yes. It's getting chilly out here." Thankful for an end to the awkward conversation, Kristin followed her sister-in-law into the parlor. She had liked Blake's wife from the beginning. Hanna was as strong as she was pretty, without an unkind bone in her body. And she was Alvar's sister, with the same blue eyes and wheaten hair—a gentle reminder of the boy Kristin had loved.

"It's been a long day for me," she said. "I think I'll turn in early, maybe read for a while. Thank you for giving me back my old room, Hanna. That makes me feel right at home."

"You are home," Hanna said. "This house is as much yours as it is ours. We'd be happy to have you stay forever."

Not that she intended to stay, Kristin reminded herself as she climbed the stairs to her cozy room at the end of the hall. As a doctor who'd taken an oath to do no harm and to keep in confidence anything she might see or hear in her practice, the last thing she wanted was to be torn between that oath and family loyalty. In the smoldering conflict between the Dollarhides and the Calders, with its history of flare-ups, she couldn't allow herself to take sides.

Nor could she live with her family in a remote hilltop house that could be out of reach for her patients, especially in case of a nighttime emergency. Finding a place close to town and getting set up with an office, a reliable auto, and maybe access to a horse and buggy was going to take time and effort. But she would take on the challenges tomorrow. Tonight, she just wanted to rest.

Dressed in her nightgown, she selected a random book from the shelf above her head—*The Last of the Mohicans,* by James Fenimore Cooper. Snuggling under the covers, she opened the book to the first chapter. When she was growing up, the story had been one of her favorites. Rereading it now brought back the memory of being a young girl again. Except that she was no longer a girl. And she'd seen horrors that, by comparison, would make the dangers faced by Hawkeye and Cora seem like a game of hide-and-seek.

By the end of the chapter, she was drowsy enough to put the book aside and switch off the bedside lamp. For a time, she lay quietly, gazing at the moon-cast shadow of the pine that grew outside her window. Little by little, her body relaxed. Her breathing slowed and deepened as the fog of sleep drifted over her—and with it came the dream.

She stood at the entrance to the hospital tent, wearing long rubber gloves, a cap over her hair, and a bloodstained white apron. The frigid winter wind carried the odors of gunpowder, raw earth, rotting animal carcasses, smoke, and blood. From the far side of the next ridge came the rumble of exploding mortar shells falling on the American soldiers in their trenches.

Her eyes scanned the crude road that had been hacked out of the hillside from the battlefield to the hospital. Anxiety tightened a knot in her stomach. Where was that ambulance with its load of wounded men?

It was a regular thing for her nurses to double as ambulance drivers. But she should never have sent Marie Farman out with the vehicle. Only a few days ago, Marie had revealed that she was pregnant by a soldier who'd died. She was set to be transferred to a safer posting. But the girl had insisted on taking her turn as driver today. Now the ambulance was overdue.

From over the ridge, she could see flashes of light against the dawn sky. The blasts seemed to be getting louder. If the troops were falling back, the hospital would need to be moved as well, wounded men and all. It would be prudent to prepare her staff for bad news.

Now, at last, she caught sight of the ambulance coming around the hill and down the road. With a sigh of relief, she turned back toward the tent to alert the nurses and doctors inside.

At that instant, a shell, flying over the ridge, made a direct hit on the ambulance. The roar of sound and flame obliterated the vehicle, the wounded men in the back, and the driver.

Abandoning all caution and common sense, Kristin raced toward the burning remains. That was when another shell struck the hospital tent. The force of the blast knocked her flat on the ground. She screamed . . .

Her body jerked awake.

She lay shaking in her warm bed. She was home, safe in the cozy upstairs room of her girlhood. But that dream, like so many lost faces, would haunt her for the rest of her life.

Forcing herself to take deep breaths, she waited for her pulse to stop racing. She had long since learned that going back to sleep would be impossible. She didn't like depending on alcohol—a habit she was struggling to break. But a drink would settle her quivering nerves.

Her father had kept a stash of Kentucky bourbon in a locked cabinet in his study. If Blake hadn't moved things around, it might still be there. She wouldn't take much—just enough to feel the burn going down her throat.

Wasn't that what she always said?

Without bothering to turn on the lamp, she sat up, swung her legs off the bed, and reached for the robe she'd left draped over a chair. The house would be dark, but she'd grown up here. She could find her way blindfolded.

She crept down the hall, the polished wood floor cold beneath her bare feet. She had almost reached the landing when an unexpected sound reached her ears. The door to one of the bedrooms stood ajar. Inside, someone was crying—not just crying, sobbing.

Blake and Hanna's bedroom was downstairs. The door to the girls' shared room was closed. It had to be Joseph she was hearing.

The boy had been fine at supper, smiling, teasing his sister a little. Now he was crying as if his young heart had been ripped in two.

What could have hurt that much?

When the truth struck Kristin, it didn't come as a surprise—nor did her awareness that she was mostly to blame.

Guilt-ridden, she rapped lightly on the open door. When no answer came, she stepped into the room. With her eyes accustomed to darkness, she could make out her nephew's huddled figure under the quilts. Leaning over the bed, she laid a hand on his shoulder.

"It's me, Joseph," she said.

"Go away, Aunt Kristin." His pillow muffled the words.

"I'm not going anywhere. Not until we've had a chance to talk." Kristin pulled a chair close to the bed and sat down.

"Tell me what happened."

At first he lay still, refusing to talk. Minutes passed before he rolled onto his side, wiping his eyes with the sleeve of his flannel pajamas. "I just wanted to tell Dad good night. I was on my way outside when I heard him talking to you."

"I understand. How much did you hear?"

"Enough. Enough to know that everything I believed about my family was a lie." His voice broke.

"Oh, Joseph." Kristin checked the impulse to take him in her arms. The boy wouldn't want that. And Kristin didn't want to treat him like a baby. It was grow-up time.

He sat up. "I've always wondered why I'm the only one in the family with green eyes. Now I know. My father isn't Blake Dollarhide. He's a man I've never seen—a man who left town because he didn't want me. And my dad didn't want me either. Grandpa forced him to marry my mom."

"That's not true. If you'll stop feeling sorry for yourself, I'll tell you the real story. Would you like to hear it?"

Joseph nodded, sniffing.

"All right. First of all, do you understand that your grandpa, Joe Dollarhide, had two wives—and two sons, Blake and Mason?"

Joe nodded. "I know that much."

"Mason lived with his mother, Amelia, on the Hollister Ranch. But while he was growing up, he spent a lot of time here, with our family. He was my brother. I loved him. We all did, even my mother. But after he became a man, he stopped coming by. We hardly ever saw him. It broke your grandfather's heart. He loved both his sons.

"Mason was handsome and charming, but I think his mother must have spoiled him. He was popular, especially with the girls. But he wasn't very responsible. He met your mother at a dance. She was young and beautiful, and very innocent when it came to men. Mason charmed her into falling in love with him. And then . . ." Kristin paused. "I hope I don't have to tell you how babies are made."

"It's okay. Boys talk. I know."

"Well, it happened. When your mother found out she was going to have a baby, your grandfather Anderson went to Mason's mother and demanded that he marry her. That woman slammed the door in their faces and sent Mason out of town on the next train. She wanted him to marry a rich society girl, not the daughter of an immigrant farmer. Mason never had the chance to choose whether he wanted you or not. And we never saw him again. We don't know where he is or even whether he's alive."

Joseph had stopped crying. Kristin had given him plenty to think about. She could only hope the boy was mature enough to deal with what he'd learned.

"I was there the night your mother and her father came to our house. Your grandpa Dollarhide wanted his grandchild to have his name and grow up in his family. It was his idea to have Blake marry Hanna. Blake could have said no. He wasn't forced. But he did the right thing. He gave her a nice wedding and treated her with every kindness. By the time you were ready to be born, the two of them had fallen in love.

"Did you know that when you came into the world, it was Blake who delivered you? When I walked into the room a few minutes later, the love on his face as he held you was so powerful that it brought tears to my eyes.

"Joseph, Blake Dollarhide *is* your father. He would do anything to keep you safe and happy. And the idea that he'd hurt you by hiding the truth would break his heart."

Joseph was silent for a long moment. "So what should I do now?" he asked.

"That's up to you. You can talk to him and your mother or keep what you know a secret. Either way, I don't intend to say a word. I know this is a big load for a boy to carry. But young as you are, you need to be a man about some things."

Slowly he nodded. Then his slumped posture straightened as if he'd come to a resolution. "I'll think about it," he said. "Thank you, Aunt Kristin. I'm not going to cry anymore. You can go back to bed."

Kristin stood. "I'm proud of you," she said. "Good night, Joseph. I'll see you in the morning."

Deciding against the drink, she walked back to her room. Maybe she could sleep now. But she couldn't help wondering. Had she done a good thing, giving comfort to a suffering boy? Or had she opened the door to a world of trouble?

CHAPTER THREE

*T*o a man who'd spent uncounted nights in the misery of freezing trenches and lying wounded on a hospital cot, the guest room in the Calder home seemed as sumptuous as the royal suite at the Ritz. But neither the mattress that cushioned his bones nor the downy quilt that warmed his body could give Logan what he craved—a simple, peaceful night's rest.

So many changes. He lay awake, his head resting on a too-soft pillow as he gazed up into the darkness. Four months ago, after the armistice, he'd made plans for the rest of his life. The injury to his leg would end his military career and give him a modest pension. He was headed home to the family farm in Texas, where he'd left his wife, Miranda, and their two little boys in the care of his parents. They would welcome him with open arms, and he would spend the rest of his days working the land, loving his wife, and watching his children grow up. The dream of that homecoming had guided him like a beacon through the darkest days of the Great War. Soon, he'd told himself, that dream would become reality.

Instead, he had come home to an empty farmhouse and five graves in the town cemetery, marked by slabs of scrap wood bearing the names.

"It was that Spanish flu," a neighbor had told him. "It came through here like a damned tornado, took your family and a whole lot of other folks. Those of us who didn't die wore ourselves out diggin' graves. We ran out of coffins and had to wrap the bodies in bedsheets. Sorry for your loss, Logan. We'd have wrote you a letter, but there wasn't time, and we didn't know where to send it. Your animals are at the Johnsons' if you want 'em back."

"Never mind the animals. Thanks."

Numb with grief and shock, Logan had wandered through the house. His eyes had taken in the unmade beds, the clothes in the closets, his father's old work shoes on the floor, the children's toys, and the dirty dishes in the kitchen. Flies had buzzed in the silent space, which smelled of rot and death.

Logan had found a jug of kerosene in the shed, splashed it over the walls of the house, and lit a match. As the place went up in flames, he'd walked away, climbed into the Model T five-passenger touring car he'd bought for the drive home, and headed back to Fort Worth. On the way, he'd noticed the oil rigs sprouting like weeds in his neighbors' fields.

He'd stayed in Fort Worth long enough to settle his family's affairs and to track down someone who knew how to find his Calder relatives in Montana. His telegram to Webb Calder had received a welcoming answer. There was plenty of land for sale, and Logan was welcome to come and start a new life.

The auction of the mineral rights to his oil-rich acreage, including royalties, had left Logan wealthy. He'd paid for a fine granite headstone to mark the graves of his family. Then he had banked the rest of the money and set out driving to Montana, with several letters to deliver. Along the way, he had spooled out his grief until it became as hard and bitter as tar on an icy winter day, its blackness filling the deepest hollows of his heart.

And now he was here, with some life-changing decisions to make. Webb had already picked out a choice land parcel for him to buy. Logan had yet to see it. But what if it wasn't suitable for him? Should he feel obligated to go along with Webb's choice?

Webb Calder was one of the most powerful ranchers in the state of Montana—but to gain and hold that kind of power called for a measure of ruthlessness. Webb would do whatever was best for himself and his legacy. Logan had gathered that much from tonight's conversation over dinner—which reminded him of another decision to be made.

That morning, he'd delivered Axel Anderson's final letter to the young man's parents in Blue Moon. He could still picture their faces as he described the fine soldier Axel had been and how he'd died bravely, charging out of the trench to meet the enemy. When Logan had told them how he'd visited their son's grave in France, Lars and Inga Anderson had barely been able to contain their emotion. They had thanked him profusely, embraced him, and even invited him to stay for lunch, an invitation Logan had declined.

And now Webb Calder was counting on him to go back to these good people and talk them into selling him their land—land that would end up belonging to the Triple C Ranch.

Logan faced a painful choice—betray the people who trusted him or defy a powerful ally—an ally who was testing him, to see whether he could be controlled.

But he already knew what that choice would be. There was no way his conscience would let him take advantage of the Andersons. It was time to draw lines, even if it meant losing his cousin's support.

As he lay pondering, an image rose in his memory. A slim, dark-haired woman in riding clothes, kneeling beside a grown-over mound of earth. He remembered the wilted bouquet and the sorrow in her eyes. Kristin Dollarhide. The name came back to him. *Dr.* Kristin Dollarhide.

Tragic, fierce, and hauntingly beautiful. He wouldn't mind knowing more about her. But he was still mourning his family. And right now, he had more pressing concerns on his mind.

What was it she'd said about the grave and the young man who was buried there? Now he remembered, and he understood why the Andersons would never sell their land. Not even to him.

The next morning, after an early breakfast, the two men saddled horses and rode out to view the parcel that Webb had chosen for Logan to buy. The dawn air was fresh and cool, a fiery sunrise fading in the east. A flock of wild geese rose from a distant field, trailing into a long V formation as they swung northward. A meadowlark warbled from a solitary fence post that was all that remained of an immigrant's deserted farm.

The prairie was like a sea, with waves of yellow grass rippling all the way to the foothills. The deep-rooted native grasses had been lost to wheat farming here. But the newer, less nourishing growth, dotted with wildflowers in shades of yellow, orange, and violet, still made a pretty sight.

"Beautiful country." Logan's gaze swept up to the peaks. "It feels peaceful, something I've missed over the years."

"Well, peace won't make you any money," Webb said. "With the war over, and not so many troops to feed, beef prices are bound to drop. But the market will survive. And that ranch land you'll be buying should support at least a thousand head. Cows may be noisy and dirty and dumb—and they're a lot of work. But that house where you spent last night was built on beef profits. I can sell you enough surplus animals to start your own herd."

"What if I don't want to raise cattle?"

Webb stared at him and snorted. "What the hell do you want to raise? Kangaroos?"

"I plan to raise horses, bred and trained to work cattle. I've seen some good animals here—like the ones we're riding. But most cow ponies are descended from the wild mustangs that were caught and broken back in the day. I want to breed and train the kind of horses that this wild country has never seen before—fast and strong and smart, like some of the horses I've seen in Texas. They're called quarter horses—fastest thing on four legs for a quarter of a mile. They're bred for working cattle."

Logan could tell from Webb's response that he needn't waste breath explaining why he wanted to raise horses. In the war, he'd seen horses—so noble and innocent—suffer and die horribly on the battlefield. There'd been nothing he could do for them. But the desire had been born in him to raise horses that would be loved and valued, not worked to death, slaughtered for meat, or thrown into the hell of a war that was none of their making.

When he'd seen his first quarter horses race in Texas, his heart had stirred with new life, and he'd known what he wanted.

He'd never imagined having the resources to carry out his dream. But the loss of his family had given him the money. He needed to make that money count for something meaningful.

"You're crazy!" Webb exploded. "You'll go broke before your horses are ready for sale. And who the hell's going to buy them? Not me."

"You'll see. Show me the land."

"Come on." Webb kicked his horse to a trot, his mouth set in a grim line. Logan knew he'd annoyed his host and would probably make him even angrier when he refused to take advantage of the Andersons. But sooner or later Webb would have to learn that Logan hadn't come here to follow his agenda.

They rode in silence for a time until Webb reined his horse to a stop. "It's just ahead. Everything from that old stump to the foothills."

Logan liked what he saw. The land was vast and rolling, covered with grass. In the hills beyond, he saw a meandering strip of willows and alders—a sign of water.

Webb made a sweeping gesture with his hand. "This land used to be the Tee Pee Ranch. It belonged to a friend of my father's, Tom Petit. Tom was a good man but after he passed away, his son, Doyle, mismanaged the place and ended up selling it to the drylanders for wheat farming. When the drylanders pulled out a few years later, Doyle bought most of the land back—for next to nothing, of course."

"So where is Doyle now? Is he the one selling the ranch?"

Webb took a long, rough breath. When he spoke again, his voice was raw with emotion. "Doyle's dead. He was responsible for killing my wife."

Logan remembered the painting of a stunning, auburn-haired woman that hung on the wall above the stairs—Chase's mother, he assumed. She'd never posed for the portrait, Webb had told him. He'd had it painted from the single photograph he kept by his bed to remember her. The glamorous gown and the jewelry had been added by the artist.

"I'm truly sorry about your wife," Logan said.

"I didn't kill the bastard if that's what you're wondering. He shot himself and saved me the trouble. The bank in Miles City owns the ranch now. If you want to buy it, you'll be dealing with them."

"I'd like to see more." Logan could make out what appeared to be a house in the near distance. Not much of a house. But if it was fit to move into, that would make getting settled easier. It would also get him out from under Webb's thumb.

They moved forward, the grass swishing around the legs of the horses. Here and there, Logan could see the remnants of barbed wire fences. They would have to be cleared away and replaced with stout logs. He was going to need corrals, a barn, and sheds as well. Getting the ranch ready for horses was going to take a prodigious amount of work. The thought was both daunting and exciting.

Logan scanned the grassland, thinking of access to the ranch house. "Are there any roads out here?" he asked.

"Most of the old wagon trails are grown over," Webb said. "But there's one. It's over there." He pointed to a break in the grassy landscape. Riding closer, Logan could see that it was a well-worn wagon road.

"That's the road Blake Dollarhide cleared to get his logs from the railroad in Miles City to the lumber mill on his ranch," Webb explained. "The big lumber wagons carried them most of the way on the main road. But a quarter mile short of Blue Moon, this road cut off across the prairie, straight to the mill. It saved distance and kept the dust and noise out of the town."

Logan studied the deep ruts, with grass and weeds growing knee high in the center. "It looks to me like the road hasn't been used much lately."

"The mill's been shut down for the past two years because of the war. But with the lumberjacks home and getting back to work in timber country, you can bet those wagons will soon be rolling again."

"That's good to know," Logan said. "If I buy this land, I'm going to need plenty of lumber for outbuildings and fences. I may turn out to be their best customer."

With an abruptness that caught Logan off guard, Webb turned on him like a striking bear. "There's lumber for sale in Miles City," he snapped. "You can get it delivered from there. But if you buy so much as a fence post from those damn Dollarhides, you're no kin of mine!"

Logan studied the wagon road, taking a moment to recover. "I'll be the judge of that," he said, measuring each word. "But first I need to know about the Dollarhides and why you dislike them so much."

Webb snorted. "Because they're low-down, murdering skunks who'll do anything to make money—even betray a fellow rancher."

"Tell me more," Logan said. "I'm listening."

"All right. But it goes back a long way, starting when a kid named Joe Dollarhide signed up as a wrangler on Benteen Calder's first cattle drive. Halfway to Montana, the kid took off on his own and hooked up with a bunch of cattle thieves. Somewhere along the line, he learned to break horses. Then he showed up in Blue Moon and married the daughter of the second richest rancher in the county. He used her money, and what he made from catching and selling horses, to build that house on the bluff and start the sawmill.

"Here. Look for yourself." Webb handed Logan the binoculars he'd hung on the saddle. "Look in the direction of the road. You can see that big log house on top of the bluff and the sawmill at the bottom. When the mill's running you can hear those damned saws halfway to Miles City. The noise scares the cows and wakes the babies. Nobody will be happy to have that racket start up again."

Logan raised the binoculars to his eyes. To the south, on a high bluff, he could make out a rambling log structure, partly raised to a second story on top. He found himself admiring the broad porch, the graceful slope of the roof, and the way the design appeared to blend with the landscape. Lower, where the road ended, he could see the sawmill. Today it was little more than a cluster of sheds surrounded by a high chain-link fence.

"Old Joe Dollarhide's gone now," Webb said. "His second wife is gone too. Their son Blake is in charge now. He runs the whole show—cattle, horses, lumber, and land. Blake's twice as greedy as his father was. But that's not the worst of it. When the home-steaders moved in, plowing up the good grass to plant wheat, Blake Dollarhide welcomed them with open arms. As long as they bought his lumber, he didn't give a damn about the rest of us ranchers. He even married one of the honyockers—got her in a family way first if you want to count the months."

That would be the Andersons' daughter, Logan surmised. But he decided not to mention the family yet. "And that's why you don't like him?"

"That's just the start. I haven't told you what happened last summer." Webb took an open cigarette pack from his shirt pocket and held it out to Logan. When Logan shook his head, he took one for himself and lit it, smoking as he talked.

"It was a dry year. One of the driest ever in these parts. The pas-tures dried up. Even our wells were in danger. We had barely enough water to fill our cattle tanks. We had to sell off some of our stock early so we could have enough water for the rest. Blake Dollarhide did the same.

"If you look to the east, you'll see a canyon cut through the foothills. The creek that runs out of it is fed by snow runoff from the mountains. The upper part is steep. It's mostly rapids. But where the slope levels out, the creek forks. One branch flows north, all the way to the Triple C. Another branch, the bigger one, goes south, toward the Dollarhide pastures."

Logan had begun to understand where the story was going. "By midsummer, we were getting desperate," Webb continued. "The Dollarhides were getting the better part of the water, but our herd was three or four times the size of theirs. We needed more water to keep our cows alive. So I did the only thing I could.

"The place where the creek forks is on government land. I took some of the boys up there one night and threw enough big rocks in the water to make a dam, diverting most of the water to the north fork and the Triple C. There was enough water trickling through the rocks for the Dollarhides. But that wasn't enough to suit them. They wanted it all.

"Two nights later Blake Dollarhide and some of his cowboys showed up with dynamite. I'd figured they might try something, so I'd posted a couple of my boys, with guns, just to keep watch on the dam. To make a long story short, there was gunplay. My men were outnumbered, and both of them got shot.

"As soon as the shooting stopped, the Dollarhide bunch dynamited the dam and blasted it to kingdom come. Then they rode off and left my wounded men lying there. By the time we found them the next morning, Jake was dead. Eddie was almost gone, too, but we patched him up and he lived. That's how we knew what had gone down."

"So what happened after that?" Logan asked. "Was there more fighting?"

"There would've been. And you can bet there'd have been more blood spilled. Water is more precious than gold in this country. But the next day the weather turned. We got enough rain to cause floods. After it stopped, the government sent a crew to repair the creek. They put up a fence and a sign threatening a big fine for tampering with the water flow. There's been no more trouble since, but I don't do business with the Dollarhides. And neither should you. Either you're a Calder, or you aren't."

As they rode, a jackrabbit bounded from under a clump of sagebrush and darted into the long grass. Right behind it, swift and determined, was a coyote. Stopping his horse, Logan watched the chase—the zigzagging flight of the rabbit, the relentless coyote, gaining ground until, with a pounce and a snap of jaws, the chase was over. The coyote trotted off through the grass with the rabbit in its mouth. Logan had almost lost sight of it when a pistol shot rang out. The coyote dropped, twitched, and lay still.

Webb replaced the gun in his holster. "Varmints," he growled. "You've never seen what a pack of them can do to a calf or an injured cow. I kill every damn one of them I see, and so should you."

Logan sensed a hidden message in what he'd seen and heard.

This land was no place for gentleness or mercy. Everything was a fight for survival—even among men.

"Let's go have a look at the house." Logan nudged his mount to a trot. It was becoming clear that if he bought this land, he'd be forced to take sides in a dispute that was none of his making. Since he'd put no money down, it might be smart to pull up stakes and look elsewhere.

But this was beautiful country. The singing grass, the mountain peaks, and endless sky were already calling to his heart. He wanted to become part of this place, to build his dream and make a life here. A life of peace—if that was possible.

But what if peace wasn't possible?

The one-story frame house was originally from the Tee Pee Ranch days. It was a far cry from the stately mansion on the Triple C, but it looked solidly built. Apart from the need of a good cleaning, some minor repairs, and a plumbing upgrade, it would do.

The barn was in disrepair, with gaps where the boards had blown away or been stolen. He would tear it down, use what he could salvage for the sheds, and build a new stable with roomy box stalls and storage for hay and tack. The corrals and chutes were missing rails, but they could be replaced. He'd need a bunkhouse, too, unless he could get by with hiring cowboys who lived in town.

The two men had dismounted to inspect the house. Now they walked the yard, checking the well and what remained of the outbuildings.

"So what do you think?" Webb finished his second cigarette and stubbed out the butt with his boot.

"I'll have to sleep on it," Logan said. "A man would be looking at a mountain of work to get the place in shape."

"Here's what I'm thinking," Webb said. "If it's horses you want to raise, you won't have the place ready with a stable and pens, and maybe some good quality grass planted, for months. By then, it'll be fall. The winters are brutal here, and hay's damned expensive. You won't want to bring in your colts till next spring. But if you can get one pasture fenced off, I'll sell you some branded yearlings. You could fatten them up and ship them with my herd in the fall. That would make some money off your land while you're building. How does that strike you?"

"Whoa there!" Logan shook his head. "You're talking like the deal's already in place. I said I'd sleep on it."

Webb chuckled. "You don't need to sleep on it. Land is like a woman. The minute you set eyes on her, you know whether you want her or not. And you want this place. I can tell."

"I said I'd sleep on it. Maybe I'll look around and see what else is available, too."

"Go ahead. But you won't find anything this good. When I heard you were looking for land, I called in a favor, put down a small deposit, and asked the bank to hold this parcel for thirty days. The time's almost up. If word gets out that it's available, somebody will buy it. Blake Dollarhide would probably be first in line."

Logan was beginning to see a pattern. "So why haven't you bought it yourself?" he asked.

"Good question. But a ranch the size of the Triple C costs a lot of money to run. We're rich in real estate and cattle, but not in cash. Otherwise, I'd buy this parcel in a minute. Choice location, manageable size, good soil, and water. Come on out back. There's something you've got to see."

The splash of flowing water reached Logan's ears as he followed Webb around the house. Striding through high grass and weeds, he found the creek bordered with willows and flowing high with spring runoff.

"That's the creek I was telling you about," Webb said. "It runs along the east property line. The far bank is federal land, but you'd have free use of the water."

Logan was tempted to ignore a prickle of warning. He wanted this land. He'd wanted it from the moment he set foot on it. But even without asking, he sensed what Webb had in mind. According to his story, the creek forked below its headwaters into two branches—one flowing north toward the Triple C Ranch, and the other south toward the Dollarhide property.

The water in this branch flowed south.

* * *

"Come on, Joseph!" Buck Haskell called as he raced out of the schoolhouse door. "Me and Chase and Cully are gonna catch us some fish."

Joseph sighed. He knew his friends would be going to Hollister's Pond. And fishing sounded like just the thing to do on a Friday afternoon. But he couldn't skip out on a promise. "Go on, Buck," he said. "I promised Miss Anderson I'd clean the boards and erasers. If I get done, I'll catch up."

"Oh, go on, Joseph." Britta Anderson waved him toward the door. If she had a soft spot for him, it was probably because she was Joseph's aunt as well as his teacher. A tall woman with a freckled face and kind blue eyes, she wasn't a beauty like Joseph's mother or her younger sister, Gerda. Maybe that was why she hadn't married. But she was one of the smartest women Joseph had ever known.

Looking at her now, he couldn't help wondering if she knew the family secret he'd learned only last night—that Blake Dollarhide wasn't really his father. Had she kept it from him all these years, like the rest of the family?

"It's a beautiful spring day," she said. "Go with your friends, Joseph. Catch a fish or two for me."

With a grin and a murmur of thanks, Joseph rushed outside.

He and his sixth-grade friends were ranch kids. On school days, they rode their horses into town to attend the two-room school. Buck and Chase lived on the Triple C. Buck's dad, Virgil, was the foreman, or at least that was what Buck said. His mother, Ruth, taught the younger children in the ranch school. Chase, of course, was the Calder heir—big for his age, handsome, and self-confident, the kind of boy to whom everything came easily.

Cully O'Rourke was the newest, and the only one of the boys who was poor. His clothes, though clean, were frayed and patched; and his boots looked too big for his feet, as if they'd been handed down from someone else. His black hair hung in strings around his thin face.

Joseph had seen the family in town. The father, who ran cattle on scrubby land in the foothills, looked like a grown-up version of his son. The mother, surprisingly neat and pretty, had been trailed by a small girl with a mop of black hair and fiery eyes. Maggie, her father had called her.

Being Irish and poor might have made Cully an outcast, but he told funny stories—most of them off-color, which boys of that age found hilarious. And he would do almost anything on a dare, from swallowing a live worm to sprinting across a bull pasture. Those qualities gained him acceptance, even admiration, from his peers.

Joseph joined his friends behind the schoolhouse, where their horses were tethered to a hitching rail. Most of the time they rode bareback. Only Chase used a saddle. Now he mounted up and swung his bay gelding in the direction of home.

"Aren't you coming with us, Chase?" Buck asked.

"Not today," Chase said. "My dad wants me to help cut some yearlings from the herd. He'll skin me if I don't come straight home."

"Hell, Chase," Buck said. "Can't one of the cowboys do that job?"

"That's what I asked my dad," Chase said. "But he told me I needed to learn every job on the ranch if I ever want to be the boss."

Joseph watched his friend ride away. Until last night he'd expected to be the future boss of the Dollarhide Ranch. But now he couldn't be certain of anything. He no longer felt sure of who he was or his place in the world.

"Let's go!" Buck kneed his horse. The other boys followed, whooping as they shot out of the schoolyard, galloping across the open fields behind Blue Moon, headed south, past the town, toward the pond on the Hollister Ranch.

The Hollister spread wasn't large, but it was one of the choicest parcels of land in the county. Deep native grasses carpeted a rolling landscape that had never been farmed by wheat growers. Ample groundwater fed wells that kept the grass green from early spring through fall.

Near the border of the ranch was a spot where the groundwater had risen to the surface to form a natural pond, overhung

by willows and stocked with thriving yellow perch. For boys brave
enough to ignore the NO TRESPASSING sign, the Hollister pond was
heaven on earth.

A quarter mile short of the ranch, the three young riders cut
back to the main road, which would take them past the ranch
house. Here, to avoid attracting attention, they slowed the horses
to a walk.

As they passed the substantial brick home with its long driveway, Joseph fixed his gaze on the road ahead. He'd known all
along that the woman who lived there was Joe Dollarhide's first
wife, Amelia. What Joseph hadn't known until last night was that
Amelia was his grandmother—and that she'd wanted nothing to
do with her son's child.

When he tried to picture her, there was no memory. Most
likely, he'd never seen the woman. He only knew that she was old
and that she lived alone except for her servants and the cowboys
who tended her cattle. He'd even heard whispers among the children at school that she was a witch. But Joseph didn't pay them
any mind. Witches were only make-believe.

Pushing away the thought, he caught up with his friends. The
house was out of sight now. A log rail fence stretched along the
road, bordering the pasture. Planted along the inside of the fence
was a thorny hedge of wild roses.

Just ahead, marked by the NO TRESPASSING sign, was a low opening where it was possible to crawl under the hedge. On the far
side was the pond.

The boys dismounted and tethered their horses to the fence.
Cully, who was the skinniest and bravest, bellied through the
opening.

"All clear," he said in a loud whisper. "Come on."

Buck, blond and husky, went next. Joseph followed him, feeling a thorn rip his shirt as he wriggled under the hedge. His
mother wouldn't be happy about that, but he dismissed the worry
at the sight of the pond that lay like a dark mirror, framed with
willows, with a gentle, grassy hill rising on the far side of it.

The boys had no poles, but they'd been here before and had a plan. Buck used his pocketknife to cut three stout willow branches. From an empty Prince Albert tobacco tin, he pulled out three cotton strings, each one tied to a small hook. Turning over a few rocks gave them enough worms to use as bait. Soon, with their makeshift tackle, they were catching fish.

Joseph had often wondered where the yellow perch came from, since they weren't found in wild streams. Someone in the past must've stocked the pond with them. They were too small to have much meat on them, but they were a lot of fun to catch.

Joseph had just landed his third fish when a sound from the direction of the house chilled his blood.

It was the sound of barking dogs—big dogs, and more than one. They were coming closer.

CHAPTER FOUR

As the hellish barking grew louder, Cully was the first to react. Dropping his pole, he dived for the opening under the hedge with Buck right behind him. Lean and nimble, Cully made a clean getaway. But Buck was slower and bulkier. Halfway through the hole, he snagged the seat of his pants on a thorny branch. Caught fast, he twisted and struggled, blocking the way out and leaving Joseph with nowhere to go.

Joseph was trying to reach his friend when two massive dogs bounded over the crest of the hill. Snarling and growling, they paused on the far side of the pond. Joseph crouched by the hedge, trying not to show the terror he felt. If he were to run, odds were that the dogs would bring him down and tear him to pieces.

Their ugly jaws gleamed with drool as they eyed him like predators sizing up their prey. With heavy bodies and brindled coats, they reminded him of the dogs in an old English painting he'd seen in a book. Mastiffs—the name of the breed sprang unbidden into his mind.

He could hear the rustling sounds of Buck moving under the hedge. Maybe his friend had managed to free himself and would get to safety. But Joseph knew better than to follow. If he were to dive for the opening, the dogs could be on him in an instant, seizing his legs and dragging him backward.

"Good boys." Standing, he spoke to the dogs in a coaxing tone. "It's all right. I don't mean any harm."

One dog growled. The other dog, hackles bristling, edged closer around the side of the pond. Joseph could sense the tension building in the beasts. Any moment now, those vise-like jaws and ripping teeth could be closing on his flesh. Maybe he should make for the pond. At least in the water, he might have a fighting chance. He braced himself for the sprint and the leap.

A shrill whistle split the stillness. Ears pricking, the dogs wheeled and loped back up the hill. Weak with relief, Joseph was about to drop to the ground and follow Buck, who'd made it through the opening under the hedge, when a rider appeared over the hilltop, flanked by the dogs and mounted on a tall black horse.

Cast in silhouette against the sun, the figure in the saddle was small, almost childlike. Was it a boy, even a girl? But no—as the horse walked closer, changing the angle of the light, Joseph realized he was looking at an elderly woman in riding clothes.

"What are you doing here, boy?" Her age-roughened voice was steely, her posture ramrod straight. In one hand she carried a coiled bullwhip. "I asked you a question," she snapped. "Answer me."

Joseph cleared his throat. "I—I'm sorry, ma'am. I was just catching a few fish. I know I'm not supposed to be here. If you'll let me go, I promise to never come back again."

For a silent interval that seemed to last forever, she studied him. Her cat-green eyes seemed to look right through his skin. The low sun cast a russet aura over her silver hair.

"What's your name, boy?" she demanded.

"Joseph, ma'am. Joseph Dollarhide."

"And your father's name?"

"Blake Dollarhide, ma'am. And my grandfather—"

"Never mind, I know," she snapped. "All right, go on back the way you came in. But if I ever see you here again, I'll set the dogs on you. Do you understand?"

"Yes, ma'am." Joseph's knees quivered with relief.

"Then get going before I change my mind!" Her voice had taken on a shrill quality. "Go on, you little bastard! Get out of here!"

Joseph dived for the opening under the hedge, wriggled through, and struggled to his feet. His heart was pounding so hard that he could imagine it slamming a hole through his ribs. As he walked back to the horses where his friends were waiting, he felt a lump rising in his throat. Tears stung his eyes. He blinked them away.

"Are you all right?" Buck asked as Joseph mounted his horse. "Did the dogs attack you?"

"No. The dogs were fine. It was just scary." He nudged the horse to a trot, moving ahead of his companions. He didn't want them to see his face or ask him any more questions.

No matter how many questions they might ask, he would never tell them the truth—the truth that roiled in his stomach, making him want to be sick.

He had just met his grandmother.

Shep, the crusty retired range cook, was still working in the Dollarhide kitchen. He was a decade older, his hair snow white and his disposition grumpier than ever. But the meals he prepared were as tasty as Kristin remembered.

Sitting down to dinner that night, she couldn't help but recall her mother's dining style—the white linen cloth and napkins, the good china and silver, and the insistence on proper manners and polite conversation. Sarah Foxworth Dollarhide had declared that her aim was to raise children who could share a table with anyone, even the president, and not feel out of place.

But times had changed. Hanna had made an effort to follow Sarah's example, but with a young family and a busy husband, dinners tended to be less formal and more practical. And that was all right, Kristin told herself. It was all right even when five-year-old Elsa spilled her milk or nine-year-old Annie argued for a later bedtime—or when Joseph sulked over his food, as he was doing tonight. This was family—what she'd yearned for during those long, bleak months of tending the wounded. And if there was mild chaos at the dinner table, there was also an abundance of love.

Only her parents were missing. They hadn't been elderly. If not for the flu, they would have been here, smiling and chatting with the rest of the family. Coming home on the train, Kristin had read a news report speculating that even more people had died of the Spanish flu than had died in the war.

"Why aren't you eating, Joseph?" Hanna asked her son. "I know you like chicken and dumplings. Is everything all right?"

Joseph nodded, his mouth set in a grim line. "Sorry, I'm just not hungry," he said. "May I be excused to go to my room?"

Hanna reached out and laid her palm against his forehead. With the dreaded flu still raging in the world beyond Blue Moon, the worry about contagion was far from over. "You don't feel feverish," she said. "But maybe you should go and lie down. Promise you'll let me know if you start feeling worse."

"You may be excused, Joseph." Blake, looking preoccupied, gave the boy his fatherly permission.

Joseph pushed back his chair, stood, and trudged off toward the stairs. He didn't look sick, Kristin thought. But something was clearly troubling him.

"I can look in on him later, if you like," she offered.

"Thank you," Hanna said. "It'll be good to have a doctor in the house again."

"As I told you, Hanna, you've made me feel welcome here," Kristin said. "But I can't stay long. Once I start my practice, I'll need to live in town—or close to town, at least."

Hanna looked disappointed but nodded her understanding.

"I'm hoping to find a house where I can have my office up front and living space in back," Kristin said. "Do you know of any place like that?"

"Nothing comes to mind. But I can ask when I go to town tomorrow. I want to see the letter that man left with my parents. What did you say his name was?"

"Hunter. Major Logan Hunter." The stranger's scar-slashed face rose in Kristin's memory. He'd mentioned that he was a relative of the Calders. Did that mean he was planning to stay? Would she see him again?

But what did it matter? Given the history of the two rival families, and what Blake had told her about the water incident last summer, the less she had to do with any Calder, the better.

"Why don't you come with me tomorrow?" Hanna suggested. "If my mother knows of any available houses, you'll be there to look at them."

"That's a fine idea. And I'll enjoy seeing your family again. It's been a long time."

With the meal finished, Hanna took the girls away to get them ready for bed, leaving Kristin and her brother alone at the table.

"You weren't very talkative tonight, Blake," Kristin observed. "And now that your family's gone upstairs, you're looking as if you'd bet your savings on a horse that lost the race."

His mouth twitched in an ironic half smile. "Hardly that. But you always were too observant for your own good."

"So, what's the matter?" she asked. "Sometimes it helps to talk. And I'm a good listener."

Standing, he opened a high cabinet behind him, took out a partly filled decanter of brandy, and poured a small amount into each of two crystal glasses. "I know alcohol's illegal now," he said. "But some nights call for a drink. Let's go into the parlor."

Kristin took her glass and followed him into the next room. A fire had been lit earlier against the chill of the spring night. As he stood facing the fireplace, the glow of its embers cast Blake's face into deepening lines and shadows. Only now did Kristin realize how much the weight of grief and responsibility had aged her brother.

"So what's the trouble?" she asked him.

"Nothing, yet. Just disappointment and worry. I've had my eye on that Tee Pee Ranch parcel, the one that used to belong to the Petits, ever since the rumor went around that it might go up for sale. I even asked the bank to let me know the minute it went on the block."

"Do we really need more land?" Kristin asked, sipping her brandy, feeling the heat of it creeping down her throat.

"We need *that* land. The wagon road from the lumber camps to our mill runs straight across it. And the creek that flows along the boundary of that ranch is the one that waters our property. The money would be a stretch—I'd need to get financing—but having the road access and the creek water under our control would be worth whatever I had to pay."

Blake drained his glass and set it on the hearth. "This afternoon I went into Miles City on business and stopped by the bank to ask about the land. The manager told me that Webb Calder had put down a deposit to hold it until the end of the month for some oil-rich Texas relative of his who was looking to buy a ranch and could pay top dollar."

Kristin stifled a gasp. "That would be the man I met. The major."

"That's just what I'm thinking. He's already here. And if the deal goes through, we'll have a Calder right on our doorstep, gating the road, damming the creek, and doing whatever the hell Webb tells him to."

"The bank's closed until Monday. Maybe the major will find a different ranch to buy. Or maybe—"

"You're grasping at straws," Blake snapped. "Barring some miracle, the deal's as good as done. And my only choice is to accept it or fight."

"No!" An image flashed through Kristin's mind—Alvar lying in a pool of blood outside the burning sawmill. "I can't condone another range war. So help me, Blake, if you start anything like that, I'll leave Blue Moon and never come back!"

Blake picked up his glass. "I may not have a choice," he said.

Logan accepted the half glass of bourbon Webb offered him and took a lingering sip. "I guess I'd better make this last," he said. "With Prohibition the law of the land, who knows when you'll be able to get more."

Webb grinned. "Hell, I'm not worried. I've got enough booze in my cellar to supply the whole damned state of Montana. And it's not like anybody's going to come looking for it."

The two men stood in Webb's spacious study after a dinner of prime beefsteak. If Webb was in a celebratory mood, it was because earlier that afternoon, Logan had told him that he'd decided to buy the former Tee Pee Ranch. The money would be wired and the deed transferred on Monday at the bank and land office in Miles City.

"Here's to your new ranch and your new life." Webb extended his glass. "And here's to our new partnership."

Partnership? Logan hesitated. There'd been no talk of any such arrangement—no money changing hands and no signing of contracts. "To our new friendship," he corrected, raising his glass to touch the rim of Webb's. If Webb had noticed the correction, he showed no sign of it. "For the record, I plan to return your deposit as soon as the money arrives in my account."

The two men drank. Webb splashed more of the amber liquid into the glasses before the two men sat down in the matching leather armchairs. "So now what's the plan?" he asked.

"You know how much work the place needs," Logan said. "I'll be starting as soon as the ink's dry on the deed. So I won't be imposing on your hospitality beyond this weekend."

"Having you here is no imposition. As for that house, you saw the inside. The place isn't fit for a clan of Irish goat herders. You can't move in till it's been cleaned and renovated."

"During the war I lived in tents and trenches, and I shared a latrine with my whole platoon. Once I've chased out the rats and spiders, I can make do in the house until I get more important things done, like fencing and a new well and a barn. I packed the Model T with tools when I left the old place in Texas, but I'm going to need more, as well as horses and a wagon and plenty of lumber and nails."

"Well, what you can't find here in Blue Moon you can get in Miles City. That place is almost civilized—a fine hotel, good meals, and a couple of saloons." Webb drained his glass. "With the Eighteenth Amendment passed, I don't suppose they'll be selling alcohol anymore—at least not in the open. But there'll still be card games and billiard tables, and a fair class of women if you're hankering for a good time. Or if you aren't too fussy, the old watering hole here in Blue Moon is a restaurant now, and the owner, Jake Loman, boards a couple of his so-called nieces in the rooms upstairs."

"I'll keep that in mind." Logan dismissed the suggestion. A meaningless tumble with a paid woman might give him a brief release; but it would do nothing to warm the frozen lump that had once been his heart. Overseas, with men dying around him, the thought of Miranda and their boys waiting for him at home was the one thing that had kept him from falling into despair. Now they were gone, and it was as if his soul had shriveled inside his body. He felt no grief, no pain, no desire. Nothing at all.

"I'll need to hire some workers," he said, changing the subject. "Is there anybody you'd recommend?"

"None that come to mind. But there are men home from the war who'd probably be glad for the work. Put up a notice somewhere. You'll get plenty of help."

"That's fine for the fences and corrals. But when it comes to building the barn, I'm going to need at least one man who knows how to do the job. I was thinking of Lars Anderson. He's a carpenter, and he strikes me as being honest and capable."

"No. Not him." Webb's tone dripped contempt. "You know that he's Blake Dollarhide's father-in-law. You'd be crazy to trust any of that lot."

When Logan didn't reply, he continued. "Speaking of the Andersons, when are you going to talk to them about buying that land parcel next to the Triple C?"

"I've decided against it," Logan said.

Color darkened Webb's features. "Well, you'd better have a damned good reason."

"I do. Talking to the Andersons would be a waste of time. Their oldest son is buried on that land. They'd never sell it. Not to anyone, including me."

"Anything's for sale at the right price," Webb said. "Since I'll be buying it from you, you can offer whatever it takes."

Logan shook his head. "The Andersons lost their only remaining son on my watch. I won't cheapen their sacrifice by pressuring them to sell their land."

Webb's face had gone florid. With a muttered curse, he stood and slammed his glass on the desk. "There's something you need to understand. The Calders were the first to settle this area, and the Triple C is still the biggest ranch in the state. That means power—power you can share. But the price of our friendship is loyalty. Don't make the mistake of forgetting that."

Logan had stood to face him. "Webb, I appreciate all you've done to help me settle here. But if there's some kind of feud going on, I don't want any part of it. All I want is to live in peace on my land, to choose my friends and the people I do business with, and to be left alone. Is that asking too much?"

Webb's gaze hardened. "Here's how it works," he said. "Either you're with us or against us. You may have Calder blood, but unless you're a Calder at heart, you're no kin of mine!"

Joseph had looked more troubled than sick when he'd left the dinner table. Either way, Kristin was worried about him. She gave him some time until the house was quiet. Then, wearing her nightgown and robe, she tiptoed down the hall to his room and tapped on the door.

"Joseph?" she whispered. "Are you awake?"

There was no answer. He was probably sleeping, but she needed to make sure he was all right. As quietly as she could, she opened the door. The room was dark, but she could make out the shape of him, lying in the bed.

"I'm fine, Aunt Kristin." His voice startled her. "I'm not sick and I'm not crying. So you can go."

Kristin hesitated, warned by the strain in his young voice. "Just let me check your temperature," she said. "I promised your mother I'd do that."

"I'm not sick."

"Let's make sure." She leaned over the bed and laid a hand on his forehead. His skin was cool. "No fever," she said. "But I can tell something's not right. Do you want to talk about it?"

When he didn't answer, she lowered herself to the chair beside his bed. After a long, tense moment of waiting, he sighed and spoke. "After school today, Buck and Cully and me snuck through the fence to the Hollister pond. We didn't mean any harm by it. Just having fun, catching a few fish."

"And was it fun?"

"At first. Then this old lady showed up on a horse with two big dogs. Cully and Buck got away. But I didn't have time. All I could do was stand there and hope she wouldn't sic the dogs on me." He stirred, shifting restlessly. "When she looked at me, I saw her eyes. They were green like mine. I could tell she was my grandmother."

"I haven't seen her since she was younger, but I'm guessing you were right. Did she know who you were?"

"She asked me my name. When I told her, she called me 'a little bastard.'" His voice wavered, breaking. "Nobody ever called me 'a bastard' before. But I know what it means. I guess that's what I am."

He was close to tears now. Kristin fought the urge to take him in her arms and rock him like the child he was. Pity was the last thing he needed. "You are whatever you choose to be, Joseph. Don't let that evil old woman choose for you. She's nothing. What she says doesn't matter. Do you understand?"

He nodded.

"You're a Dollarhide, and one day, if you make the right choices, you'll be the head of this family. Remember that when you're tempted to call yourself by the wrong name. All right?"

"All right," he whispered. "Thanks, Aunt Kristin. I can go to sleep now."

"Good." She brushed her fingertips across his curly hair. "Sleep tight. I'll see you in the morning."

She walked out of the room and closed the door behind her. At this stage of her life, it seemed unlikely that she would ever have children of her own. But young Joseph was giving her a glimpse of what it might be like to feel love for a child.

She'd known other children in the war. Their images rose in her memory now as she walked downstairs, found the brandy in the cabinet, and poured some into a glass. Ragged children with haunted eyes, huddled in the ruins of burned-out buildings. Children with injuries, dying, beyond her help. Children she'd forced herself not to love.

One boy—still a child at fourteen—had lied about his age to get into the army. Kristin had held him in her arms as he died, singing him a lullaby, fighting surges of love.

She had held love back for so long that she'd forgotten how it felt.

The glass was empty. After pouring herself another two fingers of brandy, she replaced the bottle and carried the glass upstairs to her room. Blake would probably notice how much was missing. But what did it matter? She was an adult. And maybe if she drank a little more, the dreams wouldn't come tonight.

The next day was Saturday. Kristin saddled her mare and set out for town alongside the buggy, which Hanna was driving with her two daughters. Joseph had stayed behind to help his father and the hired hands get ready for spring roundup.

Blake owned a Model T, which he used for trips to Miles City and beyond. But Hanna still preferred the one-horse buggy to the mechanics of fiddling with the engine and cranking the starter. Horses didn't break down in the middle of the road, she liked to say.

The trip to town was a treat for the little girls. They giggled and sang all the way. Kristin might have joined them in the buggy, but she'd wanted the freedom to go off on her own and check out possible quarters for her medical practice.

The town of Blue Moon had changed in the years of her absence. The land boom was over, the wheat fields gone to yellow grass and dry weeds. The railroad platform had vanished, the unused rails buried in dust. The bank, once owned by Blake's former friend Doyle Petit, was gone. Doyle was gone, too, dead by his own hand as his crooked schemes collapsed around him like a house of cards.

At least a few businesses were thriving. The general store Kristin remembered had burned, along with several other buildings along Main Street. Its replacement featured a gas station, grocery store, and post office. The hardware store now included a dry goods section. The saloon, since the passage of the Eighteenth Amendment in January, had become a roadhouse where meals were served, with pool tables in the back. Several black Model T Fords mingled with the buggies, wagons, and horse traffic on Main Street.

Hanna had planned to leave the girls with her mother and sisters while she did her shopping. Kristin followed the buggy to a neat white frame house on the outskirts of town.

Remembering the tar-paper shack where the Andersons had lived on their wheat farm, Kristin was gratified to see that they'd moved to a more comfortable place. It appeared that Lars was getting plenty of carpentry work. Britta's teaching probably brought in a little money, too.

Hanna's mother, Inga, was at home with her two younger daughters. Years of hardship and the loss of two precious sons had taken their toll. Her hair was white, her face wrinkled by age and grief. But there was vigor in her step and resilience in her smile as she greeted Kristin with open arms.

"How good to see you, dear. Hanna told me you were coming home. I hope you're here to stay."

Kristin returned her embrace, which ended when Hanna's two sisters crowded in. Britta was tall like her father, with a freckled face and a ready smile. But it was Gerda, the youngest of the family, who surprised Kristin most. The eight-year-old child she remembered had grown up to be a stunning beauty, with long-lashed indigo eyes, a tiny-waisted figure, and a wealth of golden curls tied back with a blue ribbon.

Hanna's little girls had come inside. Skipping with eagerness, they followed Britta into the kitchen where she'd promised earlier that they could help her make cookies.

"We can visit after I've done my shopping," Hanna said to her mother. "Is there anything you need from the store?"

"Nothing that I can think of," Inga said. "I've got fresh lemonade out back in the cool box. We can enjoy some when you get back."

Gerda spoke up. "I need some buttons for the new dress I'm making, but I want to choose them myself. Do you mind if I come along, Hanna?"

"Of course not," Hanna said. "Why don't you come, too, Kristin? The store's a good place to meet people. You can leave your horse here and ride with us in the buggy."

"That's a fine idea," Kristin agreed. And it was. Getting to know the townspeople would be an important first step in starting her medical practice.

The store was only a few minutes away. Hanna secured the buggy to the hitching rail next to a new-looking auto, a fine layer of dust coating its shiny finish. Kristin gave the vehicle a glance, then followed Hanna and Gerda around the corner of the store to the front entrance.

Once inside, the three women separated. Hanna, who'd made a list, set out to find her items in the most efficient way. Gerda made for the rack of button cards, trim, and sewing notions, leaving Kristin to wander among the shelves. The store was busy with customers doing their Saturday shopping. Soon she was greeting old acquaintances and meeting new people, mostly women, who'd moved to Blue Moon after she'd left.

Passing the display counter in front, she noticed a small girl wearing a faded dress that appeared to be made over from some larger garment. Her feet were bare, and her black hair hung down her back in a thick braid. Her hungry eyes gazed up at the glass candy jars on the countertop—lemon drops, candy canes, licorice, and lollipops—as if they were the very treasures of heaven.

"So here you are, Miss Mary Frances Elizabeth O'Rourke." The woman who took the child's hand spoke with an Irish brogue. She was as delicately pretty as a sparrow, her dress clean but threadbare and out of style. In her shopping basket, she carried only a few essentials—salt, baking soda, and a pint jar of molasses.

Kristin spoke on impulse. "Excuse me, ma'am, but I noticed how your little girl was looking at those candies. Would you allow me to buy her one?"

The woman's expression hardened. "Thank you for the kind offer, but we don't take charity."

"Oh, but it isn't—"

"I said no thank you. If she wants a sweet, I'll buy her one myself."

With a defiant look, she pointed to the jar of peppermint sticks. As the clerk took one out of the jar and handed it to the little girl, the woman opened her tiny pocketbook and dumped a few coins into her hand. After counting them carefully, as if she might not have enough, she laid them on the counter. The clerk scooped them up without giving her change. It was probably all the money she had. Head high, she took her purchases and left, keeping a firm grip on her little girl's hand.

A few minutes later, Kristin spotted Hanna carrying her loaded basket to the counter. Gerda was nowhere in sight. If she was still making up her mind about buttons, the girl might need to be hurried along.

Ending her conversation with a chatty, silver-haired matron, Kristin turned away and headed for the rear of the store where the fabrics and sewing notions were kept. There was no sign of Gerda.

Unease crawled along Kristin's nerves as she searched up and down the aisles. Gerda wasn't a child. Maybe she'd met a girlfriend or given her buttons to Hanna and gone outside to wait in the buggy. But something didn't seem right.

Hanna had paid for her purchases and was just going out the door. Kristin was about to follow her when she saw Gerda. The girl was backed into a rear corner of the store, almost hidden by the bulk of a broad-shouldered man in a leather jacket.

Alarmed, Kristin strode toward them, ready to send the man packing and rescue the girl. That was when an unexpected sound reached her ears. Gerda was laughing—a tinkling, musical sort of laugh. A flirting kind of laugh.

Didn't the naive little fool know that she could be in danger? Temper simmering, Kristin reached them and tapped the man on the shoulder. "That's enough, sir," she said. "You should know better than to take advantage of—"

The words died in her throat as he turned around. Chestnut hair, grown a little long. Laughing green eyes and a chiseled jaw with a dimpled chin.

It was Mason.

CHAPTER FIVE

"H ELLO, SIS." EXCEPT FOR A CHIPPED FRONT TOOTH, MASON'S charming smile was just as Kristin remembered. "I'll be damned, you're all grown up."

Despite the shock, Kristin's first thought was for Gerda. Putting her hands on the girl's shoulders, she pulled her aside. "Go help your sister, Gerda."

Gerda's blue eyes widened in a startled look. "But we were only talking. He asked me where to find the cinnamon, and I showed him."

"Not another word." Kristin shoved her toward the door. "Go. Now. I'll be along in a minute."

As Gerda fled out the front door, Kristin faced her half-brother. "What are you doing here, Mason?" she demanded.

"I've come home." His expression was all boyish innocence. "My mother's getting along in years. I've come back to help her run the ranch. But why don't you seem glad to see me?"

"You know why. Leaving town was the best thing you ever did for our family."

Again, he gave her that bewildered look he'd always been good at faking. "I don't understand," he said.

"I think you do. And if I catch you anywhere near that innocent young girl, so help me, I'll put you on the train myself—if her father doesn't shoot you first."

She turned to go, but he blocked her way, putting a hand on her arm to delay her. "We're still family. How's our father?"

"He died of the Spanish flu last winter along with my mother." Saying the words still triggered a stab of grief.

"I'm truly sorry for that," he said.

"It's too late for sorry. You broke his heart, Mason. And now the best thing you can do is leave our family alone. Blake's in charge now, and he's doing fine. So stay away from us. We'll all be better off."

Pushing her way around him, she strode toward the door. By the time she stepped outside, she was shaking. Had Mason seen Hanna? Had she noticed him? And Gerda—she'd been a seven-year-old child when Mason left town. She hadn't even known him. Had anyone ever told her what he'd done?

Mason was part of the past. Why couldn't he stay there?

Hanna had driven the buggy around to the front of the store. Kristin climbed in, squeezing next to Gerda on the front seat. As they drove through town and back to the house, she studied the two sisters. Gerda was pouting, her lower lip thrust out like a child's. But Hanna was calm and smiling. She must not have been aware that Mason was in the store. But she needed to know that he was back in Blue Moon.

When the buggy pulled up to the house, Kristin swung to the ground, giving Gerda room to climb out. Still pouting, the girl stalked up the walk to the front door, giving Hanna and Kristin a moment alone.

"Mason's back," Kristin said. "He was in the store. I don't suppose you noticed him."

"I didn't," Hanna said calmly. "But I'm not surprised. I've always known he'd come back someday."

"He could cause a lot of trouble," Kristin said.

"I know. But I'm not a silly girl anymore. I'm prepared to stand up to him and to protect my family, especially Joseph."

"Blake needs to know."

"I'll tell him," Hanna said.

"And you might want to keep an eye on Gerda. He was talking to her, and she seemed to be enjoying it. Does she know anything about what happened?"

"Not unless my mother told her. Gerda was too young to understand at the time. But I'll tell her as much as she needs to know. With that pretty face and no more sense than I had at her age, she's a worry to the family. Maybe I'll ask Britta for help. She knows everything."

"In any case, I trust you to deal with the situation," Kristin said. "I won't be coming in. A woman in the store told me about a place that might be perfect for my office. I'm going to look at it. I'll see you later at home. Good luck."

"I'm going to need more than luck," Hanna said. "But Mason is not going to damage my family. I'll make sure of that."

The house wasn't perfect, but it came with almost everything Kristin needed. Set at the edge of town on the road to Miles City, it had peeling paint and two cracked windows. But there were three bedrooms and a parlor, a handy kitchen with a big wood stove, and indoor plumbing. There was a shed for her auto, and the friendly neighbors kept a few horses and a one-horse chaise, which she could borrow as needed in exchange for free medical care.

Within the hour, she had signed a lease and paid her first month's rent. Tomorrow, even though it was Sunday, she would roll up her sleeves and get to work.

She was about to start for home when she remembered last night's conversation with Blake. The cutoff to the wagon route that ran from the main road, crossed the former Tee Pee Ranch, and ended at the lumber mill couldn't be far from here. She would do some exploring on the way home, maybe look at the parcel Blake had wanted to buy.

Mounting up, she followed the main road until she found the overgrown wagon track, cutting off to the right. It didn't appear to have been used much, but with the mill starting up again this spring, that was about to change.

She could only hope that Blake wouldn't have a problem with access for his wagons. If by some miracle he was still able to buy the land, the issue would be resolved. If not, he could only hope the new owner would accept payment for letting the wagons cross his property.

But if the new owner was a Calder, all bets would be off.

The lower part of the wagon road cut across open land that had once been planted in wheat. The old Anderson farm lay north of here. But she wasn't going in that direction today. This route headed south and east in a straight diagonal across the prairie. Taking the mare at a brisk walk, she set a safe path alongside the road, avoiding ruts made by the heavy wagons and deepened by rain and snow.

The sky was cloudless, the breeze like gentle fingers rippling through the yellow grass and newly sprouted blades of wild-growing wheat. How lonely it was out here, and how quiet. It was so still that Kristin fancied she could almost hear the beating of her own heart. Lulled by the sun's warmth and the swaying of the mare, she began to drift.

A covey of quail exploded out of the grass, bursting upward under the mare's nose. Crying and flapping, they scattered in all directions.

The mare whinnied and reared. Jerked awake, Kristin had no time to react before she was flung out of the saddle. She flew through the air and landed on her back with a thud.

For the first few moments she lay still, her breath coming in gasps, her eyes closed against the glare of the sun. She could hear the sound of the mare galloping away. Trying to catch the animal would be futile. Her mount was gone, and she was still several miles from home. Unless she wanted to be stuck out here, she had no choice except to walk—if she could.

After gingerly testing her limbs, she sat up. The vast, yellow prairie spread around her, the road barely visible through the long grass. Going back to town might be the safest choice. But it made more sense to go on. If the mare returned home on the road, Blake would come this way to look for her.

Forcing herself to move, she struggled to her feet. She was aware of a dull pain in her head. The horizon seemed to tilt one way, then another. But at least her legs worked.

The midday sun was blinding. Shading her eyes with her hand, she found her hat and jammed it onto her head. She'd had nothing to eat since breakfast, and the water canteen she'd carried was on the horse. So was the rifle. But if she sat down to wait for rescue, she could be trapped out here after dark. The only thing to do was keep moving and conserve her energy as best she could.

At least she had the road to guide her. The ruts would have been dangerous for the mare, but for her on foot, they'd be the easiest place to walk. Planting her feet, she willed her legs to move, one step, then another, making slow but steady progress.

Ahead, she could see black shapes flocking against the glare—vultures and ravens squabbling as they settled on a meal. If she kept to the road, she would have to pass within a few feet of whatever they were eating. It wouldn't be a pretty sight. But she'd seen far worse in the war, Kristin reminded herself. This was only a dead animal.

She glimpsed the remains now. The animal appeared to be a coyote—not much of a meal for the scavengers that fought over every scrap. This was nature on the prairie, a common event in the circle of life. But as she drew closer, the buzzing flies, the smell of death, and the hoarse cries of birds ripped through the floodgates of her memory. She was back behind the lines after a night of shelling, gazing out over a nightmare landscape, with black clouds of ravens—too many to drive away—flocking in to do their grisly work.

Suddenly the memory became too much.

Seized by mindless panic, she clambered out of the roadbed and plunged away from the carnage. Running headlong through the grass, she caught her boot in a tangle of weeds, stumbled forward, and fell to her hands and knees.

Stupid, she lashed herself as the dry, prickly weeds cut into her hands. She should have just kept walking.

After a few seconds to recover, she raised her head. The fall had brought her back to her senses, but she could no longer see the road or even the birds. She knew the country well enough to make her way home, but the long-neglected grass hid many hazards—scraps of wire, animal holes, even rattlesnakes. The going would be rough until she found the road again.

She was struggling to her feet when she saw the horse—not her mare, but a pale buckskin, saddled and bridled, standing like a mirage in a haze of sunlight. Maybe she was hallucinating. But if the horse was real, catching it would save her a long, painful walk. Once home, she could identify the owner and return it, or simply turn it loose and let it find its own way.

"Easy boy." She began walking toward the horse. Its ears pricked forward. "Good boy. Don't run away. I won't hurt you." She edged closer, making little clicking noises with her tongue. The animal looked vaguely familiar, but buckskin was a common color, one she could have seen anywhere.

"That's it, boy . . ." A few more steps and she was able to seize the reins. Straining against the sudden pull, the horse swung to one side. Only then could Kristin see the Triple C brand on its haunch—and something else.

Streaked down the horse's side was a long smear of drying blood.

Logan staggered through the tall grass, his teeth clenched against the pain. Damned horse—if it hadn't run off, he might've had a good chance of making it back to the ranch house. With water and shelter, he might have been able to tend the gunshot wound in his upper arm and save his own life. But on foot, the odds of getting there before he passed out from blood loss were slim to none.

The bullet, coming out of nowhere, had struck below the left shoulder—usually a survivable wound. But the flow of blood told Logan that the shot had nicked a blood vessel.

He had stripped off his shirt and knotted it around the wound as tightly as he could manage with one hand and his teeth. When that hadn't been enough to stanch the bleeding, he'd found a stick and twisted it under the knot to make a tourniquet. That had helped, but not enough. He could already feel himself getting weaker. Barring a miracle, he would die from blood loss—not on the battlefield but in the middle of the godforsaken Montana prairie.

This morning, after a night torn by doubts and questions, he'd decided to ride out alone for one last inspection of the ranch property. True, he'd already told Webb that he wanted to buy the place. But he could still change his mind—and would if he couldn't overcome his misgivings.

He had two days to make a final decision before the bank opened on Monday. The site was perfect for building his dream. It had grass and water, with plenty of space and a livable house. And its beauty whispered to his heart—*home*.

But every time he spoke with Webb, he sensed that this ranch would be used as a buffer and a weapon against the Dollarhides. If the tension escalated, he could find himself trapped in the middle of an all-out blood feud and forced to join in the fight.

He'd been riding the boundary of the ranch, imagining where he would put fences, when he'd spotted something shiny on the ground—probably just a brass shell casing, but it had pricked his interest. He'd climbed out of the saddle to pick it up when he'd heard the rifle shot and felt the burn of the bullet below his shoulder. In his military career, he'd been shot more than once, and he knew what to expect. For the first few seconds, despite the pain, he'd been more annoyed than worried. But then he'd noticed the blood.

Now his memory was beginning to fog, but he recalled trying to climb back onto the horse. Spooked by the smell of blood, perhaps, it had run off, leaving him stranded. In the near distance, he could see the black scavengers feeding on the carcass of the coyote Webb had shot. If he didn't make it to somewhere safe, he could be their next meal.

That was his last thought before the darkness closed in. He collapsed to his knees and fell forward in the long yellow grass, his blood seeping into the earth.

Cully O'Rourke whistled a tune to buoy his sagging spirits as he rode home to the family ranch in the foothills. The old Tee Pee

Ranch was usually a good place for rabbit hunting. He'd counted on bagging one or two for his mother's stew pot. But today he'd seen only one animal—and in his haste to shoot it, he'd forgotten that his dad's old lever action 30.30 had faulty sights and always shot high. He'd missed the blasted rabbit by a mile. He couldn't even see where the bullet had struck. Maybe it had just kept going.

He might have hunted for more rabbits. But in the distance he'd glimpsed a horse. Standing next to the animal, partly screened by a scraggly cedar tree, was a man on foot, who'd probably dismounted to take a piss. Since Cully was trespassing, that could mean trouble. It was time to head for home.

His mother and little sister would be disappointed, and his father would grumble, but supper would have to be carrots and potatoes. No meat for the family tonight.

Mounted on the buckskin horse, Kristin could see the distant birds flocking around the dead coyote. At least she'd have no trouble finding the road. But she couldn't turn toward home until she'd found the person whose blood streaked the horse's side.

Was that person Major Logan Hunter? He'd been riding a horse like this, with the Calder brand, when they'd met. If he was buying this ranch property, it made sense that he'd be exploring the place.

But who it was made no difference. She was a doctor, and somebody needed her help. It was her duty to find them and do what she could—even if what she could do was nothing.

Once more, the birds came to her aid. A hundred yards eastward, beyond the dead coyote, something had attracted a new flock. The vultures and ravens were circling, touching down, then rising again, as if waiting for a feast.

Nudging the horse to a brisk trot, Kristin reached the spot in seconds. The birds scattered at her approach, revealing a man sprawled on the ground.

Logan Hunter appeared to be breathing. But the blood-soaked

flannel shirt that wrapped his arm and the red stain on the earth—which had to be from a gunshot wound—told her he might not live long.

Dropping the reins to keep the horse from bolting, she grabbed the canteen from the saddle, vaulted to the ground, and sank to her knees beside him. She needed to turn him over, stanch the blood any way she could, and get some water down him. She'd tended far worse wounds in the field hospital, but this one could be just as fatal, and here she had nothing to work with.

She shook him gently on his uninjured right side. "Major, can you hear me?"

He groaned and murmured something under his breath. It sounded like "... *Miranda* ... *tthe boys* ..."

"I need you on your side," she said. "I can't turn you alone. You've got to help me."

"What's happened?" He still sounded disoriented but seemed to be coming around.

"You've been shot. Come on." She reached across and hooked her fingers into his belt. He was not fully conscious, but when she braced and began pulling his left side toward her, he helped by pushing with his legs. After a few seconds of effort, she had him on his side, where she could access the wound.

The bullet appeared to have nicked a collateral branch of the brachial artery—if it had hit the main artery, he would have died in minutes. The clumsy knot he'd tied wasn't doing enough to stop the flow. She rewrapped the blood-soaked shirt—folding the body of the garment to layer over the wound and using the sleeves for the knot. She tied it as tightly as she could and twisted the stick to function as a tourniquet. It would have to do until she got him someplace where she could clean and disinfect the wound.

The weight of the canteen told her it was about half full. Raising his head with her knee, she twisted off the lid and gave him all he would take. The water seemed to revive him. He was looking up at her now, his gaze sharp and clear.

"What are the odds that I'd be found by a doctor?" he muttered.

"Don't try to talk," she said. "We've got to get you someplace safe, where I can dress your wound. Can you mount the horse?"

"Given the alternative, I guess I'll have to." He struggled to rise. He was so weak that the effort was excruciating, but with Kristin helping, he managed to clamber onto his feet and raise himself into the saddle. He slumped over the horse's neck as she pulled herself up behind the cantle and wrapped her arms around his waist.

"The old ranch house is a couple of miles from here." He spoke with effort, his strength ebbing. "There's a well with good water. Webb gave me the key."

His mention of Webb touched off an avalanche of questions. But right now, Kristin's only concern was keeping this man alive.

He took the horse at a walk, holding the reins with his right hand. Even then, as Kristin cradled him in her arms, she could sense the pain that shot through his body with every step. A faster, more jarring gait would have been too risky for him.

"Do you know who shot you?" she asked.

He shook his head. "Never saw a soul. Just heard the shot and felt the bullet. When I came home from the war, I thought I was through being a target."

And I believed I was through watching men die, she thought.

"Could it have been an accident?"

He didn't answer. Kristin felt his body slump against hers. Was he unconscious or just weak and tired?

Reaching around him, she steadied the hand that held the reins. Ahead, over his shoulder, she could see the ranch house. Except for the ravages of time and neglect, it was much as she remembered it from her growing-up years, when Tom Petit was alive and his daughters, long gone from here, had been her playmates.

"We're here," she said, and felt him nod. Easing herself off the back of the horse, she led it to the hitching rail in front of the house. Logan Hunter pulled himself upright in the saddle. She caught his weight as he half climbed, half slid to the ground. Blood was oozing from under the shirt that wrapped his wound. She'd loosened and tightened the makeshift tourniquet as needed, but it hadn't helped much.

"Key's in my left hip pocket." His voice trailed off. She reached behind him and found the key as they mounted the porch. Supporting him with one arm, she opened the front door.

On the inside, the house had the look of a place that had stood empty for a long time. The last occupants appeared to have left in a hurry. Was there anything here that she could use?

The sofa in the parlor was probably mouse-infested, but it would give him a place to rest while she searched, starting with the horse.

The saddlebags were empty except for some spare ammunition and a small box of matches. Kristin stowed the matches in her pocket and took the rifle out of its scabbard. If some enemy had shot at Logan meaning to kill him, they could be back.

The canteen, almost empty now, hung by its strap from the saddle horn. But there was a pump at the base of the windmill. Logan had mentioned well water. Gripping the handle, she pumped and prayed with all her strength. Moments later she was rewarded with the sound of water gushing up from below. As it poured out of the tap, she filled the canteen and hurried back into the house.

Her patient had sagged into a corner of the sofa. His eyes were closed, but more water from the canteen, raised to his mouth and splashed on his face, revived him. Kristin left him long enough to do a quick search of the house. Clean linens or kitchen utensils would be a godsend. But the cupboards and closets were empty. She found little more than a dirty-looking mattress on the floor of one of the bedrooms. But the kitchen did have a plain wooden drop-leaf table. With a good scrubbing, it could be put to use.

The hospital where she'd been posted toward the end of the war had made use of the latest devices and procedures—transport by motorized ambulance, anesthetics like nitrous oxide, new methods of disinfecting, like sodium hypochlorite that killed bacteria without burning delicate tissues, and even blood transfusions. Kristin could have used any and all of these to save her patient. But here, in this isolated place, she had nothing.

The outcome here would depend on her own ingenuity and on Logan Hunter's strength and will to live.

The table, newly washed and still damp, was cold against Logan's bare skin. He lay on his side, feeling like a sheep on the butcher's block, with his arm elevated and his booted feet dangling over the end. Whatever happened next was going to hurt like hell. His only consolation was that, one way or another, it was bound to be over soon.

Kristin had removed her white blouse. The simple muslin shift she wore underneath was tucked into her divided riding skirt. The damp fabric outlined her round, firm breasts, the nipples shrunken from the cold water she'd used to splash off the dust. Too bad he was in no condition to appreciate the sight as she bent over him. She was a beautiful woman. He could only hope she was also a skilled doctor.

He'd lent her his pocketknife. She'd sterilized the blade in the fire she'd made with gathered kindling in the kitchen stove. She would use it to probe for the bullet if it hadn't passed through, and for any other needed emergency surgery.

With care, she unwound the makeshift bandage and examined the wound. "We're in luck," she said. "The bullet made a clean exit. It must've been a small caliber weapon. But you've lost a lot of blood, and you're still bleeding. How does your left hand feel?"

"A little numb. But I can move my fingers."

"Good. Now, try lifting your hand from the wrist."

He made the effort and failed. "Damn. It's as limp as a dishrag. What the hell—"

"Don't worry. We'll need to splint it for a few days. But it should heal fine. Blood loss is the big worry now. We'll have to keep using the tourniquet until that artery closes off and the bleeding stops. When that happens, the blood will find another passage— it's the body's way of healing itself. But meanwhile, if you want to survive, you'll need fluids and rest."

She tipped the canteen to his lips, supporting his head as he drank. "Take all you can. How do you feel?"

"Light-headed as hell." He tried to focus his gaze on her as she folded her blouse into a strip with the sleeves at either end. Tying it into a pad above the wound, she used the stick to tighten the makeshift tourniquet. Her image floated over him like a vision. He closed his eyes.

"Have you ever had anything like this done before?" she asked, probably trying to distract him.

He opened his eyes again to watch her. His vision swam from blood loss. "My leg," he replied. "I got hit in the Argonne Forest, the same day we lost Corporal Anderson. The doctors wanted to take it off, but I wouldn't let them. It's ugly, but at least it's still . . . attached." Putting words together was an effort.

"I was in that area, behind the front lines. But it wasn't my medical team who treated you. I'd have remembered."

"And I would certainly have remembered you."

Her beautiful face was the last thing Logan saw before his vision darkened and he floated away.

CHAPTER SIX

Kristin wet the handkerchief she'd found in her pocket with water from the canteen and used it to clean his arm below the wound. The tourniquet would have to be loosened and checked every two hours around the clock until the artery sealed off. Meanwhile, the major could still die from blood loss.

And saving him here would be an uphill battle. He needed bed rest. He needed nourishment. He could get none of that here.

She checked his pulse. It was steady, but he was still unconscious. Kristin needed to wash herself clean at the pump. But she couldn't risk having him wake up alone and disoriented on the table.

She stood gazing down at him. His eyes were closed, his lashes like smudges of soot against his bloodless cheeks. With his powerfully chiseled bones, the slanting scar down his face, and the road map of healed wounds that crisscrossed his bare torso, he could never be called a beautiful man. But Kristin found his looks strangely compelling. He was a battle-scarred warrior.

She trailed a finger down his cheek, feeling the prick of dark stubble that edged his jaw. "Don't you dare quit on me, Logan Hunter," she murmured. "I've done everything I could to save you. Now, damn it, it's up to you to live."

"Gas! Get your masks on!" Logan's body jerked. *He was running, shouting the alarm. His men were dropping around him, screaming and*

choking as the clouds of chlorine poured over the trenches. He smelled it, tasted the burn in his throat . . .

He opened his eyes as the dream dissolved into memory. Kristin was bending over him, her arms holding him down. Her face was freckled with blood. His blood.

"Thank goodness you're awake." The words emerged between breaths. "It was all I could do to keep you from falling off the table."

He exhaled, forcing his body to relax. "Dreaming . . . Did I hurt you?"

"I'm fine. And I understand." She let go of him but stayed close. "I've had bad dreams myself. Do you know where you are?"

"Montana. I got shot. You're a doctor."

"Good." She nodded. "At least your mind is clear. But you've lost a lot of blood. You'll need rest. Sleep would be even better. Here, drink this." She raised his head and tipped the canteen to his lips. The cold water sent a shudder through his body.

"If I help you, can you make it to the sofa?"

"Anything would be better than lying on this table like a side of beef."

"Let's do it. When I sit you up, swing your legs off the table and put your good arm around my shoulders. You'll be weak. You'll need to lean on me."

"I can make it fine."

"I wouldn't bet on that."

With her gripping his right arm, he sat up. The room blurred. Lord, he was as weak as a newborn lamb. But he had to do this.

Stumbling and staggering, he managed to get off the table and make it to the ragged sofa in the parlor. Dr. Kristin Dollarhide was stronger than she looked. He had to lean heavily on her, but she didn't let him fall. Every step shot pain up his shoulder and down his arm, but he'd been wounded before. He knew what to expect.

She eased him onto the cushions and paused to catch her breath. Weak as he was, Logan couldn't help noticing again that, above the waist of her divided riding skirt, she was still clad in her revealing shift. Her white blouse had been sacrificed to bandage his wound. He lowered his gaze. She didn't deserve to have him ogling her.

"How do you feel?" she asked him.

"About how you'd expect." He'd spent his meager strength just getting this far. Even forming words in his head was an effort.

"I need to do some things outside," she said. "Will you be all right alone here for a few minutes?"

"I'll be fine," he said. "In fact, you've done enough. Take the horse and go home. Somebody's bound to come looking for me. Or better yet, you can send help."

"Don't even think about it. You're too weak to be left here alone." She took the canteen and her hat, which she'd left on the back of the sofa. "I'll be close by. Call if you need me."

Her voice faded as she stepped out the door, leaving it open behind her. Questions rose like wisps of phantom smoke in Logan's mind. Who had shot him? How had the woman managed to find him out here? And if she was a Dollarhide, why hadn't she just left him to die?

Questions without answers. They floated away as he closed his eyes.

Outside, Kristin filled her hat with water and held it while the horse drank its fill. Then she tethered the buckskin where it could graze. After that, she combed the yard for every stick and scrap of wood she could find and piled them on the porch. The sun was low in the sky. Before long, the light would be gone.

That done, she stood at the pump and splashed her face, hair, arms, and chest with cold water to wash away the worst of the blood. By the time she'd finished, her teeth were chattering. What she wouldn't give for a blanket or a warm shirt. But the heat from the stove in the kitchen would have to do.

Returning inside with the canteen slung over her shoulder and her arms full of wood, she found Logan asleep on the sofa. He had moved since she'd left him. Now he was leaning against the corner, his head pillowed on the arm in what looked like an awkward position. Dropping everything, she hurried to check him.

His breathing was regular and his pulse was steady, if not as strong as it could be. The color of his left arm was healthy, which hopefully meant that the blood was circulating. But the hours ahead would be critical.

The fire in the stove had burned down to coals. Kristin stirred them with the poker and added chunks of wood until she had a crackling blaze.

Only as the warmth began to spread into the parlor did she realize how tired she was. Her legs and body ached as if she'd been carrying a heavy load.

Logan groaned, stirred, and settled again. Whether she was tired or not, it would be up to her to see that he didn't roll off the sofa or put weight on his wound. Seating herself, she lifted his head and maneuvered it gently into her lap.

He opened his eyes, gazing up at her in the last of the fading light. His lips moved. She hushed him with a fingertip. "Don't try to talk," she said. "Just rest. We'll both rest."

He gave a slight shake of his head. "I'm trying to remember what happened. How did you find me?"

"I found your horse. When I saw the blood on his side, I knew somebody was hurt. Then I saw the birds."

"You could've left me for dead. Why didn't you?"

"I'm a doctor. It was my responsibility to do what I could."

"Even if you're a Dollarhide?"

"My name has nothing to do with anything."

"And you don't know who shot me?"

"I don't—" Kristin broke off at the sound of horses outside. The beam of a flashlight shone through the curtainless front window. An instant later there was a pounding on the front door.

"Kristin, are you in there?" The voice was Blake's.

"Yes. The door's unlocked. Come on in."

The door opened. Blake, holding the flashlight in one hand, strode into the room. The beam found the pair on the sofa. "What in hell's name—" he sputtered.

"It's all right," she said. "This man's been shot. I found him after my mare bolted. That's his horse outside."

Blake exhaled. "Thank heaven you're all right, Kristin. When the mare came home on the wagon road, I was afraid I'd find you hurt somewhere, or worse. That's why I came in the buggy. I even brought Mother's old medical kit."

"Oh—Blake, you're a godsend! Now I can get this man somewhere safe."

Logan raised his head. When he spoke, the irony in his voice was subtle as a shift in the night breeze, but it was there. "I don't think we've met. I'm Logan Hunter—Major Hunter, not that it counts for much anymore."

"You must be the Calder cousin I've been hearing about." Blake's tone was courteous but cold.

"And you're Blake Dollarhide. If what Webb tells me is to be believed, you're the devil incarnate. But I like to judge people for myself. Please excuse me if I don't get up."

Blake's gaze had shifted to Kristin. "Good Lord, what happened to your blouse? You look indecent!"

"The major is wearing my blouse as a bandage. As for my looking indecent—" She shrugged. "When someone's losing blood, modesty doesn't count for much."

"Here." Blake stripped off his twill jacket and tossed it to her. "At least you'll be warmer."

"Thank you." She eased Logan's head off her lap and helped him sit up before slipping on the jacket and buttoning it down the front. "We could use a blanket if there's one in the buggy. And I'll need the medical bag."

Blake nodded and disappeared outside without another word.

"Did I get you in trouble?" Logan asked.

"He's surprised, that's all. We were apart for years, but he still thinks he should play the big brother. I suspect he doesn't know quite what to make of me."

"I can sympathize. I don't know what to make of you either."

"You don't have to make anything of me. I'm your doctor, no different from a man."

Logan raised an eyebrow. "Some might argue that. But the doctor I'm looking at is definitely not a man."

"As a doctor in combat, I've done everything a man would do.

And no wounded soldier ever refused treatment because I was a woman. As for you, Major—"

She broke off, her argument forgotten as the sound of men's voices, loud and getting louder, rumbled through the closed door.

The door burst open as if it had been kicked. Webb Calder strode across the threshold, his face a mask of fury. His glare swept the room.

"What in hell's name is going on here?" he growled.

"As you can see, Webb, I've been shot." Logan spoke calmly. "The doctor found me and stopped the bleeding. I owe her my life, so have a care how you speak to her."

Webb turned to Kristin. "So you're the woman doctor I've been hearing about. *Doctor* Dollarhide." His tone was mocking. "I remember you from years ago. Figured you'd have a husband and a passel of kids by now."

"I remember you, too, Mr. Calder," Kristin said. "It's been a long time."

Webb nodded, his frown deepening. "Well, you can pack up and go with your brother, lady. The major here will be riding home with me. He'll have a day to rest up before we go into Miles City to buy this ranch."

Kristin drew herself up to face him. She was tall for a woman, but he loomed over her. "Major Hunter is my patient," she said. "Riding a horse could start him bleeding again. It could even kill him. And he won't be fit to go anywhere on Monday. He's lost too much blood. He needs to rest, and he needs to be where a doctor can check on him."

Webb muttered a string of curses that ended abruptly as Blake walked in carrying a woolen blanket and the familiar black leather satchel. As Blake tossed Logan the blanket and handed the satchel to Kristin, Webb turned on him.

"This mess stinks," he said. "And it's got your hands all over it, Dollarhide. I'm not a fool. I know you tried to buy this place— and that the bank told you it was reserved for the major, here. So let me tell you what you did. You knew he'd likely be out here, looking the place over. So you followed him and shot him."

"Now just a minute, Webb!" Blake had gone white around the

mouth, a sign that he was struggling to control his rage. "First of all, that's a goddamned lie. Second, I was on the range all day. My men can vouch for that. So can my son."

"That's your story," Webb said. "Mine is that after you shot him, and he didn't die, you got your sister to see that he didn't make it to the bank, so you could sneak in and buy the place for yourself. For all I know, she was in on this with you all along. Prove I'm wrong."

"That's the biggest pile of bullshit I've ever heard!" Blake said.

"Is it? Unless you can prove you didn't shoot this man, I'm taking my story to the sheriff."

"You lying sonofabitch!" Blake lunged at him. Webb sidestepped and raised his fists.

"Stop it!" Kristin sprang between them, her hands on her brother's chest. "Stop it right now!"

Blake pushed her out of the way. "You've had this coming for years, Webb! Now you've crossed the line! I'm going to teach you a lesson you'll never—"

"Gentlemen!" Logan's commanding voice cut through the tension. "Stop acting like schoolboys! Put your hands down."

As if stunned by his forceful manner, the two backed off and stood glaring at each other. Even Kristin was startled, but she shouldn't have been, she reminded herself. As an army officer, Logan had years of experience handling men in emotional situations.

"That's better," Logan said. "Now we can talk. I don't know who shot me. I'd dismounted to look at something on the ground, and the bullet came out of nowhere. When I couldn't get back on the horse, I walked until I passed out. After the doctor found me, she could've left me for dead. I'm alive because she didn't."

"Maybe *she* was the one who shot you. Did you ever think of that? Why else would the lady *doctor*—" Webb's voice oozed sarcasm. "Why else would she be wandering around out here alone?"

"I was taking a shortcut home," Kristin said. "My mare shied at some birds and threw me. The rifle I had was slung on the saddle. I couldn't have shot the major."

Webb snorted. "Unless you already had."

"The mare came home with the rifle in the scabbard," Webb said. "I checked the gun before I moved it into the buggy to come back here. I'll swear an oath that there were no missing bullets. Anyway, why would my sister save the life of a man she'd shot? Your story's full of holes, Webb. I don't know who shot the major, but it had nothing to do with us."

"We're wasting time," Kristin said. "We need to get this man into the buggy and get him home where he can rest and I can treat the wound properly."

"Not so fast." Webb had moved to block the door. He hadn't drawn the pistol he was wearing, but its presence was a threat. "Nobody's going anywhere until I get some satisfaction. Blake, I still doubt your story. But I'll be willing to forget the matter on one condition."

Blake didn't respond. A muscle twitched in his cheek. It was all he could do to keep his temper in check.

"Go on." Pain creased Logan's features. Kristin saw it and heard it in his voice. While the two men argued, she opened Sarah's bag. Among other useful items, she found a bundle of clean wrapping strips and a vial of laudanum. Taking the spoon she found, she gave him enough to ease his pain and make him drowsy.

Webb was making his demands clear. "If my cousin still intends to buy this ranch, I want your promise, Blake, that you won't step in ahead of him or interfere in any other way. If you're as innocent as you say, that will be proof enough for me."

"And if your cousin doesn't want to buy the ranch?"

Webb shrugged. "Then it's anybody's game. Agreed?" Webb extended his hand to seal the promise.

Fury smoldered in Blake's eyes, but he accepted the handshake.

"Fine." Kristin moved back to Logan's side and began wrapping him in the blanket for the move to the buggy. "Now let us get the major back to our house. We've got a spare room, and a closetful of medical supplies that my mother left. He'll get the best possible care."

"No." Webb stood rooted in place, refusing to move. His hand rested lightly on the ivory grip of his pistol.

"Please, he needs care. I know he's your relative. If you have any regard for him at all—"

"Of course I do. He's my own flesh and blood. But I won't have him going to your place, where you can do anything you want with him and fill his head with a lot of lies. We'll take him to the Homestead in your buggy. If you're so all-fired concerned about his welfare, you're welcome to come inside and stay till he's stronger. Then somebody can see you home."

Clearly, Webb wasn't going to back off. And Logan's life was still in danger. The longer the delay, the more critical his condition would become. She needed to get him somewhere safe and clean and warm, where she could take care of him—even if it was the Calder mansion.

She gave her brother a pleading look. "Can you drive us there, Blake? Then you can take the buggy home. Please, a man's life is at stake. We don't have time for a standoff between you and Webb."

Seething, Blake gave her a grim nod. With the tension between the two men as volatile as gunpowder, Kristin knew that it was up to her to take charge.

"I need to tend to the major's tourniquet," she said. "I'll sit with him in the back of the buggy while Blake drives. Webb, you take the horses back to your house and meet us there. Have a bed ready and also some hot water and plenty of towels."

Logan was hovering on the edge of laudanum-induced sleep. Kristin used the wrapping strips to make a sling, looping the cloth behind his neck and under his right arm to hold everything in place. Then she bundled his upper body in the blanket. "Help me get him to the buggy," she ordered. "Now hurry!"

Mason Dollarhide studied the woman who sat across the room in the brocade-covered chair that had always reminded him of a throne. Although they'd exchanged occasional letters, he hadn't set eyes on his mother since that night twelve years ago when she'd ordered him onto the train to save him from a forced marriage to a pregnant immigrant girl.

Amelia Hollister Dollarhide was still the queen of her ranch kingdom. But time's bitter gifts had hardened her nature—the husband whose ambition had ended their marriage, the son who'd fled in disgrace, the lover who'd wearied of being her lackey. Now she was alone except for her dogs and her paid employees—a solitary monument to her own iron will.

"As I recall, Mason, I told you not to come home without a suitable bride," she said. "Surely, it couldn't have been that difficult."

Mason shrugged. In all these years, nothing had changed. His mother wanted a daughter-in-law with money, manners, family connections, and a spotless reputation. The trouble was that Mason's taste had never run to the kind of girl who'd keep her legs crossed until she had a ring on her finger. Besides, with so many ladies willing to fall into his bed, why should he tie himself to just one?

"I met your bastard the other day," Amelia said. "He looks like a Dollarhide. Nobody would guess he was yours—not until they noticed his green eyes."

"It doesn't matter," Mason said. "For all I know, there could be more of your grandchildren out there in the world. I never stuck around long enough to meet any of them. But chances are that I planted my seed in some fertile ground."

"Oh, stop it!" To Mason's amusement, she shuddered. He enjoyed needling her. It gave him a feeling of power over the woman who'd exercised so much control over his early life.

She picked up the crystal glass from a side table and sipped the wine the butler had poured for her. Her aging hand still wore the emerald ring Blake remembered.

"So what brings you home after all this time?" she asked. "It couldn't be love."

Mason lit a Cuban cigar, inhaled the mellow flavor, and blew the smoke out into the room. "Maybe I came back to help you manage my inheritance. You're not getting any younger, Mother. Maybe it's time to step back and enjoy your golden years. You could take up something like cross-stitch or china painting."

"You're joking!" She punctuated the words with a harsh laugh. "No, tell me why you're really here. If it's a loan you're about to ask for—"

"Now that's a low blow, Mother. I'm not asking you for a thing. In fact, I've done quite well for myself. What I've come for is to offer you a chance to *make* money. And you won't have to lift a finger. All it involves is the use of the barn for storage, and for you to sleep through any noises you might hear in the night."

"And there's money in that?"

"More money than you or I ever dreamed of."

She raised her empty glass for another splash of wine, then sent the elderly butler out of the room. "Tell me more," she said.

Kristin had visited the Calder mansion as a little girl, when her mother had been friends with Benteen Calder's wife, Lorna. At the time, the large, white house had seemed as elegant as a fairy-tale palace. Now that she had seen Paris, London, and New York City, the place appeared no more than ordinary. But tonight it could have been Versailles, and she would have scarcely given it a glance. All her attention was fixed on the man who lay in the bed next to her chair, his rugged face as pale as the pillow that cradled his head.

Dosed with laudanum, Logan Hunter slept deeply. The long ride in the buggy, over rough roads, had been hard on him. To cushion the jarring, Kristin had cradled him in her arms. Even so, by the time Blake left them at the Calder home, the bandage on Logan's wound had been oozing blood.

After undressing him and giving him more water, Kristin had broken into the Calders' store of medical supplies to cleanse the wound and apply a fresh tourniquet. Now she watched him sleep, hoping with every breath that his body would be strong enough to recover.

Webb stood in the doorway of the guest room, an anxious look on his face. Did he care about his distant cousin, or did he just want to make sure the Dollarhides didn't buy the ranch property?

But that wasn't a fair question, Kristin reminded herself. Like most men, Webb Calder tended to put his own interests first. But he had a genuine heart. Hanna had told her the story of how Webb had fallen in love with Lillian, the beautiful wife of a middle-aged immigrant farmer. After her husband's death, Webb had married her and fathered their son, only to lose her to a bullet in a senseless ambush. Webb had never stopped mourning his only love.

Webb walked into the room to stand by the bed. "How is he?" he asked.

"No worse than before," Kristin said. "But his condition will be touch and go for the next few hours. If he were in a modern hospital, he could get a blood transfusion. But there's no way to do that here."

"I'm his closest relative. Could he use some of my blood?"

"It's generous of you to offer, Webb. But it's a lot more complicated than that."

"Logan told me you were in the war," he said.

"I was. And tonight I feel as if I'm still in the war. Why can't you men settle things peacefully?"

"Sometimes we do. But you soon learn that if you want to keep what's yours, whether it's a piece of land or a horse or a woman, you've got to be ready to fight for it." He gazed down at Logan's sleeping face. "He's a decent man, but stubborn as hell. Maybe too stubborn for his own good. Who do you think shot him?"

"I have no idea. I only know that it wasn't me. And it wasn't my brother. Maybe it was an accident. A bullet that misses its target, with nothing to stop it, can go a long way and still be lethal."

"Hmph! That sounds mighty damned far-fetched to me." Webb shook his head. "Are you hungry? I can have the cook bring you up some soup."

"I'm too anxious to eat. But if you can ask your cook to leave some soup in the kitchen, I'll feed it to Logan when he wakes up." *If he wakes up.* She forced a smile. "He's going to need nourishment. A hearty soup will be just the thing—and beef tea, if she knows how to make it."

"Is there anything else you need?" He glanced down at her

skirt. "You've got blood on you. Some of my wife's old clothes are stored in that wardrobe over there. She was about your size before our son was born."

"I'll be fine. If all goes as hoped, Logan will be feeling better in the morning, and I'll be free to go home." Blood or no blood, she wouldn't feel comfortable wearing Webb's late wife's clothes.

"I'll leave you then," he said. "My room is three doors down the hall. If you need anything, wake me."

"I will." She suppressed the polite *thank you* that sprang without thought to her lips. She had nothing to thank him for. She'd been brought here practically by force. If anything, he should be thanking *her*.

After he'd left, she checked Logan's pulse once more. It was unchanged, steady but weak, like an engine running low on fuel. But the color in his left hand was healthy. At least the arm was getting enough blood.

Restless, she stood, stretched her cramped legs, and crossed the room to the window. When the sash yielded to her fingers, she tugged it all the way up, opening the stuffy room to the cool night breeze. The fresh air would be good for Logan, and for her as well.

Leaning past the windowsill, she breathed in the aromas of spring grass, cattle and horses, and the mellow odor of tobacco smoke rising from the bunkhouse across the yard. In her time away from Blue Moon, one of the things she'd missed most, besides her family, was the scent of Montana air. At least that hadn't changed—except that if she were at home, her senses would also be basking in the fragrance of pine.

The moon, rising over the eastern mountains, flooded the landscape with silver-blue light. From the upstairs window where she stood, she could see the long driveway that lay like a pale ribbon from the house to the ranch gate, which was literally miles away, too far to see from here. The homes of the longtime ranch hands and their families were clustered in the distance, like a small town, complete with a school and a store. The barns, sheds, and corrals covered acres, and the pastures, dotted with thousands of white-faced Hereford cattle, spread as far as the eye could see.

The Triple C wasn't just a ranch. It was a kingdom. And Webb Calder was king.

Raising a hand, she tried to rake her fingers through her tangled hair. She'd done her best to splash it clean at the ranch house pump, but she could feel the knots and snarls and the specks of dried blood that she'd missed. She probably looked ghastly. But what did it matter? She was a doctor doing her job.

The night breeze was getting chilly. Kristin closed the window and walked back to the bed to check on her patient.

Leaning over him to check his wound, she gasped. Logan's eyes were open. Wide with confusion, they gazed up at her.

"Miranda . . . where the devil am I?" he muttered.

CHAPTER SEVEN

As LOGAN'S VISION CLEARED, THE FEATURES OF THE WOMAN LOOK-ing down at him swam into focus—the eyes etched with weariness, the hair falling in tangles around a strong, beautiful face, cast into light and shadow by the bedside lamp.

For a fleeting moment he'd imagined she was his wife. But no, Miranda had been blond with blue eyes and a face like a china doll's. This woman was dark, with a fierceness that recalled the sculpted goddesses he'd seen in Europe's museums.

Strange that he could remember that, and nothing about where he was or why he felt so weak. He raised his head and struggled to sit up but fell back onto the pillow.

"Lie still," she said. "In case you don't remember, you were shot. You lost a lot of blood. That's why you're weak."

"You're the doctor." The memory was coming back, like bits of a torn poster blown by the wind.

"That's right. I gave you some laudanum to help you rest. And after we put you in bed, I took the tourniquet off and replaced it with a dressing. How does your shoulder feel now?"

He shifted his arm, which was supported by a sling. He was rewarded by a jab of pain. Someone had put a clean flannel shirt on him, leaving it unbuttoned to expose the dressing. "It hurts," he said. "But I'll pass on more laudanum, thanks. I'd rather stay awake."

"What about your hand? Can you move it?"

He flexed and extended his fingers, but still couldn't raise the hand above his splinted wrist.

"Here. Drink this." She poured water from a porcelain pitcher into a glass. Raising his head, she tilted the glass to let him take careful sips. "Since we don't have any way to give you intravenous fluids, you'll need to drink a lot. But only a little at a time for now. We need to make sure it stays down."

Logan lay back on the pillow. His eyes scanned the shadowy room from the damask-papered walls to the brass chandelier hanging from the high ceiling. The place looked vaguely familiar. "Where am I?" he asked again.

"You're in the Calder house. Webb insisted that you be brought here in my brother's buggy. Otherwise, you'd have gone home with me."

"But you're a Dollarhide. Your family hates him—and me."

"I'm a doctor first and a Dollarhide second. I agreed to stay until you were out of danger."

"And Webb?"

"Let's just say he invited me to be his guest. He looked in on you earlier. But I think he's gone to bed."

Logan's memory was clearing. He recognized the room as the one he'd stayed in as Webb's guest. Now he felt more like a prisoner, too weak to even get out of bed. Damn, but he hated being so helpless. "And you still don't know how I got shot?" he asked.

"Nobody seems to know. I can't help thinking it was an accident. Somebody hunting, maybe. Webb has different ideas, but you can ask him tomorrow." She set the glass on the table. "You need nourishment. There's soup in the kitchen. I'll warm a little and bring it to you." She gave him a stern look. "Don't you dare try to get up."

"Lady, I couldn't get up if I had to."

"I'm a doctor, not a lady. You may call me Kristin. But I meant what I said. Rest. Don't move until I get back."

She walked out through the open doorway. Logan lay still, listening to the swift cadence of her footsteps, retreating down the hall to the landing. As silence fell around him once more, he closed his eyes.

Downstairs in the kitchen, Kristin turned on the light and found the vegetable beef soup in a covered saucepan, sitting on the counter. It had cooled enough for the fat to congeal and form a layer on top. The soup would need to be heated.

The massive iron stove was barely warm to the touch. Kristin lifted away a lid on the cooktop and laid a few sticks of kindling on the coals beneath. As the kindling began to crackle and blaze, she replaced the lid and set the pan of soup on top.

Now she'd need a spoon to stir it and a bowl to take it upstairs. She was rummaging through the cabinets when she heard a deep voice behind her.

"Can I help you find something, Kristin?"

Her nerves jumped. Webb stood behind her, a brown woolen robe wrapped over his pajamas. He gave her a smile. "Sorry, didn't mean to startle you. I heard a noise in the kitchen and thought it might be you. How is Logan?"

"Awake and talking, but weak. I'm heating some soup for him. But I need a bowl and a spoon."

"That's an easy request." He opened a drawer and a cupboard and handed her what she needed. "There you are. Can I get you anything else? You must be hungry, too. There's plenty of soup. I'll keep you company while you eat."

"Thanks, but that can wait. I'll need to take the soup upstairs to Logan as soon as it gets warm enough." She used the spoon to stir the soup. It was thick and still cool.

Webb had made no move to leave her side. "I'll tell you what, then," he said. "How about sharing a drink with me. I've got a bottle of good single malt Scotch in the cupboard. There should be just enough time to enjoy a few sips while the soup gets warm."

Kristin hesitated, knowing she should refuse. But she'd had an exhausting day, and the pleasant burn of alcohol sliding down her throat would do wonders to calm her frayed nerves.

"You're aware that liquor is illegal now, aren't you?" She stirred the soup, which was barely lukewarm.

"Yes, I know. That makes it taste even better." He laughed as he opened a cabinet and took out a half-empty bottle and two glasses.

"Just a taste," she said. "I can't climb the stairs with a bowl of soup if I'm tipsy."

He poured her more than she'd asked for, handed her the glass, then poured some for himself. Standing by the stove, she sipped slowly, keeping an eye on the pan of soup.

"I know you're here for a worrisome reason," he said. "But I'm grateful for the chance to get to know you. Blue Moon hasn't had its own doctor since Simon Bardolph passed away in that awful accident years ago. You'll be a great asset to the community—and I hope I can count on your help here at the ranch from time to time."

"Of course you can. It's my job."

"And I'm aware that you don't work for nothing. I plan to pay you a generous fee for saving my cousin and staying to take care of him."

Kristin raised an eyebrow. "Even though I was practically shanghaied into coming here?"

"You'll get extra for that." Webb chuckled. He had an infectious laugh, she thought. And he was a handsome man, wealthy as Midas and charming, when he chose to be. It was a wonder some woman hadn't snatched him up after his wife passed away.

She could smell the soup getting warm. She slid the pan off the fire to let it simmer while she finished her drink. Pride tempted her to refuse payment for her services. But that would be foolish. She wasn't working on salary for the U.S. Government anymore, and setting up her practice wasn't going to be cheap. Besides, it wasn't as if he and Logan were poor men.

"You're a lovely woman, Kristin." He studied her in the stark light of the electric fixture that hung from the ceiling. "I can imagine you in a beautiful scarlet ball gown with your hair pinned up and rubies dangling from your ears. You'd be stunning."

Kristin managed an awkward laugh. "All I can say is, you've got a vivid imagination, Mr. Calder. Or maybe it's just the whiskey talking."

"Please, call me Webb, and I can assure you I'm not drunk. Why is it you haven't married? Surely you've been courted."

"Courtship takes time. And I've never had much of that to spare—or found a man worth my trouble. You might say I'm married to my career." Unsettled by his flattery, Kristin put down her empty glass, ladled some warm soup into the bowl, and added the spoon. "I need to get back upstairs," she said. "Oh—a napkin would be helpful."

"Here you are." He took a folded cloth out of a basket on the counter. "Since the stove's still hot, do you think our patient would like some coffee? I could brew some and bring it up to the room."

"That sounds fine. It should make him more alert and help get more fluids in him. But take your time. I want him to have the soup first." She gave him a tired smile. "As long as you're making coffee, I could use a cup myself."

"No trouble. I'll make an extra."

Kristin placed the bowl, spoon, and napkin on a tray and turned to leave the kitchen. He stepped into her path, his gaze holding her a reluctant captive.

"Kristin, you're exhausted. You need to get some rest. The room next door has a bed you could use. I'd be willing to give Logan the soup and sit with him for an hour or two."

She shook her head and stepped back. "Thank you for the kind offer, Webb, but Logan isn't out of danger. As his doctor, I need to stay and check his vitals in case he shows any signs of getting worse. I'll be fine. I've been in a war, remember? I'm accustomed to long nights."

"I understand." He nodded. "Sometime, when you've got time to talk, I'd like to hear the stories of your war experiences."

"You wouldn't want to hear my stories, Webb. And I wouldn't enjoy telling them. Some memories should be buried and forgotten. That's what I'm trying to do."

Turning away before he could keep her longer, she hurried back to the stairs. With light filtering down from the hallway above, it was easy enough to see her way without stumbling.

Had Webb been flirting with her? If so, it was the last thing she'd expected. She was a member of the family he hated. And after her harrowing day, she looked like a red-eyed, frowzy, blood-stained walking nightmare.

Experience had taught her that a man didn't say the kind of things she'd heard without some purpose in mind. But Webb Calder? That didn't make sense. Maybe her exhausted mind had read too much into their conversation.

She found Logan sitting up in bed against her orders to lie still. She was tempted to scold him, but his color looked all right, and the dressing on the wound appeared to have stayed in place.

"I hope you're hungry," she said.

He cast her a defiant look. "I could be—as long as you don't plan on spoon-feeding me. I'm not as helpless as you seem to think I am."

"Be my guest." She laid the tray across his lap. He took the spoon with an unsteady hand, dipped it in the soup, and managed to get it to his mouth. "How does it taste?" she asked.

"Good. My compliments to Webb's cook." He took another spoonful, then more, making a visible effort not to spill.

"Webb will be bringing up some coffee," she said.

"Good. I hope he remembers that I like it black and hot." The spoon paused as he studied her. His gaze narrowed. "You look like you've been dragged across the prairie behind a galloping horse. Have you been here with me the whole time?"

"Yes. It's my job."

"But you didn't have to stay here. You could've gone home with your brother and left me to take my chances."

"I couldn't do that. You'd lost too much blood. Somebody had to watch you and check the tourniquet. And what if you'd needed more laudanum for the pain? I couldn't depend on anyone else to know how much to give you. You could have died."

"I've survived worse."

"But you can only die once. I couldn't let it be on my watch."

His mouth twitched in a wry half smile. "Sometimes I think that would be no great loss. My family is gone. There's no one left to

mourn me—except Webb, who mostly seems intent on my own-
ing that ranch property. Even if I were to die, he could set himself
up as my next of kin and claim everything I own."

They stared at each other as the same possibility struck them
both. "Good Lord, you don't think—" he began.

"No. Of course not. Webb may be ruthless, but I can't imagine
he'd commit murder. He's got too much to lose. Besides, according to my brother, Webb is an expert shot. If he'd wanted to kill
you, you'd be dead."

"Now there's a comforting thought." Logan finished the soup,
laid the spoon on the tray, and touched the napkin to his mouth.
"That was good. I'm feeling stronger already."

"Would you like more? There's plenty left in the kitchen."

"Thanks, but that's enough soup for now. I'll wait for the coffee
if Webb's still planning to bring some."

As if on cue, Webb stepped through the open doorway with
two mugs in his hands. Kristin moved the tray with the empty
bowl to the nightstand.

"Black for you." Webb handed Logan the blue mug. "And I assumed the lady would want cream and sugar." He handed the
white mug to Kristin. She took it, even though, while serving in
war zones, she'd learned to like it black, the way the soldiers
drank it.

"Thank you, Webb." She sipped the brew, which was so sweet
she could barely swallow it.

"Anything to please a lady." Webb's hand brushed her shoulder. "If you could use a break, I need to talk with your patient—
not long, let's say, about fifteen minutes."

"Of course. A breath of fresh air would do me good."

She set her mug on the tray, then carried the tray down the
stairs. This time Webb had turned on the light. Now she noticed
the nearly life-sized portrait of his late wife which hung on the
wall in an ornate gilded frame. Lillian Reisner Calder had been a
stunning woman. Dressed here in creamy brocade with an emerald necklace setting off her rich auburn curls, she was as regal as
a queen—in spite of having come to Webb straight from an immigrant farmer's shack.

Her death must have crushed him. But almost ten years had passed since the tragedy. And Kristin's shoulder still tingled from his not-quite-casual touch. She was experienced enough to sense when a man was interested in her. And whether for a place at his side or a night's romp between the sheets, Webb was interested.

She left the tray in the kitchen. Still carrying the coffee, she crossed the entry hall and walked out the front door, onto the porch. The night air was just chilly enough to be refreshing. She could hear the distant lowing of cattle and the cry of a barn owl. The windows in the bunkhouse had gone dark, but the moon, drifting among the clouds, flooded the yard with its pale light.

What if Webb had serious intentions? Would she want this life of security, luxury, and power—and the chance to make peace between their families? Would she want *him*?

But this was no time for such imaginings. For now, all she could do was give the situation time to run its course. During the war and afterward, at the military hospital, she had dreamed of coming home to Montana and setting up her practice. If she failed to make that dream come true, she would never forgive herself.

Tomorrow, if Logan continued to improve, she would ask—or demand if necessary—to be delivered home. On Monday she would start work on the house she'd rented. She'd be too busy to think about Webb Calder or any other man.

She took a sip of the coffee Webb had given her. Now that it had cooled, its sweetness was more revolting than ever. Reaching past the edge of the porch, she emptied the cup on the roots of Lorna Calder's roses.

"You're looking better," Webb observed. "I take it you're going to live."

"I've had a good doctor." Logan sipped the strong, black coffee.

"You have. It's hard to believe someone so beautiful could be so competent. So much education—when all a woman with her looks needs to do is find a good husband."

"Beauty doesn't rule out ability. Women doctors were rare in the war, but I saw plenty of pretty nurses." Logan had seen those nurses die, too. They'd been as brave as the men they cared for. But he didn't want to veer into that subject.

Webb settled into the chair next to the bed. "Will you be strong enough to take a car into Miles City with me on Monday? That's assuming you still want to buy that ranch."

"That remains to be seen, on both counts." Logan handed the empty mug to Webb, who set it on the side table.

"I understand. You came here to settle down, and the next thing you know, some bastard is shooting at you. I wouldn't blame you if you packed up and headed back to Texas—but of course I'm hoping you won't. Working together, you and I could accomplish some great things—like driving the Dollarhides, with their noisy sawmill, out of business. Trust me, you won't want to raise horses with that racket going on."

"I'll admit I like the property. It's perfect for my needs. But I didn't come here to fight a war, Webb. I got my fill of that overseas. All I want is to be left in peace."

"And with my backing, that's possible. We just need to settle a few scores first. After that, once people accept you as a Calder, they won't take a step out of line—and that includes Blake Dollarhide." Webb leaned closer to the bed. "You met that sonofabitch at the ranch, after you got shot. I'd still bet good money that he was responsible. He claimed to be working cattle all day, but he could've ordered one of his men to do it—maybe not to kill you, but to give you a good scare. And to hear you talk now, I'd say that's just what he's managed to do."

Logan felt the anger rising in his body. He welcomed its strengthening heat. "I don't scare easily, Webb, and I've got the scars to prove it. If I decide to pass on that parcel, it won't be out of fear. It'll be because I want to check out something else—something without so many complications attached."

Webb rose to his feet. "Damn it, every place has complications. You can pick land around Miles City or Missoula, or anyplace you want. There'll always be somebody else wanting it, or wanting to control it, or somebody who just plain doesn't like your being there. But one thing you won't have is blood kin to support you when you need help. You'll only have that here. Think on it."

Only as Webb turned to leave did the two men see Kristin standing in the open doorway. Logan couldn't help wondering how much she'd heard, or whether it mattered to her.

"You told me fifteen minutes, Webb," she said. "Have I come back too soon?"

"Not at all, my dear," Webb said. "I was just leaving. You can have your patient back. He seems to be doing better."

"I'll be the judge of that." She swept a tendril of hair from her fatigue-shadowed face. "He'll still need plenty of rest. But if he's doing better in the morning, I'll be ready for a ride home."

"I'll keep that in mind," Webb said.

"But if you don't get some sleep," Logan added, "you'll be the patient by tomorrow. Go to bed, Kristin. I'll be fine."

"Maybe later." She settled onto the edge of the chair. "You're a stubborn man. I don't want you trying to get up. You could get light-headed, fall, and reopen your wound. Then we'd be right back where we started."

"Is there anything else you need?" Webb asked Logan.

"Not right now. You might as well go back to bed, Webb. I'm in capable hands."

"Fine. I'll see you in the morning. Sleep on what I told you." He ambled out of the room and down the hallway. His bedroom door opened and closed with a faint click.

Logan sank back against the pillow. Kristin studied him with a knowing expression, as if waiting for him to speak.

"So how much of that conversation did you hear?" he asked her.

"Enough. But none of it surprised me. I know that Webb hates my brother and would do anything to ruin him. What I don't know is where you stand."

Logan took a slow breath, measuring his words. "Where would you stand if you were me, Kristin?"

"Why should it matter? You'll do whatever suits your purpose. It's none of my business."

"That's where you're wrong," he said. "I'm asking because I respect your opinion. And because you know the situation and the people involved. What would you do if you were me?"

She answered without hesitation. "I would pack my bags, load my auto, and drive to someplace where I'd never have to hear the name Calder or Dollarhide again."

Her jaw tightened as she finished speaking. Her eyes glimmered with anger—or could it be tears?

"Can you tell me why?" he asked.

"Because Webb will use you," she said. "He'll get you in his debt and then expect you to do anything he wants. If you refuse, he'll find a way to make you sorry. All my brother wants to do is make a living. But you'll be expected to stop him—cut off the road, cut off the water . . ." She shook her head. "Blake is a good man, but believe me, you don't want him as your enemy. You think you can be neutral—treat both sides the same. But you can't. If you buy that land, you'll be forced to choose, and if you don't choose Webb, heaven help you."

Logan couldn't help feeling touched by the passion in her voice. But she was advocating for her brother, he reminded himself. If he decided not to buy the ranch, it would be Blake Dollarhide's for the taking.

"One more question," he said. "Webb mentioned the racket that the sawmill would make when it starts up. He said that folks could hear it all the way into Blue Moon, and that it would spook the horses I'm planning to raise. Is that true?"

"I grew up listening to that saw," Kristin said. "It's loud if you're close, but the sound barely carries as far as the main road. As for horses, we have them on the Dollarhide Ranch. Cattle, too. They've always done fine." She sighed. "Maybe I should have lied and told you that the noise makes livestock crazy. That would give you one more reason not to buy the place—or maybe to buy it and shut the mill down. I'm sure that was what Webb had in mind."

"Either way, I appreciate your honesty," he said. "You've given me a lot to think about."

She stifled a yawn. "Sorry, I'm getting sleepy. I guess I should've drunk that coffee Webb brought me. It was so sweet that I poured it out."

"You've got to get some rest," he said. "Go on in the other room. I'll be fine."

"You know better than to suggest that. You're still weak, and having no way to take your blood pressure, I can only guess how low it might be. And I'll need to check your wound. If anything were to go wrong, I'd never forgive myself."

"Then I have another suggestion. If you don't like it, feel free to slap my face. This bed is wide enough for two people. If I shift over a few inches, there'll be room for you to stretch out next to me. I swear my intentions are honorable—and even if they weren't, I'm in no condition to carry them out."

Logan had expected a ladylike rebuke. Instead she laughed. "Believe me, it wouldn't be the first time. In a hospital tent, with shells exploding outside and wounded soldiers to tend, if you get a chance to close your eyes for a few minutes, you'll lie down anywhere, next to anybody."

He shifted toward the edge to give her room and smoothed the quilt while she walked around the bed and kicked off her boots. "So I shouldn't feel flattered," he joked.

"Hush. I'll turn off the lamp."

In the darkness, she slipped off her brother's twill jacket. Clad in her shift and riding skirt, she lay down on top of the quilt with her back toward him and the coverlet pulled over her body. "Don't worry, I don't snore," she said.

"I wouldn't care if you did. You saved my life, Kristin. I wouldn't be here if you hadn't found me. I want you to know how much I appreciate it."

"I told you, it's my job," she muttered. "Now go to sleep."

Logan slid lower in the bed and lay still, listening to the gentle cadence of her breathing. Even chastely separated by the quilt that covered him, he felt the urge to pull her close and spoon her warm body against his. He held himself in check. He wanted her to stay. He wanted her to trust him.

He'd almost forgotten how it felt to lie next to a woman. Unlike some of his friends, he'd been true to his wife while he was overseas. He'd wanted nothing more than to come home and spend his nights making love to her. He'd wanted to wake up to their laughing children and share an early breakfast with his aging parents. Coming home to find them all dead had been a hundred times worse than anything he'd endured in the war. It had crushed the life out of his soul, leaving him empty.

So why, when he had nothing left to lose, was he dragging his feet at the prospect of a new challenge? Building his ranch on the land he'd found wouldn't be easy. He'd be dealing with a troublesome neighbor, a controlling relative, and a blood feud that was not of his making. He'd also be facing bad weather, treacherous fate, and a lot of damned hard work. But he'd taken on worse. The ranch was the only dream he had left. If he took the coward's way out, he would regret it for the rest of his life.

Decision made, Logan closed his eyes. Lulled by the sound of Kristin's breathing, he allowed himself to drift.

Time passed—Logan had no idea what hour it was when he was awakened by the sound of Kristin whimpering and gasping beside him. Her body jerked as if struggling against some invisible enemy. She was dreaming, he realized, most likely the same kind of hellish war dream that made a torment of his own nights.

"Kristin?" he whispered, hoping to wake her gently. When she continued to moan and tremble, he reached out with his uninjured right arm and pulled her against him. "It's all right," he murmured against the damp tangle of her hair. "It's only a dream. You're safe."

She clung to him, as if seeking refuge, her head nestled in the hollow of his throat. Beneath his hand, her skin was warm through the rumpled shift, her breasts pressing his ribs through the quilt. He cradled her close, savoring her nearness and the faint heat of arousal that shimmered through his body. Her tremors had eased. She was weeping softly, breathing in low, gasping sobs. "It's all right," he whispered, resisting the urge to bend his head and kiss her. "Don't be afraid, Kristin. You're safe with me."

As she settled back into restful sleep, he knew that it was time to let her go. Moving carefully, he slipped his arm away and tucked the coverlet around her. Exhausted, she slumbered on. Logan lay back against the pillow and closed his eyes, lulled by the memory of her warmth and the soft cadence of her breathing.

Kristin woke at dawn with a dim memory of her nightmare. She couldn't recall how it had ended, except that it was over. Beside her, Logan still slept. His breathing was deep and even. His color, what she could see in the thin light, looked healthy. When she touched his wrist, his pulse was strong, his skin cool. All good.

She eased off the bed without waking him and pulled on her boots and the jacket Blake had lent her. For now, she would let him sleep. When he was awake, maybe Webb could have one of the men help him out of bed and see to his needs.

Feeling grubby and sticky with sweat, she found the bathroom and washed her face and hands before going downstairs to the kitchen. She craved a bath and some clean clothes, but that could wait until she got home—which she hoped would happen today. If not, she might have to swallow her pride and accept some of Webb's late wife's castoffs.

Downstairs in the kitchen, the middle-aged cook, who was married to one of the older ranch hands, greeted her with a smile. "So you're the doctor. Goodness, you're so young and pretty, I never would have guessed it. Are you hungry?"

"Starved, actually. And that coffee smells wonderful."

"Here." The woman filled a steaming mug and passed it to her. "I'll fix you a plate to go with it. Mr. Calder is eating in the dining room with his son. I know he'd be happy to have you join them."

"Actually, I'm such a mess, I'd rather eat in here with you. Is that all right?"

"Sure. Have a seat at the table. How's our patient upstairs?"

Kristin took a seat. "He was sleeping when I left him. He seems better, but I'm hoping he'll stay in bed today. After he's awake, I'll take him a tray."

"Let me know what you think he'd like. Here you are." The cook set a plate of bacon, scrambled eggs, and thick buttered bread in front of her. Every bite tasted wonderful. It was all Kristin could do not to wolf it down.

Finished, she carried her plate and mug to the sink. "Thank you so much. I'm going back upstairs now. I'll let you know about the tray."

She hurried upstairs to find Logan sitting up in bed, face washed, hair combed, and wearing a fresh nightshirt. The dark stubble on his jaw gave him a roguish look that set off an unexpected quickening of her pulse. She remembered lying next to him last night. Tired as she was, she'd been very much aware of him. But then she'd gone to sleep, and the dream had come and gone. Nonetheless, she'd awakened feeling calm and rested.

"Webb sent a man to help me up," he said. "I'm still unsteady on my feet, but I don't want to stay in this bed any longer than I have to."

"How's the pain?"

"The shoulder's sore. But not as bad as yesterday."

"Excellent. Let me get you some breakfast. When you're done, I'll check the dressing."

In the kitchen again, she prepared the tray in only a few minutes. Kristin carried it up the stairs, taking slow steps to keep it from spilling. She remembered last night's conversation about the ranch property. Had she convinced Logan not to throw in his lot with Webb Calder?

He'd listened, but she couldn't be sure what he was thinking. She only knew that if he bought the ranch, he'd be in a position to cause no end of trouble for Blake—trouble that could lead to conflict, violence, and bloodshed.

She could push and ask him whether he'd made a decision— but no, she'd said her piece. That would have to be enough.

Logan was eating his breakfast with the tray on his lap. Kristin was at the window, about to open it and let in some fresh air, when Webb stepped into the room. At the sight of his face and the flinty look in his eyes, her throat tightened as if someone had jerked a noose around her neck. Even before he spoke, she knew it was decision time.

He walked straight to Logan's bedside. "You're looking better today," he said.

"I feel a lot better. But my doctor's insisting that I stay in bed for one more day."

"Good idea," Webb said. "By tomorrow, I want you well enough to go to Miles City and buy that property from the bank. You do plan to buy it, don't you?"

In the beat of silence that followed, Kristin forgot to breathe.

"Yes, I do," Logan replied.

Kristin's heart dropped.

"You're sure now?" Webb said. "You're not having second thoughts, are you?"

"No. My mind is made up."

Webb grinned for the first time. "Well, now, that's good news. I was afraid you were backing out, but I should have known better. You may have a different name, but you're a Calder at heart."

Kristin turned away and walked out of the room.

CHAPTER EIGHT

*E*ARLY SUMMER ON THE MONTANA PRAIRIE BROUGHT KNEE-HIGH grass and long, sunlit days. Spring roundup was over. In the pastures, new white-faced calves frolicked beside their mothers. With school in recess for the season, there was no better time to be a boy.

After the daily chores were done, Joseph would grab a few apples from the cellar, wrap some bread around a slab of roast beef, and ride down to the crossroads to meet his friends.

Sometimes Chase would join them. But with his father often keeping him busy at home, it was usually just the three of them—Joseph, Buck, and Cully. A world of innocent fun awaited them. They could ride into the foothills for a picnic, fish in the creek, or shoot birds and rabbits with Buck's BB gun. If the day was warm, they could swim in one of the cattle ponds that dotted the pastures or gig frogs in the patch of swampland that bordered the road south of town. But those adventures paled beside their new discovery.

Joseph had forgotten which of his friends had suggested sneaking out of their homes at night, after their families were asleep. But once they'd tried it, the lure of darkness called to them like a siren's song—the beauty and mystery of night, the danger, the risk, and the thrill of being unseen. There was always the chance that they could be caught and punished. But that only heightened the sense of adventure.

It took some planning to get it right. All three boys lived some distance from town. Getting together meant setting a time and place and riding their horses to the rendezvous. For Joseph, it meant listening for the chime of the downstairs clock, arranging a pillow dummy in his bed, and sneaking out the kitchen door to the stable. Bridling his calm horse and mounting it bareback, he would ride down the hill to the main road. Somewhere along that road, his friends would be waiting.

Once or twice a week, from late May into early June, they enjoyed their forays into the sleeping community. The few pranks they played were innocuous enough—a dead rat on a girl's doorstep, an opened gate on a pigpen, a harmless snake slipped into a Model T parked outside the roadhouse—the usual boyish mischief.

But then came the night when everything changed.

It was after midnight. The boys had met on the south road from Blue Moon. They'd tethered their horses to a fence and were plotting their adventure when an army surplus–style truck pulling a canvas-covered flatbed came rumbling along the road from the direction of town.

The truck was traveling without headlights. Only the sound of the engine and the crunch of wheels on the rough dirt road warned the boys to get out of the way. They melted into the shadows, calming their nervous horses as they waited for the rig to pass.

Fifty yards down the road, the truck stopped, its engine idling. The driver climbed out and walked to the roadside. The boys could see him in silhouette as he relieved himself in the weeds that grew along the ditch bank.

"Where do you think he's going?" Buck asked quietly.

"And what do you think he's got in that truck?" Joseph wondered out loud.

"Hey, let's follow him and find out," Cully said.

By now the truck had started to move again. The boys mounted and followed at a distance. The rig's speed had slowed to a crawl, as if the driver might be watching for something.

The truck passed the turnoff to the Dollarhide Ranch and kept going. A shiver passed through Joseph as he realized where it was headed. There was only one large property between here and the end of the road—the Hollister Ranch where his grandmother lived with her whip and her monster dogs.

"Maybe we should go back," he said. "Remember what happened last time we came out here?"

"You're not turning chicken on us, are you?" Buck teased.

"We'll be careful. Come on," Cully said.

Joseph stayed with his friends. They didn't know the truth, he reminded himself. And he would never tell them.

The truck was nearing the ranch gate. Joseph could see a glowing lantern, hung as a signal, perhaps, from one of the gateposts. Slowing further, the truck swung left and rolled through the open gate.

The boys had halted their horses in the road, a dozen yards back from the gate. Joseph's danger senses raised the hair on the back of his neck. "This is far enough," he whispered. "Let's get out of here."

"Hell, no." Buck had dismounted and was tethering his horse to a clump of saplings. "You can stay here if you want, but I want to see what's under that canvas. This is a real adventure."

"Don't be a scaredy cat, Joseph," Cully said. "Come on."

The challenge was too much for Joseph's pride. He left his horse and followed his friends along the outside of the fence as far as the open gate. Hidden by shrubbery, they peered through, into the yard.

A second lantern flared in the darkness, lighting the way to the barn. As the lantern moved, guiding the truck as the driver turned the rig around and backed up to the open barn doors, Joseph glimpsed the man holding it. He was of medium height with broad shoulders, his features shadowed by the fedora hat he wore. His dress and manner suggested an air of authority. Maybe he worked for the old woman—as a foreman or boss of some kind.

At least there was no sign of the old woman or the dogs.

As the man vanished from view, along with the lantern, the truck stopped. Still visible in the moonlight, the driver, a swarthy fellow in work clothes, opened the door, jumped to the ground, and trotted around to the back of the rig.

In the instant before he disappeared, the light caught something that chilled Joseph's blood. Tucked into the driver's belt was a deadly-looking pistol.

Joseph was staring after the two men when Buck nudged him. His friends were on the move. Pulling him along with them, they rounded the gatepost and crept through the shadows into the yard.

Keeping low and close to the bushes, they could see the two men untying the ropes that held the canvas over the load. From somewhere beyond the house, Joseph's ears caught the barking and baying of the dreaded dogs. He froze. But after a few seconds he realized that the barks weren't coming any closer. The dogs were probably penned or chained. He forgot about them as the canvas fell away to reveal stacks of wooden boxes, all of a size for a man to carry. Some of the boxes were plain. Others were embellished with a black stamp, like a brand. The two men began unloading them from the flatbed and carrying them into the barn.

"Hot diggity!" Buck muttered under his breath. "I know what that is! It's booze! Hauled down from Canada, I'll bet. There must be fifty thousand dollars' worth on that truck. Maybe a hundred."

"How do you know so much about it?" Joseph asked in a whisper.

"I listen to the cowboys talk. It's against the law to have booze these days. But folks are bringing it into the country or brewing homemade hootch in stills—and the ones that don't get caught are getting as rich as kings."

"Well, we won't be getting rich," Joseph said. "You saw that gun. If we get caught, we could end up dead. Come on. Let's get out of here."

"If I could get my hands on just one box, I could make a bundle," Buck said.

"That's crazy," Cully hissed. "Joseph's right. Those men could kill us. Let's go."

Joseph was about to lead the other boys back through the gate when he became aware of a sudden silence.

The dogs were no longer barking.

"Run!" He grabbed his friends. They burst out of their hiding place and sprinted for the gate. But the two huge mastiffs were already loping around the corner of the barn. Snarling and drooling, they closed around the terrified boys, not attacking them, but cutting off their escape.

"What the devil?" The broad-shouldered man Joseph had seen earlier strode out of the barn. The lantern he carried shed a circle of light around the three boys who clung together, shrinking from the dogs.

"Well, what have we here? And what am I going to do with you?" The man's face was shadowed but his calm, cold voice struck fear into their young hearts.

"Please, mister." It was Joseph who spoke. "Call off your dogs and we'll go. We didn't mean any harm. We were just curious."

"I'd say you were too curious for your own good." The man gave a low whistle. The dogs backed off a few paces and settled onto their massive haunches. "How about I give you a choice," he said. "Either I can let these dogs have at you, or I can put you to work. What do you say?"

The boys exchanged furtive glances. Their agreement was a given. "We'll work, sir," Joseph said.

"Fine." With a command and a hand gesture, the man ordered the dogs back. They settled next to the barn door, alert for any reason to strike.

"Tell us what to do," Joseph said.

The man nodded. "You boys look strong enough to help unload these boxes. Get around behind the trailer. When my friend, here, hands you a box, you'll carry it to the stack in the barn and then go back for another one. Clear?" He paused long enough for the boys to respond. "Then, unless you want to be dog meat, get to work."

The inside of the barn was lit by a single lantern, hanging from a hook on a long chain. The truck driver stood on the flatbed, handing each box down to a boy, who lugged it to a growing stack in the rear of the barn. As expected, the boxes were heavy. Staggering under the weight, the three friends trudged back and forth. Their arm and shoulder muscles throbbed, but they knew better than to complain or even speak a word to each other. They were lucky to be alive.

The man in the fedora stood watching from the shadows. Joseph could sense his gaze every time he passed, but the man said nothing.

At last, after what seemed like a long time, the last box was unloaded from the flatbed and placed on the stack. By the time the truck started up and headed out of the gate, Joseph and his friends were so tired they could barely walk. They sank onto the floor of the barn, where they huddled together, rubbing their sore arms, too scared to speak.

Still wearing his hat, the man stepped out of the shadows and walked into the circle of light. For a long moment, he stood looking down at the boys. At last, Joseph summoned the courage to speak up.

"We're done with the work, sir. Is it all right if we go now?"

"Soon, after I've finished with you." His expression was unreadable in the shadow cast by his hat brim. "Tell me your names. You first." He nodded at Buck.

"Buck Haskell." His voice quivered.

"Now you." Singled out, Cully muttered his name.

"And you."

"Joseph Lars Dollarhide, sir." Joseph willed himself to hide the fear he felt. "Now can we go?"

"Not until I say so. First, I want to pay you all for a hard night's work." Taking his wallet out of his hip pocket, he slipped out three crisp bills and handed one to each of the boys. Joseph stared at the bill. Ten dollars! More spending money than he'd ever had in his life. Buck and Cully were equally amazed.

"Wow, thanks, mister!" Cully said.

"Not at all. You earned it. But before you leave, we need to have a little talk." Pulling up a nearby wooden crate, he sat down. "First of all, you boys need to understand that you weren't invited here tonight. You sneaked onto the property. That's trespassing. It's against the law. Nod your head if you understand."

The boys nodded. Were they about to be turned over to the sheriff?

"You did something else tonight that's against the law," the man said. "I'm guessing you know what's in those boxes you helped unload."

"It's booze," Buck said. "I already knew that."

"I'm assuming all three of you know that—and that you also know it's illegal to have it stored in this barn." His voice lowered to a hoarse whisper. "Here's where our talk gets serious. If you tell anybody about tonight, I'll be in trouble, but so will you. Knowing what it was, you chose to help unload that illegal liquor, and you got paid for it. That means you've broken the law. If anybody finds out, you boys will all be headed for the state reform school. You'll be locked up, away from your families, for years. Do you understand?"

"Yes, sir." Joseph felt vaguely ill. "Don't worry, we won't tell a soul. And we'll never come back here."

"That's your choice," the man said. "But here's another thing. I could use some smart boys like you when I've got a shipment coming in or customers showing up. If you wanted to earn some money, you could be my messengers and lookouts, or help unload the product, like you did tonight. Would any of you be interested in a job?"

"I would," Buck said.

"Me too," Cully echoed. "I've never had money of my own."

"And what about you, Joseph?" The man spoke the name slowly, as if tasting it on his tongue.

"I don't know," Joseph said. "My folks are pretty strict. I might not be able to get away."

"Well, think about it." The man stood. "When I'm going to need help, I'll tie a black ribbon on the fence where that road takes off to the Dollarhide place. If you show up that night, I'll put you to work."

"So can we go now?" Joseph asked. "We need to get home, before our folks wake up."

"Go ahead. Don't worry about the dogs—they're in their kennel now. Remember to look for the black ribbon." The man stood. He hadn't mentioned his name, Joseph realized. Maybe he didn't want them to know it.

Sore and tired from the night's hard work, the boys rose, stretched, and trudged out of the barn. As Joseph followed them, something compelled him to pause and turn back.

The man was standing in the circle of the lantern light. He had taken off his hat and was raking a hand through his thick, chestnut hair. For a moment, his gaze locked with Joseph's—green eyes looking into his, green like his own.

"Good night, Joseph," he said.

Joseph wheeled and hurried after his friends. His heart was pounding so hard that he feared it might break through his ribs.

When had he known? Was it just now when their eyes had met, or had he sensed it all along—the kinship of blood calling to blood?

When had he known that the stranger was his father?

As the whine and blast of artillery fire faded into memory, Logan opened his eyes. For a long moment he lay still, blinking himself back to reality. This time the dream had been so vivid that he could have sworn it was real. He could almost smell the cordite and feel the shrapnel tearing into his leg. But it had only been a dream, thank God. He was home, on his own ranch, in his own house, with the dawn light slanting through the window and meadowlarks trilling their morning songs.

He had thought long and hard before buying the ranch that lay like a bridge between the Triple C and the Dollarhide spread. But since the transfer of the money and the signing of the papers, he'd been too busy for regrets.

The house was livable, barely. He'd hauled away the mouse-infested couch and mattress but kept the table and kitchen chairs, which were solid oak. After scrubbing the place down, he'd bought a brass bed with a mattress and a minimal supply of bedclothes. Other purchases, made at a mercantile in Miles City, included a tin washtub, soap and towels, and a few dishes, pans, and utensils for the kitchen. Everything else, including the rugs and living room furniture, would have to wait until the ranch was further along.

He'd also stocked the kitchen with basic food supplies and hired a local widow to pick up and return his laundry, with extra pay for the distance. It was still dawning on him that he had enough money to buy anything he wanted. He'd grown up poor and been frugal all his life. Old habits would take time to change if they ever did.

He rolled out of bed, washed, dressed, and ambled into the kitchen to make coffee. His shoulder had healed—Kristin Dollarhide had done a good job of patching it. But his left leg, the muscles ripped by shrapnel toward the end of the war, would pain him for the rest of his days. Scarred and ugly as it was, at least he'd managed to keep it.

When the coffee had boiled, he filled a mug and carried it out onto the porch. For Logan, this had become the best part of the day, watching the sunrise paint the sky above the mountains, enjoying the peace that had eluded him for such a long time.

The fifty head of steers Logan had bought from Webb were grazing in the single fenced pasture. Fattened up, they should bring a good price in the fall. For now, Logan was taking care of them himself. Later, when he got more animals, he would hire some help, but for now it didn't seem worth the trouble.

The old barn was gone. Where it had stood, a new one would soon be built by Lars Anderson, with later plans for a stable wing attached. Looking across the pastures, Logan could see the wagon coming from town, bringing Lars and his two apprentices.

Employing Lars had been a good decision. The big Swede was as honest as he was capable. The structure, still in the framing stage, would be finished by late summer. Lars had promised it would be built to last for generations.

Webb had objected to Logan's choice of hiring a Dollarhide in-law, who insisted on buying only Dollarhide lumber. But the boss of the Triple C was learning that he couldn't call the shots. Whether Webb liked it or not, Logan would be his own man.

From the south, across the wide expanse of grasslands, came the faint shriek of the sawmill, cutting timber into boards. These days the mill was running from dawn till dusk, six days a week. But Kristin had spoken the truth. At a distance of several miles, the noise wasn't loud enough to be troublesome. And it stopped when the sun went down.

Even the issue of the road had been settled for now. Logan had set Blake Dollarhide a price for every wagonload of logs that cut across ranch property. It wasn't so much that Logan needed the money, but that Blake must not be allowed to assume he had free access.

Again Webb had objected—vehemently this time. But Logan had held firm. Blocking the road would limit his own use of it. And a fight over road access would benefit no one, especially if it led to spilled blood.

For now, while the pastures were green and the creeks flowing high, the fragile peace was holding. But Logan knew he was walking a tightrope. Even a minor incident could upset the balance and throw the situation into conflict, forcing him to choose sides.

And he had no doubt which side he'd be forced to choose.

The wagon rolled into the yard, with Lars driving the team of draft horses. Not only were the massive Belgians, on loan to Lars from the Dollarhides, used for hauling and transportation, but they also powered the winch that would be rigged to raise the framed walls of the barn and hold them while they were secured in place. That task would take place today, with all hands helping.

The two apprentices, Pete and Ezra, were town boys who'd been too young to go to war. The skills they'd learned from Lars would serve them well when the time came to marry and raise families. Pete, a natural jokester, had ginger hair and a freckled face. Ezra, the serious one, was a handsome young man with dark hair and brown eyes. As soon as the wagon had stopped, they jumped to the ground and began setting up the ropes and pulleys to raise the first wall.

Lars, who was getting on in years, climbed slowly out of the wagon. Today his weathered features wore a troubled look.

"Is something wrong, Lars?" Logan had come out to help unload the wagon.

The older man's only answer was a sigh.

"Is there anything I can do?"

Lars shook his head. "Nothing that won't get you arrested. Yesterday I saw a man I hoped would never show his face in Blue Moon again. He passed me on Main Street, in his fancy automobile. If I'd had a gun, I'd have shot him."

"Knowing you to be a fair man, you must have had a good reason."

"I had every reason. Years ago, the man dishonored my daughter. When I demanded that he do the right thing and give her baby his name, he left town. Now he's back, and probably up to no good."

"Who is this man?" Logan picked up a keg of nails and handed it to Pete, to take to the barn site.

"Mason Dollarhide." Lars spoke the name like a curse. "My daughter was lucky. His half-brother, Blake, agreed to marry her. They have a fine family now. But that bastard Mason—my Hanna was as innocent as a flower. He didn't care. He ruined her, not because of love, but just because he could."

Logan remembered something Webb had claimed—that Blake Dollarhide had gotten Lars's daughter pregnant and was forced to marry her. But this was the real story. Blake had done the decent thing, saved the girl's honor, and claimed his brother's child. And, so it appeared, all had ended well.

Not that any of this was his business, Logan reminded himself. But he couldn't leave it without saying more.

"I know you didn't ask for my advice, Lars, but I'm going to offer it anyway. Forget the man. What he did is in the past. All the hate and anger in the world can't change that. It will only eat away at your heart."

Lars sighed again. "Wise advice, I know. I tell myself that my

Hanna is happy. She married a good man. She gave me a fine grandson. I should put away my anger. But yesterday when I saw Mason Dollarhide, I remembered how he treated her—using her and throwing her away, like something of no worth. Like a . . . a whore! He didn't have to pay the consequences for what he did. And he didn't care!"

"But he did pay, Lars. Or at least he will. He lost a good woman and all claim to his son. Someday he'll look back and regret that."

"But it's not enough!" Lars's huge hands clenched into fists. Then he shrugged and turned away. "Come on, let's get to work."

The job of raising the barn's framed walls from the ground, where they'd been assembled, was strenuous and risky. Back in Texas, where Logan had grown up, whole neighborhoods or communities would come together to lift and brace the walls, then celebrate afterward with a feast hosted by the barn's owner. But in this country of isolated ranches, other ways had to be found.

Lars, who might have been a brilliant engineer in a different life, had devised the method of using pulleys and a team of horses to haul each assembled section upright. But before it could be lifted, the long ends of the vertical studs had to be precisely placed so they would drop into slots at the edge of the floor. Once raised, temporary braces would be nailed into place to hold the wall until it could be joined with the next section.

Lars drove the team of Belgians—massive horses with golden hides and creamy manes—while Logan and the two apprentices balanced the load and made sure it settled into the right place. The morning was cool, but by the time the first section was braced solidly into place, the men were sweating.

With something to stand against, the other sections went up more easily. Still, the work was grueling. By the time the final section was ready to be raised into position, it was early afternoon.

The apprentices were tired and hungry, and Logan was gritting his teeth against the pain in both his leg and his shoulder. But just one more piece remained to be lifted into place. Then the job would be done for the day.

With the pulleys rigged to the last section, Lars nudged the horses to a steady walk, raising the frame to fit in the single open-ing. Everything was going well—too well, Logan was to reflect later. Was the disaster that happened next a twist of fate or just a careless moment gone wrong?

The section was in position and sliding into place when a shriek of pain shattered the air. Ezra had reached around the side of the frame to steady it while it was being lowered. Before he could pull back, the structure had dropped, pinning his arm.

"Pull it forward, Lars!" Logan shouted as he raced to help the young man. "Break it loose any way you can!"

Lars slapped the reins on the horses' backs. The team plunged forward, pulling the frame out of line, giving Logan just enough room to pull Ezra free.

The young apprentice collapsed in Logan's arms, groaning with pain. Beneath his shirtsleeve, the upper arm was bent at an awkward angle—broken too badly to be set and splinted here.

Logan helped Ezra to the house, lowered him to the porch steps, and used one of his own clean shirts to fashion a sling. He had nothing, not even whiskey, for the pain. The ride to town in the Model T would be jarring and take time. Cutting across the grassland on horseback would be even rougher but a good deal faster.

"Do you think you can ride, Ezra?" he asked.

The young man's face was white with shock and pain, but he nodded.

Logan saddled and bridled Sky, the buckskin gelding he'd bought from Webb. After a moment's thought, he boosted Ezra onto the saddle, then mounted behind the cantle with his long legs forward in the stirrups and his arms reaching around the young man's body to hold the reins. The position was awkward, and not easy on the horse, but it would be the safest and least punishing way for Ezra to ride.

"Ready?"

Ezra nodded, using his good right arm to cradle the injured left one.

"Let me know if I need to slow down." Logan eased the horse

from a jog to a ground-eating lope. He felt Ezra's body tense, and he knew the young apprentice was in excruciating pain. But the sooner they reached the doctor, the better.

The doctor.

He hadn't crossed paths with Kristin since the morning she'd left Webb's house. She'd given his wound a final check, pronounced it free of infection, and departed in a buggy driven by one of Webb's hired men. With her parting words, she'd ordered him to come by her office later for a follow-up. But Logan hadn't done so. He hadn't seen the need, and he knew that his decision to buy the ranch property had angered her.

Even now, she wouldn't be glad to see him. But Logan knew that would make no difference. Dr. Kristin Dollarhide was a professional. Her only concern would be for her patient.

CHAPTER NINE

KRISTIN WAS IN HER SURGERY, CLEANING UP AFTER STITCHING THE gashed scalp of a venturesome six-year-old named Lester, who'd tumbled out of a tree and scraped a sharp limb on the way down. The damage wasn't serious, but like most head wounds, it had bled profusely. The child's young mother had been frantic; but all had ended well, with a smile and a cherry lollipop.

She'd wiped down the table and was putting the stained towels into a basin to soak when she heard the sound of a horse pulling up outside.

"Open the door and show them in, please, Gerda," she called toward the front office, which doubled as both parlor and reception. "Tell them I'll be out in a minute."

"Yes, Doctor." Gerda was doing her best to sound professional. Kristin had hired the girl as an assistant, mostly as a favor to her family. But Hanna's sister had proven as eager and sharp as she was pretty. She was becoming an asset to the practice.

Kristin was washing her hands when she heard the front door open and a cry of dismay from Gerda. "Ezra! Oh, no! No!"

Shaking the water off her hands, Kirsten rushed into the front room. Logan was lowering a white-faced young man into the armchair nearest the door. The young man was cradling his arm, which was supported by a sling. Gerda was weeping.

"What happened?" Kristin directed the question at Logan.

"He was working on my barn when a frame slipped. Don't worry, I'll pay for whatever it takes to treat him."

She shot him a cold look. "That's the last thing I'm worried about. Get him into the back room. He can sit on the edge of the table while I check the arm."

Kristin stepped back and held the door, allowing Logan to support Ezra as he struggled to the table. Kristin avoided Logan's gaze, focusing her attention on her patient. If things were awkward between them, that couldn't be allowed to matter right now.

With Ezra sitting on the edge of the exam table, and Logan steadying him on the right, Kristin untied the sling and used a pair of sharp scissors to cut away the left shirt sleeve. Ezra was biting his lip to keep from crying out. His upper arm was bruised, bent, and beginning to swell, clearly a compound fracture. At least the broken bone hadn't pierced the skin. But the arm would need to be set, splinted until the swelling went down, then encased in a plaster cast.

Gerda, still teary-eyed, fluttered around them as Logan eased Ezra into a supine position on the table. "I know what you're going to do," she said. "It'll hurt a lot, won't it?"

"Yes. I'll give Ezra something to lessen the pain but he'll still feel it."

During and after the war, Kristin had worked with advanced anesthesia machines that could deliver measured combinations of ether, nitrous oxide, chloroform, and oxygen to render patients safely unconscious. Nothing like those was available here, of course. All she had was a canister of nitrous oxide, also known as laughing gas, with a simple valve, a hose, and a face mask that she'd ordered from a dental supply house. Using it to put Ezra all the way under would be too risky. But she could give him enough gas to make him light-headed and less aware of what was happening.

"Don't worry, Ezra." Gerda leaned over and kissed his lips. "I'll be right here, holding your hand. I love you."

Ezra forced his colorless face into a ghost of a smile. "I love you, too," he whispered.

Kirsten placed the mask over Ezra's nose and mouth and examined the break using her fingertips to find where the bones had separated. Steeling herself, she took a firm grip on the arm. "Hold him," she ordered Logan.

* * *

Setting the bone didn't take long, but the process was brutal. Even with the laughing gas pleasantly clouding his mind, Ezra screamed as the two broken pieces came together. Holding him in place, Logan could sense the jolt of pain that shot through the young man. Memories flashed—the hospital tent, the broken bodies, the odors of sweat and disinfectant, and the sounds of suffering.

Then it was over. Kristin had removed the gas and was wrapping the arm in soft cotton, binding it to the wooden braces to make a splint that would be replaced with a cast in the next few days. Ezra, pale as bleach, lay with his eyes closed.

"Somebody should sit with him until he feels steady enough to get up." Kristin glanced at Gerda, whom Logan had met when he visited the Anderson family.

"I'll do it." The pretty girl was more than eager.

"Fine. Don't try to help him up yourself. Call me when it's time," Kristin said.

"If you'll allow me to stay, I'll see him home to his family," Logan offered.

She gave him a sharp glance. "Fine. But he lives at the far end of town, and you shouldn't take him on horseback. My Model T is in the shed behind the house. Use that and bring it back when you've delivered him."

She walked into the parlor, leaving the door ajar behind her. Logan followed. He could tell that she was still upset with his decision to side with Webb and buy the ranch. But that shouldn't give her cause to treat him like the enemy.

"We need to talk, Kristin," he said.

"All right. Have a chair. You've got until my next patient shows up." She motioned him to an armchair while she perched on the arm of the sofa. The room was plain but tasteful, with leather seating and a Persian rug on the floor. Her framed medical license hung next to the door of the surgery. A set of shelves held an assortment of classic children's books and medical texts. On the coffee table—

Logan swallowed his surprise. On the low table, in a glass vase, were six fresh, perfect pink roses. As far as he knew, roses like that only grew in one place—the flower bed below the porch of the Calder mansion, where Webb's mother, Lorna, had planted them.

Logan felt his heart drop—but for no reason, he reminded himself. He had no claim on Kristin Dollarhide. He was in no position to court any woman. He was still mourning his lost family and building his ranch. Webb, on the other hand, was free to wed again if he chose. And as his bride, Kristin would step into a world of luxury and power. Maybe Webb had already asked her. Maybe she'd already said yes. But that was none of his damned business.

"You never came around to get your wound checked," she said.

"The wound had healed. My wrist was fine, too. I saw no need for it. And I wasn't sure I'd be welcomed."

"Being welcomed has nothing to do with it. You were my patient—for all your being 'a Calder at heart,' as Webb put it."

"My decision had nothing to do with being a Calder. I bought the ranch because it fit my plans. And if you've talked to your brother, you know that we've made an arrangement for his use of the road. No matter what you think, Webb doesn't own me."

But does he own you?

Logan bit back the question. He'd be damned if he was going to ask her about her relationship with Webb—or about that vase of roses, which he was tempted to pick up and hurl out the front door. He needed to leave before he made a fool of himself.

He stood. "Where do I find that auto of yours? In the shed, did you say?"

"Yes. The tank's full and it ran fine the last time I drove it. Ezra's mother should be home. But if she isn't, let somebody know. I don't want him left alone."

Her moist lips trembled slightly. Logan imagined kicking the flowers off the table, sweeping her into his arms, and devouring that soft, firm mouth with kisses.

But it was no more than a fleeting thought. She was Webb's woman, and he didn't need that kind of trouble. Opening his wallet, he withdrew a generous handful of bills. When she didn't reach out to take them, he laid them on the table. "That should cover the charges for now. I'll start the auto and bring it around," he said. Then he turned and strode out the door.

As the door closed, Kristin exhaled the breath she'd held too long in her body. She'd noticed the way Logan's gaze had fixed on the roses, and she'd half expected him to question her about them. To her relief, he hadn't.

Webb's cook had dropped off the flowers that morning on her way to do some errands in town. They were from Webb, of course, and they'd come with an attached note in a sealed envelope. At the time, she'd been busy with young Lester and his head wound, so she'd tucked the envelope in the pocket of her white lab coat. She'd hesitated to put the roses on display. But they were so pretty, she'd resolved to leave them out for the enjoyment of her patients.

Now she took the envelope out of her pocket and ran her finger beneath the flap to open it. Inside was a single sheet of paper with a brief message.

Dinner at the Roadhouse tonight. I'll pick you up at 7:30. Wear something pretty.

Kristin replaced the note with a sigh. It was like Webb to make plans without consulting her and expect her to go along with them. But dinner at the Roadhouse was an even bigger concern. Unless she could talk Webb out of going there, it would mean taking their slow-budding relationship public. Everyone in the popular dining establishment would see them together, and the talk would spread like a prairie wildfire. A Calder and a Dollarhide keeping company. What a delicious tidbit of gossip. And Blake—Kristin didn't even want to imagine what her brother would say.

She wasn't ready for this.

Since home telephone service had yet to reach this part of Montana, she had no easy way to contact Webb at the ranch. She could only hope to talk sense into him when he showed up on her doorstep tonight.

Sooner or later, she knew, their friendship would come to a

crossroads, and he would demand more than she was ready to give. But right now, the sound of the Model T pulling up in front of the house reminded her that she had more urgent concerns.

Stepping into the surgery, she found Ezra sitting up on the table. He was pale and unsteady, but when she checked his vitals, Kristin judged him stable enough to rest at home. She could stop by and check on the young man tomorrow.

When Logan knocked on the front door, Kristin let him in and helped him get Ezra to the car. They said little except for the brief, polite exchanges essential to the situation. Remembering their easy closeness the night she'd slept beside him in the Calder house, Kristin couldn't help feeling that a door had closed between them—one that might never open again.

Perhaps he'd recognized Webb's roses. But nothing could be done about that now.

As the Model T drove away, Kristin went back inside to find Gerda collapsed on the sofa, sobbing her heart out.

"What is it, Gerda?" Kristin leaned over the girl, laying a hand on her shoulder. "Don't worry about Ezra. He'll need to wear a cast for a couple of months but after that, he'll be as good as new.

"I know . . ." Gerda gasped out the words between sobs. "But we were going to get married. He was going to ask my father. Now he says he can't marry me . . . It's because he can't work. He can't support a wife."

Kristin stroked the girl's quivering back. "But surely you can wait two months to get married. Lars will take him back, especially since Ezra is going to be your husband."

Gerda cried harder, sobs racking her body. "No, it's worse than that. Ezra's family is moving to California. His father can get a good job there. Ezra was going to marry me and stay here. Now . . . now he wants to go with them." Her fists pounded the sofa cushions. "I think he wanted to go all along. Now he's got an excuse. What am I going to do? I love him. And I don't want to be an old maid like Britta. I'd rather die!"

"My dear girl!" Kristin pulled Gerda up and gathered her close.

"You're so young. You've got your whole life ahead of you. When the time comes to marry, you'll have your choice of fine men. Meanwhile, you've got time to make something of yourself. You could learn things by working here. You could even go away to school, like I did. There's more to life than just getting married."

But wise as the words were meant to be, they were clearly not what the girl wanted to hear. Her tears soaked the lapels of Kristin's jacket. Her shoulders heaved with heart-rending sobs. Glancing out the window, Kristin saw her next patient, an elderly woman, hobbling up the sidewalk.

"That's enough, Gerda." She thrust the girl away from her. "Go into the bathroom and wash your face with cold water. If you can't stop crying, leave. Take a walk or go home. And don't come back until you've got yourself under control. Do you understand?"

"Yes." Gerda fled down the hall to the bathroom. As Kristin escorted her elderly patient back to the surgery, she heard the water running, followed by the opening and closing of the back door. The girl would be all right, she told herself. She just needed some fresh air and a little time to calm down.

Kristin had finished examining the woman and was refilling the bottle of iodine tablets her patient was taking for goiter when she heard the Model T pull around the house and into the shed. Logan had said he would leave the key under the seat without coming back inside. Still, she couldn't suppress a flicker of hope that he'd change his mind. Maybe if they had a chance to talk, they could at least remain friends. But that wasn't to be. Moments after the auto stopped running, she heard the sound of his horse trotting away, fading into silence.

The sunlight made rainbow blurs of Gerda's tears as she trudged back toward the main part of town. She didn't know where she was going, and she didn't care. This was the worst day of her life.

She'd been so sure that Ezra loved her. He'd told her so when he'd asked her to marry him. But he'd lied. He'd only wanted one thing, and now he was leaving.

How could she face her friends? She'd told them all that Ezra was going to marry her. She'd even made drawings of the wedding dress she planned to make. How could she face the town when the gossip spread, as it always did? She wanted to die. Maybe if she wished it hard enough, she would.

A shiny, black automobile, heading north out of town, passed her on the far side of the road. Gerda, who'd forgotten her hat at the doctor's, turned away to hide her face from the driver.

But he'd already noticed her. Twenty yards up the road, he slammed on his brakes, swung the auto around in a cloud of dust, and approached on Gerda's side of the road. When he came abreast of her, he stopped.

"Are you all right, miss?"

Gerda hadn't turned to look at him, but his deep, mellow voice sounded familiar. She didn't reply.

"Wait, I know you," he said, chuckling. "We met a few weeks ago in the store. You told me where to find the cinnamon."

She turned her gaze toward him then, recalling the broad-shouldered stranger in the leather jacket. He was as handsome as she remembered. "Did you find it?" she asked, cocking her head and giving him a coy smile. She might be disgraced, but she hadn't forgotten how to flirt.

He laughed. "I guess it's confession time. I wasn't looking for cinnamon or anything else. I just wanted an excuse to speak to the most beautiful girl I'd ever seen. You looked like an angel standing there, with the sunlight shining on your golden curls. You still do." His gaze narrowed. "But I know tears when I see them. Is something wrong?"

She shook her head. "Just a bit of bad news. I'll get over it."

"I'd be glad to help you do that," he said. "I'm going to Miles City on an errand for my mother. If nobody's waiting for you at home, why don't you come along? The hotel there has an elegant restaurant. We could enjoy a late lunch and get to know each other. Then I could drive you home. What do you say?"

Gerda hesitated, but only for a moment. Why shouldn't she go with him? He was only offering her a ride and a nice lunch. She was a free woman now. And since she was supposed to be at work, her parents would never find out. "All right," she said. "As long as we come right back after we eat."

"Of course we will." He stepped out of the automobile and walked around to open the door for her. "My name is Mason Dollarhide, by the way. And I can't wait to learn all about you."

Mason sighed as he gazed across the table at the vision who was polishing off a strawberry tart with the gusto of a lumberjack. *Gerda Anderson.* Lord help him. He should have guessed that she was Hanna's sister. She had the same cornflower eyes and spun gold hair. But she was even prettier than Hanna had been at that age—pretty enough to be in the movies or on stage at the Ziegfeld Follies.

But Mason had learned some hard lessons in the dozen years since he'd seduced Hanna and fathered her baby. And those lessons had taught him the value of caution. Her smile, the tilt of her lovely head, and the not-quite-accidental nudge of her foot against his under the table assured him that the lass could be made willing. But she was too young for him—and worse, she was the daughter of big Lars Anderson, who would skin him alive if Mason were to lay a hand on her.

Did she know about the past? Probably not. She would have been a child when he was involved with her sister. But now that he was back in Blue Moon, other family members would likely tell her, and that could mean trouble. One more reason to give this tempting morsel a pass.

And there was another reason. The business he'd started at the ranch demanded his full attention. One slip-up could land him in jail. The last thing he needed right now was the distraction of a woman in his life. Still, she was so pretty, and so adorably naive. A little flirting, maybe even a few kisses wouldn't do any harm—even if he had to draw the line at that.

She put down her dessert fork and dabbed her mouth with a linen napkin. "Thank you for the delicious lunch," she said, a glint of invitation in her eyes.

"You're very welcome." He helped with her chair and offered an arm to escort her outside to the waiting auto. "And now, my angel, it's time to drive you home," he said.

Even on weeknights, the Roadhouse, run by a burly man named Jake Loman, was the busiest place in Blue Moon. The food was good, especially the choice cuts of beef, bought from local ranches. The booths and tables were usually full, and there was plenty of activity at the billiard tables in the back.

The place had become a gathering spot for the community, where families could dine together, neighbors could exchange gossip, couples could court, and men could discuss business. And after hours, a man able to pay could visit one of Jake's so-called nieces who lived upstairs and helped in the kitchen.

No one was paying much attention when Kristin and Webb entered and followed Jake to the corner booth he'd reserved for them. Still, it was all Kristin could do to keep from ducking her head. Her efforts to dissuade Webb from taking her to this very public place had met with a wall of resistance. What was wrong with his wanting to show her off? he'd demanded. It was time the townspeople knew that they were a couple.

A couple? Was that what they were? But Kristin had known better than to challenge him and cast more discord on their evening together. In his own commanding way, Webb was making an effort to please her. She had resigned herself to a minor scandal. Let the chips fall where they may.

Webb was good company. She liked his intelligence, his determination, and his raw honesty. They'd enjoyed a few rides on his ranch and meals at his home, along with some pleasant conversations. But Webb Calder wasn't a patient man. He was rushing her, seemingly unaware of her need to slow things down.

Did he love her?

Maybe he wanted to. Kristin understood that he was lonely and liked the idea of having an attractive, accomplished woman on his arm. But her instincts told her that Webb's true heart had died with his wife. Any woman he chose would take second place to the portrait on the wall. Just as any man who chose her would have to respect her need to serve the community as a doctor.

Many successful relationships were built on compromise. Was it possible that this might be one of them?

Now, across the table, he smiled as he studied her in her simple yellow dress. "Every man in the room is jealous of me tonight," he said. "If I didn't know better, I'd have you stand up and take a bow, just to show you off."

"Thank you for not doing that," she said, smiling.

"And thank you for agreeing to come with me tonight. See, it's not so bad, is it?"

People were starting to notice them now. As Jake took their order, a head turned in their direction, then another and another. A low buzz of conversation drifted through the room, like the hum of bees hovering over a blooming clover patch.

Fixing a polite smile on her face, Kristin willed herself to ignore the onlookers. She was managing all right—until she glanced across the room and saw Logan.

He was sitting alone at a small table, making a visible effort not to look at her. Kristin resisted the urge to shrink behind the table. Why did he have to be here? Why tonight?

But why should it matter? He'd seen the roses. He shouldn't be surprised, seeing her with Webb. Should he?

After a long, frustrating day and with nothing worth cooking in the house, Logan had decided to treat himself to a steak dinner. He'd gone early and had almost finished his meal when Kristin walked in with Webb.

So that was how it was.

He'd suspected the truth when he'd seen the flowers on her table. But suspecting and knowing were two different things. Seeing her with Webb now, smiling as she leaned toward him in her pretty yellow dress, stirred dark emotions that an officer and a gentleman had no right to feel.

He gave himself a mental slap. Webb and Kristin were good

people, and they were his friends. They deserved to find happiness. If they'd found it in each other, all he could do was wish them the best.

But a Calder and a Dollarhide together? That was going to cause some ripples.

What was left of his appetite had fled. Standing, he laid a bill on the table and stepped away. Now he had a choice. He could head straight for the door, pretending to ignore the happy couple, or he could take the high road.

He made the second choice.

Making his way among the tables, he walked up to their booth. "Well, this is a surprise," he said. "Are congratulations in order?"

"Not quite yet." Webb was beaming. "But I finally talked the lady into letting me show her off in public."

"I was afraid we might cause a stir." Kristin's smile was strained. "It appears I was right."

"Well, I wouldn't let it bother me," Logan said. "What happens between you two is nobody else's business—including mine. I wish you both the best."

"Thanks, friend." Webb's smile broadened. "When I get time, I plan to come out and see how the work on your ranch is coming along."

"You're welcome anytime. No invitation needed. You too, Kristin." He gave her a nod. Her lips parted as if she were about to speak, then closed as if she'd changed her mind.

Trying not to show his limp, Logan went outside to his horse. He would take his time riding home, enjoying the peace of night and watching the stars come out. As for the woman who had saved his life, the woman who'd slept in his arms as he cradled her close to ease her nightmare, she had never been his to lose. He would lock away his fantasies and forget her.

After dinner at the Roadhouse, Webb drove Kristin home. The evening had been pleasant enough in spite of the curious stares and the inevitable talk. She could have managed fine if only Logan hadn't been there. The discomfort between them as he congratulated her and Webb had thrown her off balance and lingered for the rest of the evening.

Webb, however, was oblivious to her unease. He clearly saw their first public date as a triumph. As he turned to her on the porch for their usual chaste good night kiss, his arms tightened around her. His mouth lingered on hers, seeking and demanding. Kristin tasted the usual after-dinner cigar he'd enjoyed. Pulling back a little, she gave him a smile.

"Thank you for a lovely evening, Webb," she said. "I know that I argued against our being seen in public, but it was probably a step in the right direction."

"Then maybe it's time for another step." His big hand rested firmly at the small of her back, holding her fast. "I've been hoping you'd invite me in tonight. It's early yet. We've got plenty of time."

Kristin had known the moment was coming. Still, it caught her by surprise. She stiffened against him. If she were to give him what he wanted, their relationship would take a whole different turn. So, perhaps, would her life.

"I'm not a child, Webb," she said.

"I know. And I'm not sixteen anymore. We both know what we want. I'm in love with you, Kristin. And I want you. If that's what you need to hear, there it is."

She gazed up at him. Either the man had just offered her his heart or he was lying, something men were prone to do. But why should he lie, when he was powerful enough to get his way with a word? Only one question remained: What role did he have in mind for her, wife or mistress?

Either way, she wasn't prepared to give him what he wanted.

So how could she make a graceful exit? She could protest that she had a headache, or that she was tired and had a busy day of appointments scheduled for tomorrow, or even that it was the wrong time of the month. But that would only delay the real issue. And Webb deserved better. He deserved the truth. Even if it made him angry.

His arms tightened around her, pulling her so close that she could feel his hardness through the layers of clothing that separated them. "Well, how long do you plan to keep me standing here?" he demanded.

Steeling herself, she looked up at him and shook her head. "I'm not ready, Webb," she said. "You're a fine man, and given time, I might come to love you. But that time isn't now."

His arms dropped, releasing her as he took a step backward. His eyes were cold. "So how much time do you need?"

"I don't know. I'm not in a position to promise anything."

"I see." His face wore the expression of a man unaccustomed to refusal. "I'm willing to give you some time, Kristin. But I'm not known to be long on patience. I won't wait forever."

"I understand. And you must know how much I've enjoyed our friendship."

"Screw friendship! Good night, Kristin." He turned away and stalked back to his automobile.

CHAPTER TEN

THE NEXT MORNING, LARS REPORTED THAT EZRA WAS PLANNING TO leave town with his parents and wouldn't be coming back to work. Logan was tempted to ask him how Gerda was taking the news, but remembering the big man's protectiveness toward his daughters, he held his tongue. The family was none of his business.

Ezra's injury left the crew shorthanded. Until a replacement could be found, Logan stepped in and took his place. Hammering, sawing, and bracing the frame as it went up were hard work. Logan didn't mind that part. He was learning new skills that he could put to use. But it took him from other needed tasks like the planning and management of his ranch.

On the third day after Ezra's accident, a stranger rode up to the site of the barn—a man with stringy black hair under a droopy, grease-stained hat. Mounted on a dappled horse that appeared as thin and poor-looking as its rider, he came up quietly and sat watching the work for a few minutes before he spoke.

"Looks to me like you blokes could use some help." Logan recognized his brogue as lower-class Irish. "Angus O'Rourke's the name. I own the spread up there in the foothills. Raisin' some cows and such."

"Of course." Logan laid down his hammer and turned to introduce himself to his neighbor. "Webb's mentioned you. I was wondering when we'd have a chance to meet."

"Webb, the almighty Calder." He spat a stream of tobacco off the far side of his horse. "I heard you was some shirttail kin of his. But I won't hold that against you. Since we're neighbors, I'm hoping we can be friends." He swung off his horse and stepped forward to shake Logan's hand. He was a small man, the crown of his hat not much higher than Logan's shoulder. But his sinewy hand was surprisingly strong. The eyes that squinted up at the rising barn were a startling shade of green.

"That's a mighty big barn you're buildin'," he said. "It appears that you could use more hands on the job. Are you hirin'?"

"Maybe. If we can find somebody who's not afraid of hard work." Logan glanced toward Lars, who'd paused to listen.

"How about me?" O'Rourke asked. "I got me a fine ranch, with plenty of cows, but I'm short on cash. My little girl, my Maggie, she's got a birthday comin' up. I'd like to buy her a doll like the one she saw in the store. And my boy, Cully, he's growin' like a weed and needs new shoes. I done plenty of building on my ranch, so I know what to do. What d'you say?"

Logan glanced at Lars again. He was in charge of the crew; it was his decision to make. The big man hesitated, then nodded.

"We'll try you out," Logan said. "If Mr. Anderson here thinks you've proven your worth, you can stay on. If not, we'll pay you for your time and send you home."

O'Rourke grinned, showing yellowed teeth. "When do I start?"

"You can start right now," Lars said. "Take one of those hammers. If you can pound a straight nail, you're hired for the day. After that, we'll see."

Angus O'Rourke proved to be a hard worker and smart enough to follow instructions. If any fault could be found with him, it was that words flowed out of his mouth like water from a broken pipe, mostly about his ranch, his growing herd of cattle, his pretty wife and daughter, and the strapping son he was grooming to take over the dynasty one day. Logan had heard enough from Webb to know that most of what O'Rourke said was blarney. The ranch was short on water and grass, his cattle were in poor condition, and his family struggled to keep food on their table and clothes on their backs.

O'Rourke had more to say as he and Logan took a break on the porch, drinking cold water and looking out over the pasture, where the white-faced yearling steers grazed on fresh spring grass.

"Now, take those steers of yours," he said. "I can see from here, they're all branded with the Triple C. I can tell you right now why that isn't a good idea."

"I don't see the problem. I bought them from Webb. Since I plan to sell them in the fall along with Webb's herd, I didn't think it worth the trouble of rebranding them. There are only fifty head—I don't have fenced pasture for more. Webb said he'd pay me for the number I turned back to him."

"And you're trusting him to keep his word? Hell, you don't know Webb Calder like I do. He'll cheat you as sure as you're born—claim you shorted him, or that he didn't get as much for the steers as he expected. Or that yours were underweight. You can bet on it."

Logan scowled. The man was clearly a troublemaker, trying to win him as an ally against Webb. There was a lot of that power game going on in this new home of his—choosing sides, taking sides, lining up support for the next conflict whenever it came. But he wasn't going to be taken in.

"I'll take your advice for what it's worth, O'Rourke," he said. "But I've no cause to believe Webb would cheat me, especially for fifty head, when he's got thousands of animals."

O'Rourke gave him a sly look. "I can't force you to believe me. But when it happens, don't say I didn't warn you."

"Let's get back to work." Logan turned and walked away. Common sense told him that the man was lying. But the words had soured his day. What if it wasn't safe to trust anyone? Webb might not cheat him. But he'd tried to manipulate him. Blake Dollarhide resented him for buying the ranch and would move to take it if given a chance. And Lars was firmly allied with Blake's family. Even Kristin—the image of her smiling up at Webb flashed in his memory. She had saved his life. But he couldn't trust her—not anymore. In this hostile land he had no real family and no true friends. He could depend on no one but himself.

* * *

Gerda hummed a lively polka as she tidied the surgery, wiping down the exam table, arranging the instruments, and laying out clean towels before the next patient arrived. What a fool she'd been to weep over a boy like Ezra. Let him go to California. She had found herself a *man.*

Only yesterday, as she was walking home after work, Mason had come by in his auto and offered her a ride. They'd ended up on a quiet lane, exchanging kisses that made her heart gallop and her head spin. Beyond that, nothing had happened. But she could tell he'd wanted more. So had she.

Everything was going as she'd hoped. If Hanna could catch herself a rich, handsome Dollarhide husband, by heaven, so could she.

"Goodness, but you're cheerful today." Kristin had walked into the room. "Is there some special reason?"

"Yes!" Gerda knew it would be wise to keep quiet, but she couldn't help herself. She spun like a dancer, making her skirt flare prettily around her. "I'm in love! Really, truly in love!"

Kristin's dark brows came together in a frown. "Isn't this a little sudden?"

"Perhaps. But when you know, you know. And he loves me, too. He hasn't said so, but I can tell."

Kristin's frown deepened, although she looked more worried than angry. "So who is the lucky boy?" she asked.

"He's not a boy. He's a man."

Dismay flashed across Kristin's face. She shook her head, muttering something under her breath. Too late, Gerda realized she should have kept her secret.

"Gerda, is it Mason you're seeing?"

Gerda didn't answer, but Kristin clearly took her silence as a yes.

"Listen to me." She seized Gerda's arm, gripping hard. "Mason is my brother. I know him. He has a terrible reputation with women."

"But he's not like that with me," Gerda said. "He loves me. And I love him."

Kristin took a sharp breath. "Hasn't anybody told you what he did to your family? Ask your mother, or Hanna, or Britta."

Gerda squared her shoulders and lifted her chin. "I already know what he did to Hanna. I remember hearing people talk about it. But that was a long time ago. He didn't really love her. But he loves me."

"Mason only loves Mason," Kristin said. "But if you really care for him, you'll break this off. When your father finds out—and he will—you know what will happen. This could end with one of them dead, and it would be your fault."

Before Gerda could reply, a rap on the front door signaled the arrival of the next patient—young Lester, who was here to have the stitches in his scalp taken out.

"Think about what could happen—think hard." Kristin's words followed Gerda as she hurried to the front door.

At the end of a busy afternoon, Kristin sank onto the front room sofa. She'd been too busy for more talk with Gerda. But the girl had left promising to weigh the consequences of her involvement with Mason. Kristin, in turn, had agreed not to tell her family for now—but only if Gerda ended the relationship. Had she made the best decision? Right now, she was too tired to think about it. Blast Mason. He deserved to be horsewhipped for taking advantage of yet another vulnerable young girl.

A fresh bouquet of Lorna Calder's pink roses sat on the coffee table in their glass vase. A peace offering from Webb, delivered this morning by a rider from the ranch. She hadn't seen him since their tense parting on the front porch. But the flowers were a clear message that she could expect him soon. For now, she would let matters run their course. Soon the season for roses would be over. What would happen then?

She had promised to join Blake's family for dinner tonight at the big log house on the bluff. They'd be celebrating little Elsa's sixth birthday. The occasion was a happy one, but Kristin had mixed feelings about what might be said—or not said—at the table. As the promised keeper of secrets, first Joseph's and now Gerda's, she would need to watch her words. And how would she respond if Blake, ever the dutiful big brother, were to lecture her about seeing Webb?

Never mind—a glance at the clock told her that she barely had time to clean up and change before making the journey through town, down the south road, across the pastures, and up the hill to the house. She would leave the noisy, unreliable Model T in the shed and take the neighbors' horse and chaise. At least the ride, with the sun fading in the west, might calm her nerves and settle her mind.

Blake's family welcomed her as warmly as ever—although Blake's narrow-eyed glance told her he'd heard the rumors about her keeping company with Webb Calder. And Joseph seemed to be avoiding eye contact with her. Was there more going on than he'd told her when they'd last talked in private? And did it have anything to do with Mason?

Hanna had set the table with a linen cloth and Sarah's good china, crystal, and silver. She'd even picked a bouquet of wildflowers for a centerpiece. Clearly, she'd wanted to make tonight a happy occasion for her family, and especially for little Elsa.

Kristin would not have spoiled the celebration for the world. She kept silent about the things she knew. Still, she could sense the specter of Mason's return hanging over them all. Her half-brother had the power to destroy two families. And he was capable of doing it without a thought for anyone but himself.

After dinner, birthday cake, and the opening of a few gifts, including the little sailor dress Kristin had ordered from Sears Roebuck, the children went to their rooms to get ready for bed. Hanna followed Elsa to help her get undressed and tuck her in.

When Blake beckoned her out onto the porch and closed the door behind them, Kristin felt like a naughty child being taken to the woodshed. She was a grown woman and not answerable to her brother, even as head of the family. Still, she wasn't looking forward to facing him.

"I suppose you've heard the reports," she said, breaking the silence first.

"The whole town is talking," he said. "You and Webb Calder. What are you thinking?"

"Maybe that this is my life, and I'll live it as I choose."

"But it isn't just your life. Everything you do reflects on our family." He paused, taking a deep breath. "Are the two of you lovers?"

"No. Not yet. If it happens, I'd say that's my business."

"He won't marry you, you know. He'll string you along and parade you in public just to embarrass me."

"Only if you choose to be embarrassed—and only if I choose to be strung. I'm not a fool, Blake. And I'm not a child. Damn it, I'm not even a virgin. When you're in a war, with people dying all around you, and you know you could be next, you take comfort any way you can find it."

He turned away from her, shaking his head. "This isn't the Western Front. This is Blue Moon, Montana. And so help me, I'm not sure I even know you anymore."

The words stung. Kristin forced herself to accept the pain. "War changes people," she said. "Time changes people. You've changed, too. But I'm still your sister, and I still love your family."

He didn't turn around. "You've thrown in your lot with my sworn enemy. And nothing you've said gives me any hope that you'll change your mind. I think you'd better leave."

Shocked, she froze where she stood. She'd never meant to push Blake this far. She'd only meant to make it clear that he couldn't tell her how to live her life. Now she'd opened a rift between them—one that might never heal.

When he didn't speak or turn around, she took a ragged breath, walked down the porch steps, and followed the path around the side of the house to the stable yard, where she'd left the horse and chaise. Climbing onto the seat, she picked up the reins and headed the horse down the hill. The risen moon was bright. There was no need to light the lantern that she'd put under the seat.

Rounding the first bend in the road, she looked back toward the house. Blake was standing on the porch where she'd left him, gazing out at the night, his arms folded across his chest in a pose that was the very essence of stubbornness.

By the time she reached the bottom of the hill, where a side road cut off to the sawmill, the tears had begun to well in her eyes and spill down her cheeks. If only she could take back the defiant words she'd spoken. But it was too late for that. All she could do was move on and hope for some way to make peace with her brother.

Stopping the chaise where the two roads merged, she rested the horse for a moment, thinking. She could go home the way she'd come, back across the fields to the main road that led straight through town, or she could go around the sawmill and take the logging road that cut through Logan's ranch, then swung toward town to emerge just north of her house.

The logging road was shorter but rougher and more isolated. But the moon was bright, and in case of any trouble, she had a loaded Winchester .73 behind the seat.

Recalling the tragic story of Blue Moon's previous doctor, who'd been killed at night when a speeding truck hit the back of his buggy on the main road, she made her decision.

The sawmill had shut down for the night, the chain-link fence higher and stronger than she remembered. Electric lights mounted on poles provided extra security.

Mr. Garrity, the old man who'd once kept watch over the place, had passed on, along with his faithful dog. Kristin remembered the day Alvar had been working at the mill when a log had splintered under the blades and driven a shard of pine through his leg. With Alvar's mother gone, Kristin had been called to treat the injury. It had been Garrity, a veteran of the Indian wars, experienced in extracting arrows, who'd talked her through the process of removing the shard. That had been the day she and Alvar had fallen in love.

Even now, Kristin found herself wondering if she would ever love anyone as much as she'd loved Alvar. They'd been so young and innocent, heedless of the forces that would tear them apart. She was no longer young and no longer innocent. She'd learned through sad experience that love—like a song or a summer day— is good only for the brief time it lasts.

Could she love Webb? Did she want to let him back into her life? Tonight, there were no answers. All she wanted was rest.

The road had changed over the past weeks, with the heavy log wagons passing over it every few days. The ruts were cut even deeper, the weeds in the high center worn away. For the safety of the horse, she chose a parallel course along the right-hand bank. The night was quiet, the moon-silvered grass whispering in the breeze. From somewhere in the darkness, a coyote called. Farther away, another answered. The chaise swayed gently with the motion of the wheels over the ground.

Kristin was getting drowsy by the time she saw the light, faint with distance, like a fallen star below the eastern foothills. Impulsively, she swung the horse to the right and headed in that direction. Logan's ranch was out here somewhere. The light was most likely coming from there. But in case she was heading into danger, she reached behind the seat, retrieved the Winchester, and laid it within reach.

She and Logan hadn't parted on the best of terms, and it was mostly her own fault. First, she'd warned him against getting involved with Webb. She'd even walked out of the room when he'd announced that he was buying the ranch Webb had chosen. Then, the next time he saw her, he'd learned that she and Webb were courting—or at least appeared to be. If Logan wanted nothing more to do with her, she could hardly blame him.

But tonight's clash with Blake had brought home the need for a calm, impartial friend, someone who would demand nothing from her. She had some fence mending to do—if only Logan was in a mood to accept her apology.

As she neared the light, she could see the frame of the unfinished barn and the fenced pasture with its grazing cattle. Reflected moonlight gleamed on their white faces as they turned to look at her.

The house lay beyond the barn. A lantern, hanging from a post by the door, cast shadows across the yard. Halting the chaise, she climbed down and hitched the horse to a leg of the windmill tower. She was about to start for the house when a voice out of the darkness riveted her in her tracks.

"Stay right where you are, stranger. Both hands in the air, now."

Even though she recognized the voice, Kristin did as she was told. "It's me, Logan," she called. "For heaven's sake, don't shoot!"

He stepped into sight, lowering his rifle. "Making a house call, are you, Doctor?"

She chose to ignore his tone. "I was taking the short way home from my brother's house. When I saw your light, I decided to stop by." She paused, scrambling for a way to break the ice. "I don't suppose you have any whiskey, do you? I could use a drink right now."

"Sorry, not a drop. But I know somebody who does. Maybe you should've gone that way." He exhaled a long, slow breath. "If you'll settle for coffee, I can brew some. It won't take long."

"Thanks. I was getting sleepy."

"You're welcome to come in, but there's no place to sit except the kitchen table."

"That'll do. I don't plan to stay long. I was just hoping you'd give me a chance to clear the air."

"No need for that. I figure everything's been said. But if you've got something to get off your chest, I'll listen. Since you saved my life, I owe you that courtesy."

She followed him through the empty living room and into the kitchen, where he set the lantern on the table, then pulled out one of the two wooden chairs and seated her. Turning, he added a stick to the stove, measured a scoop of Arbuckle's into the enameled coffeepot, and added water.

"For whatever my opinion's worth," he said, talking as he worked, "Webb is a good man. True, he can be pushy when it comes to getting his own way. But his heart's in the right place. When I congratulated the two of you, I meant it. You could do worse. So could he—in fact I can't think of how he could do any better than you."

Kristin gazed down at the wood grain in the table. She knew the words were well meant, so why didn't they give her any satisfaction?

"Logan, I can imagine what you're thinking," she said. "But I've made Webb no promises. We're friends. He'd like to be more than friends. But I didn't go to medical school, survive a war, and come back to Blue Moon just to be a rich man's wife. In fact, I'm not even sure that a wife is what Webb wants. I'm giving it time, but I honestly don't know what's going to happen."

"Do you love him, Kristin?" He kept his gaze fixed on the coffeepot.

"Not yet. Maybe I could if I were to let myself. But I'm not ready to take that step."

"Then why are you here?" He turned to face her. "What makes you think that I'd give a damn what you and Webb decide to do with your lives? It's not as if I can help you make up your mind."

The words hit Kristin like a slap. She stood, her voice quivering as she spoke. "You can move that coffee off the heat. I won't be here long enough to drink it. I came because I thought you were my friend. And I didn't plan to talk about Webb. I only wanted to apologize for the way I behaved at his house when you said you were going to buy this property. Now that I've said it, I'll be on my way."

He slid the coffeepot to the cooler side of the stovetop. "I'll take the lantern and walk you to your buggy," he said. "We've got boards and nails scattered around the yard. It's not safe to be out there in the dark."

He came around the table and took her arm, his hand cupping her elbow as he steered her toward the front door. "It's probably best that you don't come out here again," he said. "Especially at night. You don't want talk that could damage your reputation— or give your boyfriend the wrong idea."

"Stop it!" Temper flaring, Kristin pulled away and spun to face him. "You sound like my brother, and I've heard enough. I'm tired of being lectured and judged by men who have no business telling me what to do. *You* were the one who brought up the subject of Webb. And when I gave you an honest reply, you started in on me. If I didn't know better, I could almost believe you were jealous!"

"*Jealous?*" His dark eyes burned into hers as he loomed over her. "You're damned right I'm jealous! Watching the two of you that night at the Roadhouse, every time he touched you, every time you looked at him, I had to grind my teeth. And short of starting a fight, there wasn't a blasted thing I could do about it. So let's get you on your way before I lose control and do something I shouldn't."

Only as he spoke did Kristin realize that *those* were the words she'd wanted to hear. A wild recklessness surged in her—and with it a hunger that could only be satisfied one way.

As he reached for her arm, she caught the back of his neck with her hand. Pulling him down to her, she pressed her mouth against his in a desperate kiss.

For an instant, he went rigid. Then his arms went around her, crushing her close against his hard-muscled body. Desire raced through her veins like fire through parched grass. She'd been drawn to Logan from the first moment they met, but only after he confessed his jealousy did she realize how much she needed him—and wanted him.

His kisses tasted of the fresh water he'd been drinking. She softened her mouth to the passion in them, the thrust of his tongue, the quickening of his breath. Where her hips molded to his, she felt his arousal jutting against the fastenings of his jeans. A moan rose in his throat as she moved against him, touching off shimmers of unspeakable pleasure.

She freed her mouth from his long enough to whisper, "Please, Logan, right now I need . . ."

"Need what?"

"I need you to do what you said . . . lose control and do something you shouldn't . . ."

"I can manage that." With a mutter, he scooped her up in his arms, carried her into the bedroom, and flung her onto the bed. Undressing was out of the question—the hour was late and the need too urgent.

As he leaned over her in the darkness, her fingers fumbled with his belt buckle. He helped her, shoving down his jeans before he reached through the tangle of her skirt, petticoat, and drawers to find her waiting for him, wet and open. She bucked against his hand, her breath coming in eager gasps. "Now," she whispered. "Hurry."

He moved between her legs and entered her in one long push. Big and hard and powerful, he filled the emptiness inside her, the length of him pushing deep. She thrust her hips to meet each driving stroke, flesh against flesh, sending bursts of sensation through her body. She came once, then again, her legs pulling him deeper as he drove toward his own climax. He gasped, shuddered, and lay still.

Spent, they sprawled on the bed, side by side. Tenderness lingered like an aura between them. But Kristin knew that it couldn't last.

"Will you be all right?" he asked her.

She knew what he meant. "Yes, I'm quite sure of it."

She could hear him breathing in the darkness, probably wondering what to say next. Maybe she'd shocked him. Most so-called ladies were more restrained.

"We shouldn't do this again," he said. "Not at least while things are unsettled between you and Webb."

"This isn't about Webb," she said. "And just in case you're wondering, no, I haven't done this with him, and I don't plan to."

He drew a deep breath. "If you had, it wouldn't be any of my business. I don't intend to tell him, or anybody else about tonight. But I'm a bit old-fashioned when it comes to some things, Kristin. I believe in playing for keeps. And I'll be damned if I'm willing to share you with another man. If I see you back here— ever—I want it to be because you're ready to be my woman.

"If you make a different choice, I'll understand. Webb can offer you anything you and your future children might need. Right now, all I can offer you is a dream of what this ranch can become. If you don't come back, as far as I'm concerned, tonight never happened."

His words hurt—but they were wise, tough, and fair. Tonight had been like a sky full of fireworks, but it had happened too fast. They needed time apart to come to terms with what was between them.

"Understood." She sat up and began rearranging her clothes. "It's time I was getting home. I don't like staying away too long.

You never know when some emergency will show up at my door."
She was babbling, making excuses to fill the awkward silence.

"I can saddle up and ride alongside you. You never know what
could be out there in the dark."

She shook her head. "I'll be fine. The moon's up, and I've got
a rifle in the wagon. Believe me, I know how to use it."

"Fine, but I'll walk you to your buggy." He was ready by the time
she stood and pulled her skirt down. Taking the arm he offered,
she let him lead her outside to where her horse waited by the
windmill tower.

As he helped her into the chaise, she battled the urge to fling
herself into his arms for a passionate farewell. That would only
make things harder.

"Be careful, and don't forget me, Dr. Kristin Dollarhide." He
smiled up at her in the darkness.

"Not much chance of that." Tearing her gaze away from him,
she forced herself to give the horse a light slap of the reins. The
moon lit the way as the chaise rolled out of the yard and over the
open prairie toward the road home.

CHAPTER ELEVEN

A FEW DAYS LATER, LOGAN LOOKED UP FROM FILLING THE CATTLE tank to see a rider approaching from the direction of the Triple C. Even through the blur of distance, dust, and summer heat waves, there was no mistaking the erect figure of Webb Calder.

Logan finished filling the tank, then strode to meet his visitor at the house. Webb hadn't been here since the day Logan had purchased the ranch and made it clear that he would run the place his own way. Tension had escalated between them when Logan had negotiated the road access with Blake Dollarhide and hired Lars to build his barn. Maybe Webb had decided it was time to make peace.

Or maybe Kristin had confessed her late-night visit.

Standing on the porch steps, Logan watched his relative dismount, hitch his horse to the rail, and walk across the yard, his bootheels raising little whorls of dust behind him. The silence was broken only by the sound of hammers from the barn, where Lars, Pete, and Angus had begun layering long, flat boards over the roof beams.

"Welcome, neighbor." Logan stepped off the porch. "I've been wondering when you were going to pay me a visit."

"I'm just on my way back from town," he said. "Kristin asked me to give you her best."

Logan willed his pleasant expression to freeze. If Webb had come for a confrontation, he could expect anything.

But Webb simply turned toward the hammering sound. "Nice barn," he said. "Big."

"Yes, and the stable addition will make it even bigger," Logan said. "Come on in if you want. I can't offer you anything to drink except water, but at least it's cold."

"Thanks, I'll take it out here," Webb said. "Next time I'll bring you some Scotch. I've still got a good supply."

"I won't tell a soul." Logan went back into the house and filled two glasses from the canvas bag he kept wet to cool the water by evaporation. Taking a glass in one hand, he hooked his arm through the back of a chair and carried it out to Webb.

When he came out a second time with another chair and a glass for himself, Webb was seated, sipping from his glass and studying the barn again.

"Looks like they're doing a decent job," he said. "But are you sure you want that scrubby little Irishman on your property? If you'd asked me, I'd have warned you about him."

"O'Rourke?" Logan shrugged. "He seems okay. We were short a man when he showed up asking for work. He's done all right, except that he never stops talking. Why? What would you have warned me about?"

Webb finished his water and lit a cigarette from the pack in his shirt pocket. The pungent smoke curled upward as he exhaled. "Let's just say you'd best keep a careful count of those steers," he said. "If any come up missing, look for them on the O'Rourke place. That's where I've found a few of mine."

"Isn't stealing cattle a hanging offense?"

"It is. But I've never caught the little buzzard red-handed. He always claims the cows wandered onto his place and got mixed in with his own, and that he was planning to herd them back onto the Triple C. I know that's so much hogwash, but the man's got a wife and two kids. As long as I get my cattle back, I give him the benefit of the doubt."

"Thanks for the warning. I'll keep an eye on him." Something told Logan that Webb hadn't come here to make small talk. But he'd get around to what he really wanted in his own time.

After going on about the hot, dry change in the weather and the prospects of a serious drought, Webb straightened in his chair and cleared his throat. "I actually came to ask for some advice," he said. "You're a widower like I am, Logan. How much do you know about women?"

Caught off guard, Logan barely managed to hide his surprise. It wasn't like Webb to ask such a personal question—not unless he was having woman troubles.

"I can't claim to know much," he said. "My wife was a good woman, but with a career in the army, I was barely home for enough time to sire my children. We never really got to know each other the way most couples do. But I was faithful, and I loved her."

"I loved my Lilli with all my heart and soul," Webb said. "For years, I thought I'd never find another woman I'd want to marry. But then I met Kristin."

Logan felt his heart plummet into the pit of his stomach. He waited for Webb to go on.

"Last night I asked her to marry me," Webb said. "I thought she'd be happy. I thought she'd say yes. Instead . . ." He shook his head. "The way she looked at me, I thought she was going to bolt like a spooked mare. She said it was way too soon for that question. Not only that, but she asked for some time apart to concentrate on her practice and think about the kind of future she wants. And then she sent me packing like a whipped dog. I've never been so humiliated in my life! I should have walked away and left things at that. But I can't stop thinking about her. What the hell am I supposed to do now? Give her time? Give her another chance? I know everything there is to know about ranching and cattle and how to handle men. But I can't understand a woman who turns down an offer of everything she could possibly want—money, respect, a beautiful home, and a damn fool man who worships the ground she walks on."

He fell silent, clearly waiting for an answer—one that Logan was in a poor position to give him. Webb was a man in love. And now Logan had stepped between him and the woman he wanted.

Logan couldn't—and wouldn't—change what had happened between him and Kristin. But he owed Webb as much truth as he could spare.

"I can't tell you what to do, Webb," he said. "But Kristin has faced challenges that you can't even imagine. She's learned to be strong and independent, to be in charge, and she doesn't want to let go of that. If you mean to win her, the one thing you mustn't do is take away—or even threaten to take—her freedom. Does that make sense?"

Webb sighed. "It does explain why my proposal made her skittish. But damn it, all I want is to make her happy. I want to protect her, take away her worries, give her the best of everything."

"Then all I can do is wish you luck."

Webb stood. "Thanks for your advice. It goes against my nature, but if it works, we'll name our first boy after you."

Logan watched him ride back toward his ranch, keeping Webb in sight until he disappeared in a haze of heat and dust. Webb Calder was a good man. He was also a forceful and persuasive one, capable of wearing Kristin down until she agreed to marry him. If that were to happen, Logan could only accept the loss graciously, nurse his battered heart, and hope that Webb had the wisdom to take his advice.

Kristin deserved to be happy—even if it was with another man.

On the lower part of the Dollarhide Ranch, in a pasture where the cattle grazed, there was a spot where the creek had been widened to form a pond. Over time, cottonwoods had sprouted and grown tall, with branches that overhung the water. On one side, where the bank was too high for the cattle to trample it getting to water, the grass was dotted with wildflowers.

The creek was cold; but on a day like today, with the summer sky blazing overhead and heat waves shimmering above the pastures, the four boys—Joseph, Buck, Cully, and Chase—welcomed the chill. With their clothes strewn on the bank, they swam naked, splashing, ducking, swinging on the rope they'd slung from one of the overhanging limbs and joking about how the cold water shrank their dicks.

When their teeth began to chatter, they climbed out of the water, pulled on their clothes, and sat on the high bank, tossing pebbles in the pond and talking.

"Will you two be showing up tonight?" Buck nodded toward Joseph and Cully. Earlier, on their way here, they'd all noticed the black ribbon tied to the fence, Mason's signal that a shipment would be coming in. This would be the third time the boys had been summoned to help.

"I'll be there if I can sneak out," Joseph said.

Cully nodded. "I'll be there for sure."

"You should come with us, Chase," Buck said. "We get ten dollars for less than two hours of work. Where else can you make that kind of money?"

Chase shook his head. "Not me. I don't need the money, and my dad would kill me if he found out. Anyway, you three might want to think about quitting. There's a new sheriff in town. His name's Jake Calhoun. Dad says he's sworn to put a stop to the illegal booze smuggling. He'll be watching, and if he catches you, you'll be shipped off to reform school, probably till you're eighteen."

Joseph felt a chill that had nothing to do with his damp clothes or the light breeze that rippled the surface of the pond. Chase was probably right. The money and the thrill of doing something dangerous were hardly worth the risk of disgracing his family and ruining his future.

But something else—the allure of the man with the broad shoulders, chestnut hair, and riveting green eyes—drew him like a spell. Mason Dollarhide. Blood of his blood. Bone of his bone. His father.

They hadn't talked privately since that brief exchange the first night. But Joseph knew that Mason was watching him—how he worked, what he said, and how much the other boys respected him. Joseph wanted his father to like him, or at least accept him. And he wanted to know the man who, in his eyes, appeared as glamorous as the swashbuckling pirate from a movie he'd seen in Miles City.

Dangerous or not, he would be there tonight.

Joseph's escape from the house had gone as planned. As he reached the junction in the road, he could see his two friends in the moonlight, waiting on their horses. "Did anybody see you?" he asked as he joined them. "With that new sheriff in town, we can't be too careful."

"Nobody saw us," Cully said. "And even if they did, hell, we're just kids out fooling around at night. All they'd do is send us home. Come on, let's go."

The road was empty as they rode south to the Hollister Ranch. There was no sign of the truck and no settling dust or odor of fumes to suggest that it might have passed. They tethered their horses by the gate and crossed the yard to the barn, where they found Mason waiting alone.

"I knew I could count on you boys to show up," he said. "There's been a change of plans. With that new sheriff prowling around at all hours, we can't have the truck going straight through town. I've told the driver to come here by the back road, the one the lumber wagons take to get to the mill."

"Cully and I know that road," Joseph said. "You pick it up north of town. After the sawmill, you can cut back to the main road and head south. No need to go through town at all."

"Good, that's helpful." The barest hint of a smile tugged at Mason's mouth. "The driver is new. He'll have his lights off, and he doesn't know the way. Joseph, I want you and Cully to meet him north of town, on the main road, and guide him. Can you do that?"

"You bet," Cully said.

"What about me?" Buck demanded.

"You'll stay here and help me move some boxes to make room for the new shipment. Now, is everybody straight?"

The boys nodded, although Buck looked disappointed that he wouldn't be getting in on the action.

Joseph and Cully cut through fields and back lots on their way to the rendezvous point with the truck. If that new sheriff was watching Main Street, they didn't want to be noticed, which might lead to their being stopped and questioned.

"Do you think Chase would ever tell on us?" Cully asked as they waited in the shadows for the truck to show up. "I know his dad hates your family. And he doesn't like mine much better."

"Chase is our friend," Joseph said. "He wouldn't tell on us—not unless we did something to make him really mad."

"I know. But what if he did? He could get us in a lot of trouble."

"Don't worry about it," Joseph said, looking down the road. "Listen. Hear the engine? The truck's coming."

As the truck rumbled closer, driving without headlights, Joseph dismounted, walked to the roadside, and waved the flashlight Mason had lent him. He had to jump out of the way as the driver pulled onto the shoulder of the road. The man who rolled down the window was a stranger. But Joseph had no doubt that he was armed, just as the last driver had been.

"Turn off that damned light and show me where to go," he growled.

Joseph switched off the flashlight. "Yes, sir. Follow me and my friend."

The sky was cloudy, but the moon shed enough light for what was needed. The boys rode a few yards ahead and the truck followed, swaying over the deep wagon ruts and grinding the axles against the high center. Joseph could imagine the driver cursing as he alternately gunned and slowed the engine. He would be in a foul mood when they arrived at the Hollister Ranch.

When the truck lurched hard to one side or the other, Joseph could hear the sound of clinking, sliding bottles. If any were broken, there could be trouble. But that wasn't his worry or Cully's, he reminded himself. They were only doing their jobs.

Sometime after midnight, Logan was awakened by what sounded like a racing engine—loud but muffled by distance, as if coming from the wagon road. Still muzzy from sleep, he raised his head.

His first thought was that the road, rutted by wagon wheels, and carved even deeper by rain and snow, was no place for a heavy motor vehicle. Then, as he sat up and swung his legs off the bed, it came to him that anyone driving along that road in the middle of the night was probably up to no good.

Bootleggers. Wasn't that what the new sheriff had told him when he'd stopped by the ranch a few days ago? Rumor had it that a well-connected gang was smuggling liquor over the Canadian border and hauling it south to a ranch, from which the cases could be sold to distributors at a premium price. Could that be what he was hearing?

Picking up the loaded .44 that he kept within reach of the bed, he walked outside and stood on the porch, listening. By now the sound of the engine was fading. After a few minutes, he could barely hear it moving off in the direction of the sawmill and the Dollarhide Ranch.

Could Blake Dollarhide be involved in smuggling? That didn't sound like Blake. But Logan couldn't rule it out—any more than he could rule out an innocent explanation for what he'd heard— like a late-night delivery of equipment for the sawmill. Maybe his imagination was working overtime. In any case, when he went to town, he'd report what he'd heard to the sheriff. If nothing was done, he'd deal with the problem himself. He was a peace-loving man, but he drew the line at smugglers cutting across his property.

The truck had made it to the Hollister Ranch almost an hour later than expected. By the time the driver backed up to the barn, Mason was in a lather. "What the hell happened?" he demanded as the driver climbed down from the cab. "I was imagining you behind bars and the law coming after me next!"

"That road ain't fit for a herd of buffalo, that's what happened," the driver said. "We met right on time. But I couldn't drive more'n five miles an hour without gettin' stuck or bustin' an axle."

Joseph and Cully had started unloading when Mason called

Joseph over. "We can't let this happen again. Is there a better way for the next shipment to get here?"

"Not for anything as big as a truck," Joseph said. "But the going would've been easier if he'd driven alongside the road, through the grass and brush, instead of in the wagon track."

"So why in hell's name didn't you tell him that?"

"I'm sorry, sir. We should have told him. But he didn't ask."

Mason scowled. "Next time, for God's sake, say something. Now get back to work. You too." He pointed to the driver. "We've got to get this truck unloaded and out of town before first light. Move it!"

He picked up a box and almost threw it onto the stack. Joseph felt small and stupid. He'd never wanted to make Mason angry. He would do better next time, he vowed. Whatever he had to do, he would make his father proud of him.

The major's lower leg was damaged beyond repair, the bone shattered, the flesh shredded by shrapnel. Even if she could dig out every scrap of metal, there was so little muscle left that the leg and foot would be useless. Or gangrene would set in and do even more damage. With sirens wailing and shells bursting outside the tent, she made her decision. "I'm sorry. The leg's got to come off. I'll do my best to save the knee joint, but I can't promise."

"No! You're not taking my leg." She'd heard the protest before, more times than she could count. This time the voice was calmer and more resolute, but her answer was the same.

"If I don't take it off, you'll die." She nodded to the nurse who stood by with the ether mask. The tray with the scalpel, bone saw, and antiseptic solution waited behind her.

"I said no! I'll die first!"

"It's my job not to let you," she said. "As the property of the U.S. Government, it's not your choice anymore."

"To hell with the government!"

"You'll be put to sleep. When you wake up, it'll be over. Nurse, go ahead."

But the nurse had stepped away. The mask, connected to a valved can-
ister by tubing, lay next to the table. She would have to administer the
anesthetic herself.

So far, she'd avoided looking at the officer's face. Seeing it in her mind
would only make things harder when the time came to start cutting. But as
she turned with the mask, she met his gaze. She gasped.

It was Logan.

Kristin's eyes jerked open. She was shaking beneath the quilt
that covered her bed. The dream had been shockingly real. She
could almost hear the echo of exploding shells and smell the
odors of disinfectant and soiled bandages. The last time she'd
had such a disturbing dream had been in Webb's house. Logan
had been lying next to her on the bed. In her half sleep, she'd
been aware of his arm pulling her close, calming her and making
her feel safe. But tonight there was no one to hold her.

The craving for a glass of whiskey to blur the awful images was
like acid in her gut. Since the war, she'd learned to depend on alcohol to dull the dreams and the awful memories. If she were to
marry Webb, she could have all the liquor she wanted. She could
drown her demons anytime she chose. All she needed to do was
say yes to him.

And what then?

She lay back on the pillow, closed her eyes, and tried to bring
back the sensation of Logan making love to her—the delicious ur-
gency, the surrender that was like jumping off a cliff and sprouting
wings. Logan, filling the cold, empty places inside her, warming her,
loving her.

What if she were to saddle a horse and gallop out to his ranch?
Would he welcome her? Would he take her to his bed? Or, knowing Logan, would he remind her of their resolve to remain apart
and escort her firmly back to her horse?

She craved him even more than she craved a drink. But Logan
was right. If she were to go to him now, without resolving things
with Webb, anything could go wrong. If Webb were to discover

their tryst and believe she'd been stolen from him, he was capable of destroying the man he'd brought here as a friend and ally.

Kristin's thoughts were interrupted by a frantic banging on the front door. She swung her legs off the bed, reached for her robe, and pulled it on as she hurried to answer.

A young husband, wide-eyed and disheveled, with his coat on over his pajamas, stood on the doorstep. As soon as she saw him, Kristin knew why he'd come.

"It's Belinda," he said in a breathless voice. "Her water broke and she's having pains. I've got the buggy out front."

She gave him a reassuring smile. "It sounds like things are happening just the way they're supposed to. Wait in the buggy, Charles. I'll get some clothes on, grab my bag, and be right with you."

Closing the door, she rushed back to the bedroom to get dressed. Belinda Poulsen was a healthy young woman. Kristin had examined her two days ago and found the baby in good position with a strong heartbeat. Tonight's delivery showed every sign of having a happy outcome.

Kristin's spirits rose as she picked up Sarah's old doctor's satchel and hurried outside. Times like this were the reason she'd come home to Blue Moon; and right now, that was all that mattered.

More than two weeks had passed without the sight of another black ribbon tied to the fence. Once, in town, Joseph had passed Mason on the street. Mason had pretended not to see him. It was the smart thing to do, Joseph told himself. Still, it stung not being acknowledged by the man he idolized.

Had he and his friends been dismissed from their so-called jobs in the Hollister barn? Or had there simply been a lull in shipments? Maybe the truck had been stopped somewhere and the driver was in jail—perhaps naming names. There was no one the boys could ask. All they could do was wait.

As the rainless days grew hotter, the grass yellowed and crackled underfoot. Windblown dust rose from the fallow pastures, creating a gritty haze that stuck to people's teeth. Here and there, grass fires sprang up—easily put out but frightening reminders of what could happen if the right conditions came together.

Around the dinner tables there was talk of selling off cattle early to save precious feed and water. The creeks that had been filled to overflowing in the spring ran low and sluggish, trapping trout in rocky pools, where they were scooped up and eaten by hungry families. On the ranches, tensions rose over water rights.

The creek that crossed Logan's property was getting dangerously low. But the well was still good. Because he had only a small number of steers, he was able to let most of the water flow downstream to the Dollarhides, who needed it more. This had infuriated Webb, who'd been urging him to build a reservoir and divert water into it.

"So when the Dollarhides run out, and their cattle start dying, they'll be over here with dynamite, just like before," Logan had responded. "I fought my war in Europe, Webb. I'll be damned if I'm going to fight another one here."

"Then you don't know how things work here in Montana," Webb had grumbled before walking away. "If you want to survive, you have to fight for what's rightfully yours, not give it away. I'd hoped that I could teach you a thing or two, but it appears that you'll have to learn the hard way."

Logan hadn't seen his cousin since that conversation. But even at a distance, the tension between the two men was palpable. There were no more invitations to supper, no more visits, no more exchanges about Webb's woman troubles—and no word from Kristin.

The nights had been quiet as well, with no more passing trucks on the road. Logan had alerted the sheriff to what he'd heard, but nothing had come of it. After this much time, he'd begun to wonder if the engine sound had even been real.

At least the barn was coming along. The sides were covered with sturdy boards, and the tarpaper-covered roof was more than half shingled. When it was done, the framing for the stable extension, with twelve box stalls and a tack room going off the west side, would begin. Next spring, as soon as the weather warmed, Logan was planning to bring in his first young quarter horses for breaking and training. Some he would sell to the ranches. The best he would keep for breeding.

It was the first week in July when Pete mentioned the Blue Moon Independence Day celebration. "Are you going?" the freckle-faced young man asked Logan. "It's this Saturday. Food, fun, dancing—it's the best thing that happens all year."

"I have no idea what you're talking about." Logan passed a bundle of pine shingles up the ladder to where Pete was working his way along the roof's edge.

"The celebration started twelve years ago—or was it thirteen?" Pete spoke between hammer blows. "The immigrant farmers and their families put on the first one, with a picnic, games, and a dance. They invited the whole town. It was such a success that after the drylanders moved on, the town took it over. Blue Moon's not as big as it used to be, but this Saturday they'll have people coming from all around. They've even hired a band from Miles City."

"I take it you're going," Logan said.

Pete grinned. "I wouldn't miss it, 'specially the dance. My girl's going with me. We'll be dancing till the band packs up to go home." He glanced down at Logan, who was moving the ladder to bring up more shingles. "You should go. The war's left some good-looking widows in town. A couple of them have already asked me about you."

"I can't say I'm much of a dancer with this leg." Logan carried another bundle of shingles up to the roof.

"You wouldn't have to dance. Just smile at them. You'd have those ladies bringing you pot roast, home-baked bread, and apple pie every day of the week."

Logan shook his head. There was only one woman he cared about. Would Kristin be at the celebration? Would she be with Webb? All the more reason to stay away, he thought. Seeing her in another man's arms at the dance would be torture.

"Aw, come on," Pete teased. "You're turning into a hermit out here. It wouldn't hurt for you to make some new friends in town. Besides, think about the food. The best of Blue Moon kitchens. Hey, the war's over. Live a little!"

"I'll think about it. No promises."

Pete hammered down another shingle. "At least buy a ticket. The money's going toward a new schoolhouse that the townfolks want to build."

"I can go along with that. Bring me a ticket tomorrow and I'll pay you. Whether I use it will be up to me."

"Oh, no you don't." Pete grinned. "You can only buy tickets in town, on Saturday. Now that you've promised to buy one, you'll have to go."

"I guess maybe I will." Logan felt a gust of wind on his perspiring face. Looking west, beyond the barn, he could see a cloud of brown dust sweeping across the pastures in its path toward them.

"Time to get down," he told Pete. "Take any loose shingles with you, and let's hope the others are nailed down tight. You can put the horses in the barn and ride it out in the house or head on home. Work's over for the day."

Pete had seen the dust. "I'm right behind you. Doesn't look like a big storm, but it could be a nasty one." He called out a warning to Lars and Angus, who were laying the first section of floor in the stable.

"I'm heading for home." Angus swung onto his horse. "I need to make sure the wife and kids are safe."

Logan watched him ride away. In the pasture, the steers had huddled close together and bedded down, the way a herd did on the trail. That morning Logan had counted them. There were forty-nine, not fifty. He remembered Webb's warning, but he didn't want to believe Angus would steal from him. After the dust storm, he would check the fence for breaks and give the missing animal until tomorrow to show up.

Lars was moving the horses into the barn. Pete was taking down the ladder and gathering up anything that could blow away. Logan thought briefly of Kristin, hoping she wasn't caught in the open somewhere. She was a strong woman and knew how to take care of herself. Still, it was frustrating to imagine that she could be in danger when he was unable to help.

He scanned the yard for anything that might have been left outside. Then, with dust blowing around him, he hurried to close the windows and secure the house.

Mason checked the stacked boxes in the barn to make sure they were concealed with canvas and hay. For the hired help on the ranch, he'd concocted a story about setting up a mail-order business to sell pest extermination supplies, with stock that included some dangerous poisons. The uneducated cowhands had actually bought the story, along with the admonition that they weren't to go near the barn. Still, Mason knew he couldn't be too careful.

After bolting the barn doors from the inside, he left by a side door, locked it, and headed for the house. Dust storms always made his mother nervous. She would have already brought the dogs inside—the filthy, drooling beasts. He would find them crouched like stone lions on either side of the chair he called her throne.

He'd never had much affection for the old woman. When he'd headed home after twelve years, he'd hoped to find her frail and fading, ready to surrender her ownership of the ranch. But no such luck. She was as sharp as a tack and as tough as old boot leather. For all he knew, she would outlive *him.*

On the front porch, he took a moment to watch the dust storm sweeping across the lower pasture. Business was good, with plenty of customers showing up in the dead of night. But his store of liquor was getting low, and the shipment he'd ordered appeared to be stalled somewhere. Next week, if nothing had shown up, he would make a trip to the Western Union office in Miles City and use their telephone service to make a call.

Meanwhile, he was due for a little old-fashioned fun. The town's annual Fourth of July celebration would be going on this Saturday. He could show up at the dance and twirl the ladies around the dance floor—give them a thrill. He might even steal a few kisses from that pretty little Anderson girl. Blue Moon didn't have much to offer in the way of a good time. But who knew? He might be pleasantly surprised.

The storm was getting close. Opening the front door, Mason braced himself to ride it out with his mother and those damned dogs.

CHAPTER TWELVE

THE PASSING STORM HAD LEFT A PATINA OF BROWN DUST EVERY-where—a portent of disasters to come, people said. By Saturday, however, most of the dust had either been swept up or blown away. Blue Moon was dressed in its festive best with bunting and banners strung along Main Street.

The festivities would begin at eleven o'clock with a children's parade from the log schoolhouse to the site of the picnic and dance, which had been set up at the far end of Main Street. The children, dressed in their holiday best, would wave miniature flags and march in unison to the beat of a toy drum, played by Miss Britta Anderson, who would follow along in the rear to keep them in line. When they reached the bandstand, they would sing several patriotic songs and lead the audience in the Pledge of Allegiance. Even the ranch children who were homeschooled, like Elsa and Annie, were invited to take part.

Lunch would follow, served from a lavishly laden buffet table. Afterward there would be family activities and a baseball game set up in a vacant lot. After a break, the band would tune up, and the dance would begin.

Kristin had arrived early to cheer her nieces as they passed in the little parade. She was also hoping to find Blake and make peace with him. Growing up, despite their age difference, they'd been close. And Hanna was like a sister to her. They were all the family she had. It was time she moved to mend the rift between them.

She was scanning the crowd for her brother when she heard the children's parade coming from the far end of the street. She stood at attention, hand on her heart, to show respect for the flags and the youngsters who carried them. The sixth-grade boys— Joseph, Cully, Buck, and Chase—were missing. They'd declared themselves too grown-up to march with the younger children. According to Gerda, Britta had excused them; but she'd made it clear that they wouldn't be sharing the cookies and punch that were waiting to reward the marchers after the program.

Gerda would be here today, doubtless looking her prettiest and keeping an eye out for Mason. Every time she thought about the girl, Kristin wanted to shake her. Not that it would do much good. The little fool thought she was in love and there was no convincing her that she'd made a bad choice.

Kristin had promised to keep Gerda's secret if she ended the relationship. But every instinct told her that the girl was still sneaking around. Somebody—maybe Blake—needed to corner Mason and read him the riot act. Or better yet, maybe she and Blake should confront their half-brother together.

The children were lining up in front of the bandstand to sing when Kristin caught sight of Blake and Hanna. Slipping through the crowd, she managed to reach them before the program started.

Blake gave her a sidelong glance as she came up to him. "Are we on speaking terms yet?" she asked.

His gaze narrowed. "That depends. Where's Webb?"

"Do you see him anywhere?"

"Oh, stop it, you two. We're family." Hanna reached out and gave Kristin a hug. "We're always glad to see you."

"And just so you won't have to ask," Kristin said. "Webb hasn't gone away. We're friends. But I'm not giving him any encouragement. My hopes are that he'll get tired of waiting and give up on me. Meanwhile, maybe it's time the two of you shook hands like grown-ups and ended your fight."

"That's what Logan Hunter told me, too," Blake said. "But you can't shake hands with a rattlesnake. As for Logan, he's been fair with me, but he's got Calder blood, too. I know better than to trust either one of them."

At the mention of Logan's name, Kristin's pulse quickened. But her expression betrayed nothing. "Blake, I need to talk to you about our brother," she said.

"If it's about Mason and Gerda, we already know," Hanna said. "Britta found out and told me. I've tried to talk sense into the girl, but she won't listen, not even to me. She says he's changed and that she loves him."

"Then you and I need to talk to Mason, Blake," Kristin said. "I'm hoping he'll show up here today. If he does, are you with me?"

"Of course," Blake said. "But we won't be here tonight. The girls will be tired, and we don't care about the dancing. If Mason doesn't show up before then, you're on your own."

"I understand," Kristin said. "If I see him, I'm prepared to tear a strip out of his hide."

The children had begun singing "America the Beautiful," ending the buzz of conversation as the short patriotic program began. Once the songs and readings had ended, people collected their children and, along with latecomers, flocked to enjoy the luncheon buffet of donated casseroles, sliced ham, rolls, salads, and desserts. There were a few tables, but most families ate in their buggies or on blankets spread on the dry grass.

Kristin glanced around for Webb. Last week he'd told her that he was busy at the ranch but might come for the food and the dance. It was a relief not to see him here. She wasn't looking forward to his clashing with Blake. She didn't see Mason either. If past history was any indication, he would show up to dazzle the ladies at the dance, but otherwise he wasn't much for mingling with the townspeople.

Gerda, in a blue dress that matched her eyes, was here with her parents and sister. Her gaze searched the crowd, her expression first anxious, then disappointed.

The line for the buffet table was thinning. Kristin was about to fill her plate and join Blake's family when a well-remembered figure caught her eye. Her pulse skipped.

Logan was standing at the fringe of the crowd, his Stetson tilted to shade his eyes from the sun. His face was in shadow, but she could tell he was watching her.

The surge of yearning was so powerful that her knees weakened beneath her. How long had he been here? Did she dare go to him, or should they do as they'd agreed and pretend to ignore each other in public?

But her feet had already answered that question. She was weaving her way through the crowd, her heart pounding as she neared him. She'd told herself that she could keep him out of sight and out of mind. But she'd been wrong.

He remained where he was, letting her come to him, his expression revealing nothing. Only his eyes showed emotion as she stopped within a pace of him, close enough to speak but not to touch.

"I didn't expect to see you here," she said, making a show of conversation.

"I got talked into buying a ticket to support the new school, so I thought I might as well use it. At least the food looks good." He bent slightly closer, lowering his voice. "Damn it, Kristin, I don't know how much longer I can stand this."

"I feel the same," she whispered. "But Webb could do you a lot of damage if he thought you'd stolen his woman—even though that wouldn't be true. I know him. He can be generous, but he can also be vindictive. Trust me, you don't want him as an enemy."

"I'm almost past caring about that. Is he here?"

"I haven't seen him. But even if he were to show up and see us, we're only talking."

"Talking isn't what I've had on my mind, lady."

"You're not helping." She gave him a smile and a slight shake of her head. "I'd invite you to share lunch with my family, but Blake just declared that he doesn't trust any man with Calder blood."

"I understand." He exhaled. "But it's so damned childish, this whole blood feud. You and I have been through a real war, Kristin. We know what it's like to face a real enemy. This . . ." He shook his head. "It's like some kind of game with two teams."

"I hate to tell you this," Kristin said. "But if water gets much scarcer this summer, it won't be a game anymore. It'll be a real war. Tempers will be hair-trigger; and if anybody gets hurt—or killed, God forbid—things will get serious fast. It's happened before. It could happen again. And it's not just over water. An accident, a legal dispute, or even a fight over a woman—anything can touch off violence, like a spark to tinder."

"And that's why you're worried about Webb?"

"Exactly."

"You know I'm not afraid of him. I'm only keeping my distance for your sake."

"Maybe you should be more worried about yourself. Webb wouldn't just challenge you to a fistfight. That's not his style. He's got hired men who would burn your ranch, kill your stock, and do whatever else he ordered."

Logan glanced around as if to see whether anyone might be listening. Then he leaned closer. "Let's get out of here," he said. "Come with me. Not for long. Just a few minutes to be by ourselves. My horse is tied behind the hardware store."

Kristin understood the risk involved in what he was asking. But she needed a moment in his arms—needed it too much to be cautious. "Go on," she said. "If I can get away, I'll be there in a few minutes."

She turned to check the crowd as he walked off. There was no sign of Webb. Blake and his family, including Joseph, were picnicking on the blanket they'd brought. They'd be expecting her, but they wouldn't be concerned if she didn't join them. No one else appeared to be paying her any attention. Taking her time, she slipped away, walked back down the street, and around the far side of the hardware store.

Logan was waiting with his buckskin horse. He mounted and swung her up behind the cantle with her skirt bunched over her knees. Taking a back road through the fields, they emerged onto open ground, where Logan nudged the horse to an easy lope.

With her arms wound tight around him, Kristin laid her head

against his back. As she listened to the beating of his heart, she remembered the last time they'd ridden double, when he was weak from blood loss, and she had to hold him on the horse. So many things had happened since then—not the least of them falling in love with him.

He stopped the horse in a spot she recognized, where cottonwoods and willows grew around a seeping spring. The place was on the border of the Dollarhide Ranch—but he would know that. After easing her off the back of the horse, he dismounted and took her in his arms. His kiss was long and slow and deep, his tongue tasting her, stroking the sensitive tissues inside her mouth. Waves of molten desire poured through her, pulsing deep in her body. Through layers of clothing, his arousal pressed hard against her hip. But they both knew that nothing was going to happen here, not today.

"The next time we make love, I want it to be where we can take our time," he murmured between kisses. "I want to memorize every curve and hollow of your body, to love every part of you. But I don't know how long I can stand this waiting. Webb needs to know. We need to tell him before he figures things out for himself."

"Not yet. I need to make a clean break with him—and it will go easier if it's his idea. Trust me, I know him. My family knows him. This could come back on all of us, not just you and me."

He sighed and released her. "Is there a chance he could hurt you?"

"I've never known him to hurt a woman. Not physically, at least. But he could damage you or take his anger out on my family."

"You make him sound like a madman."

"He's not. But he's a very proud man, accustomed to having his way. Nobody defies Webb Calder and gets away with it."

"We're defying him now. He just doesn't know it." He pulled her close in a quick, hard hug. "Come on. It's time you were getting back to your family. I'll let you off somewhere safe."

"You're not going back to eat, at least?"

"Better for me, and safer for you if I don't make an appearance. Don't worry, I already got what I came for."

They rode back in silence, both of them aware that they couldn't risk more time together. Not until she made things right with Webb.

He let her off near her house. From there she could walk back to the celebration without anyone questioning where she'd been. Kristin watched him ride away, feeling his frustration as she felt her own. This tangled mess was hers to resolve. She had to find a way.

The sun was low in the sky when the musicians from Miles City—a fiddler, a guitarist, and a bass player—took their places on the bandstand and began warming up. Years ago, when the immigrants had put on the celebration, accordion players from the Old World had played mostly polkas and waltzes. When the band on stage broke into a lively foxtrot, the younger couples flooded onto the dance floor.

Blake's family had gone home. But Kristin had stayed in the hope of talking to Mason. So far, he hadn't shown up. But the hour was early yet. He might be planning to come later and make an entrance. That would be like him—or at least like the Mason she remembered.

Kristin wasn't the only one watching for Mason. Gerda had no end of partners, but even when she was on the dance floor, her gaze searched the crowd, looking for the one face she wanted to see.

As the twilight deepened, electric lights, strung above the dance floor, twinkled on, lending a magical effect to the darkness. Faces glowed. Skirts and petticoats swirled to the music. Even the shadows seemed to dance.

The men, mostly cowhands, outnumbered the women at least two to one, so no willing female lacked for partners. When a homely young cowboy asked Kristin to dance, she gave him her hand and let him whirl her around the dance floor. He was polite and shy and surprisingly light on his feet. When he returned her to her place, she rewarded him with a genuine smile. There was still no sign of Mason. Maybe he wasn't coming after all.

Two tall figures stood in the shadows off to one side of the dance floor. One of them was Britta. The other was her father,

Lars. Kristin studied them with furtive glances. Big Lars, with his hulking frame and craggy features, kept a fierce eagle eye on Gerda as she danced and flirted. His expression said clearly that if he had his way, girls would be locked up at home until suitable husbands showed up to claim them.

Tall, like her father, Britta towered over average-sized men. But there was a grace about her slender figure that Kristin had noticed and admired. Her strong features, freckled by the sun, failed to meet the day's standard of dainty, porcelain beauty. But her blue eyes lit her face with kindness. Now in her mid-twenties, she'd already been dismissed as an old-maid schoolmarm. But she deserved better, Kristin thought. She deserved a man's love and a family of her own.

Now she stood well back from the dance floor, as if to avoid the humiliation of not being asked to dance. Her face, in this unguarded moment, wore a wistful expression. Was she here to keep watch on her popular sister—or maybe to control her volatile father? It was hard to believe that she would choose to be here for herself.

The catchy foxtrot tune had ended. There was the usual shuffling of partners, a buzz of conversation. Then a hush fell as a tall figure strode across the floor—long legs clad in jeans, trail-worn boots, a holstered pistol—the only one allowed here—slung from his belt, and a leather vest emblazoned with a star-shaped badge. It was the new sheriff, Jake Calhoun, and he was walking straight toward Britta.

He was a handsome man with dark hair and chiseled features that hinted of his ancestry—Cherokee, perhaps, or Spanish, or even Creole. When he faced Britta, he was tall enough to look straight into her eyes.

She looked surprised, then seemed to recover. "Am I under arrest?" she asked.

A smile tugged at his thin mouth. He held out his hand. "May I have the honor of this dance, Miss Anderson?" he asked.

She looked skeptical for an instant, as if she thought he might be joking; but then she gave him her hand and allowed him to lead her onto the dance floor. The musicians glanced at one another, then took up a slower blues beat.

He took her in his arms, leaving the proper nine inches of space between them. Britta wasn't an expert dancer, but she must've practiced, perhaps with her sisters, because she was able to follow his lead. They made a stunning couple, elegant in their height and grace. For the first few beats they were alone on the floor. Then other couples moved in around them.

Kristin had been watching them when she noticed a subtle stirring on the far side of the floor. Heads turned as Mason stepped into view.

Tastefully dressed in twill pants, a matching vest, and a raw silk shirt, he surveyed the dancers like a sheikh making a selection from his harem. Gerda had already seen him come in. She was looking past her cowboy partner, wriggling her fingers to catch Mason's eye.

The dance ended. A radiant Britta was returned to her father's side. Gerda, breathless with anticipation, stood in plain sight as Mason took his time, eyeing other girls, playing her, making her wait.

Damn his arrogance! Kristin thought.

At last he turned and, with a smile, walked toward her with his hand extended. Visibly wilting with relief, she took it and let him lead her onto the dance floor. The band broke into a newly popular jazz tune.

Clasping Gerda's waist, Mason drew her close, arching her back over his arm in a scandalously daring series of steps and moves. The crowd on the dance floor drew back to watch. Was this the way they danced in glamorous places like New Orleans, San Francisco, and Hollywood?

Startled, Gerda was rigid at first, but she soon adapted, letting Mason be the star while she played the manipulated doll. The crowd was cheering them on when a roar of incoherent rage erupted from the sidelines.

White-faced with fury, Lars charged onto the dance floor.

"No, no, Papa!" Britta pleaded, clinging to the back of his shirt.

But she was no more than a trailing feather as he pulled her along behind him. The crowd parted as he headed straight for Mason and Gerda and yanked them apart.

Gerda screamed as his huge fist slammed Mason in the side of the jaw and sent him reeling. "You are the devil!" Lars bellowed. "You ruined one of my daughters! Now you ruin this one! I will kill you!"

Staggering from the first blow, Mason was vulnerable. Gerda flew to him, trying to protect him. Lars flung her aside and waded in for another punch that struck him full in the face. Mason doubled over, clutching his nose. Blood seeped between his fingers as Lars raised his fist for another crushing blow.

"Stop it right there, Mr. Anderson." The sheriff had drawn his pistol. His voice was cold. "Don't make me shoot you to save this man's life."

"You would shoot me for defending my family honor?" Lars had dropped his hands. He stared at the sheriff, a bewildered expression on his face.

The sheriff holstered his gun. A pair of handcuffs seemed to appear from nowhere. "Lars Anderson, I'm arresting you for your assault on Mr. Dollarhide. Put your hands behind your back."

Meekly now, Lars complied.

"No! Don't arrest him!" Britta sprang to her father's side, facing the man who'd held her so gently on the dance floor. "He doesn't understand. Let me take him home."

The cuffs clicked into place, painfully tight around Lars's massive wrists. "I'm sorry, but he's broken the law," the sheriff said. "Now please step aside, Miss Anderson."

Britta shot him an angry look, then hurried to comfort her sister, who'd broken into heart-wrenching sobs. As Lars was led away, Kristin pushed through the crowd to aid her brother. He was on his feet, still clutching his broken and bleeding nose. Someone passed her a clean, white handkerchief. She gave it to Mason to soak up the blood.

"We've got to get you to my surgery," she said. "I came on foot. How did you get here?"

"My auto's out by the street," he muttered. "I don't know if I can drive. Can you?"

"I can. Come on." She took his arm. "Tell me where to find it."

Unsteady and hurting, he leaned on her for support as they walked back toward the street. Behind them, the band had started up again. In the faint glow cast by the electric lights, she glimpsed Britta shepherding Gerda toward their buggy. By now their father would be behind bars. Poor, humiliated man. Someone needed to speak up on his behalf.

"That old bastard damn near killed me," Mason said as he climbed into the passenger seat of his auto.

"With good cause, I'd say." Kristin took the key from him, set it in the ignition, and got out to crank the starter. They spoke little until she had him propped on her operating table and was washing the blood from his face and hands. His expensive vest and trousers were hopelessly bloodstained. His silk shirt was soaked down the front.

"So help me, sis, except for a few kisses, I never touched that old man's daughter. Oh, I know that I crossed the line with Hanna. And look what she's got now—a rich husband and a right fine boy. You could almost say I did her a favor. But that was in the past. I know better now."

Kristin used a speculum to guide the crooked nose back into shape. Mason cursed as he felt the painful pressure begin.

"I could leave it the way it is," Kristin said. "I've been told that some women find a broken nose attractive on a man."

"Just get it done," Mason muttered between clenched teeth. "I could've had that girl anytime I wanted, you know. More than once, she practically threw herself at me. At first, I was tempted. She's a pretty little thing. But then it struck me that she was out to get knocked up and land herself a husband, like her sister did. No way did I want to be a part of that scheme." He winced as she applied a dressing to hold the straightened nose in place. "Anyway, I don't know if I could survive having that giant Cro-Magnon as a father-in-law."

"Our brother gets along with him just fine. All done. You'll need to leave that dressing on for at least three days, and be very careful after that. Make sure you sleep on your back, with a pillow or two to raise your head.

Mason sat up, touching the dressing gingerly. "So how much do I owe you for this, *Doctor*?"

"Not a cent, if you'll do me a favor."

"Name it. Anything for my baby sister."

"Just this. The one thing Lars Anderson prizes most is the honor of his family. Years ago, what you did to Hanna cast shame on them. He's never forgotten. And seeing you with Gerda, he lost control. I want you to go to the jail tomorrow and tell the sheriff that you won't be pressing charges."

"What?" he stared at her, his face beginning to swell from the punch to his jaw.

"You heard me, Mason. Keeping that good man in jail and forcing him to stand trial would only cause more pain to his family. As for you—forgiving him would be a step toward paying down your own debt."

"My debt to the devil?" His roguish smile was lopsided.

"If you want to put it that way." She gathered up the soiled cloths, her instruments, and the remnants of the dressing she'd applied to his nose. "Will you be all right driving home? I have a cot for patients who need to stay. I could make you a bed."

"I'll be fine. In fact, I'll enjoy giving my mother a good scare when I walk in tonight—if she doesn't sic her dogs on me."

"And tomorrow you'll go to the jail? The sheriff won't know why Lars hit you. It might help to tell him."

"I'll go. It should give me a few points on the plus side of the heavenly ledger." Battered and bloodied, but still cocky, he made his way out the door and down the sidewalk to his auto.

Standing on the porch, Kristin watched him drive away. Could she believe him about Gerda? Mason had been known to lie in the past. But she wanted to trust her brother—just as she wanted to believe he would show up at the jail tomorrow to drop the charges against Lars. Still, she would follow through to make sure it happened.

As she turned to go inside, another thought struck her—one that froze her where she stood. It was something Mason had mentioned in passing, a phrase that had barely registered when he'd said it. Now it hit her like a bomb.

. . . *look what she's got now—a rich husband and a right fine boy.*
A right fine boy.

Why would he say that about Joseph unless the two of them had met?

CHAPTER THIRTEEN

BY MIDMORNING THE FOLLOWING MONDAY, LARS WAS BACK AT WORK on the barn. By then, Logan had heard about his arrest from Pete, who'd been at the dance. Wisely, Logan chose not to mention anything to the big Swede. Lars's pride had suffered enough.

And Logan had more pressing concerns. The steer missing from his herd hadn't shown up. The animal could have escaped the pasture, become lost or injured, and maybe fallen prey to coyotes. Or, as Webb had warned him, it might have been stolen. The fence was sound, which meant the steer had most likely been herded out the gate.

Acting on Webb's advice, he decided to pay a discreet visit to the O'Rourke Ranch. Angus was working on the far side of the barn with Lars and Pete. He wouldn't see where Logan was going when he rode out the back way and took the trail that wound into the foothills.

The day was already warm, the sky a cloudless blaze of blue. Yellow grass swished against the legs of his horse. Two vultures circled overhead, riding the updrafts on outstretched wings. Here and there, Logan began to see cattle wearing O'Rourke's shamrock brand. They looked poor, as Webb had described them, probably because the grass on this part of the range tended to be thin and scraggly.

Logan didn't see his missing steer among them, but he did take note of how easy it would be to over-brand a Triple C with a shamrock. When he got his own brand—one more item on his long mental list—he would be sure to design one that couldn't be easily changed.

In the distance, he could see O'Rourke's house, a low-slung clapboard structure that leaned a few degrees to the west. A ramshackle barn stood behind it. Laundry flapped from a wash line. Someone, probably Angus's wife, was hanging up more pieces. She waved, a sign that he'd been spotted. Nothing to do now but ride up and introduce himself.

As he approached, a small girl who'd been standing beside her broke away and raced toward the house, probably something she'd been taught to do when a stranger approached. But the woman seemed friendly enough. She was delicately built, with black hair and gray eyes. She'd probably been a beauty once, but poverty and hard work had worn all the softness from her face and body. The unhealthy flush in her otherwise pale cheeks suggested that she might not live to see her daughter grow up. Maybe he should suggest that she pay a visit to Kristin. But that would be intrusive, and there were some things, like consumption, that even a doctor couldn't cure.

He dismounted and walked toward her. "Mary O'Rourke." She held out her hand. "And I know who you are. Thank you for giving my husband some work, Mr. Hunter. Even though we've got land and cattle, cash in these times can be hard to come by."

Logan shook her work-roughened hand. "No need to thank me. Your husband's a good worker. I'm happy to have his help."

Looking past her, Logan could see an open shed where a large, white-wrapped object hung from a rafter by a hook. He recognized it at once. It was a skinned and dressed beef carcass, wrapped in cheesecloth to keep away the flies.

Was that his missing steer? He'd bet money on it. Why would Angus slaughter one of his own animals when he needed every one of them to sell in the fall?

But Logan had no proof. The hide had probably been buried or burned to conceal the evidence. And without positive proof, no man with a heart, not even Webb, could take away this family's father, husband, and provider.

"Is there something I can do for you, Mr. Hunter?" the woman asked.

"Just trying to track down a missing steer. White face. Triple C brand." Logan swung back into the saddle. "If it shows up here, have your husband bring it back to my place."

"Yes, I'll do that." She looked uneasy—she'd have to know the truth. But none of this was the poor woman's fault.

"I'll bid you good day and leave you in peace, Mrs. O'Rourke." He turned the horse back toward the trail. "Thank you for your time."

He headed out, knowing better than to look back. This time, the hungry family could have the beef. But he wasn't about to lose another steer, or anything else, to thievery.

Firing Angus would only worsen the situation. For now, he would keep him on. But he would watch the shifty little Irishman like a hawk. He would also need to keep an eye on the livestock at night, especially once he began shipping horses in. It might be a good idea to get a dog or two. He liked dogs. They were good protection and good company. He would think on it.

All in all, he had plenty of distractions to keep his mind off Kristin. But no concern was pressing enough to end his frustration with their waiting game. He wanted her—and he wanted the freedom to let the world know she was his. If she didn't end things with Webb soon, he would take matters into his own hands. He would go to Webb and tell him the truth—consequences be damned.

Every day Joseph had checked the roadside fence for the black ribbon that signaled plans for another shipment. He was getting anxious. Not because of the money—the forty dollars he'd earned, a princely sum for a boy, was stashed between the pages of *Treasure Island,* which he kept on the shelf above his bed. The worry was that the man who'd cast a magic spell over his life—his dashing father—might somehow be finished with him.

Last night he'd stolen out of the house, met his friends, and spent a couple of hours roaming the countryside. But the fun had

gone out of their nighttime adventures. Now it was all about waiting for the signal that had yet to come.

He'd made it home without waking his parents, but this morning he was exhausted. All he wanted to do was sleep. But his
dad—so called to distinguish Blake from his *real* father—would
have none of it. He was shaking Joseph awake at first light.

"Come on, son. We've got a fence down and cows getting out in
the lower pasture. I need you to help."

"Not now . . ." Joseph muttered into his pillow. "Lemme sleep."

"No, you don't." Blake jerked the covers off the bed, exposing
Joseph to the morning chill. "I've let you get away with running
loose all summer. You've barely done a lick of work, and you've
grumbled anytime you were asked to help. I don't know what's
going on with you, but it stops now. Get up, get dressed, and meet
me outside the stable in ten minutes. Your horse will be saddled
and waiting."

Joseph sat up. "What about breakfast?"

"Not until we've rounded up the cows and fixed the fence.
Someday, God willing, you'll be running this ranch. It's time you
started learning what it's all about."

You're not my real father! Joseph knew better than to say the
words out loud. For all his dad knew, one day he could be running the Hollister Ranch as well as this one. He'd be rich, maybe
even richer than the Calders.

"Get a move-on. I'll see you downstairs." Blake strode out of the
room. As the sound of his boots faded down the hall, Joseph
hauled himself out of bed and pulled on the clothes he'd piled
on the floor barely three hours ago. What would his dad do if he
found out he was not only in touch with Mason but working for
him? That would be the end of everything.

But never mind. A new day had started; and maybe by the end
of it, he would see that black ribbon tied to the fence.

Kristin buttoned her white coat, surveyed her immaculate
surgery, and prepared herself to face a full day's schedule of appointments. For now, she would put aside her suspicions about
Mason and Joseph. She would forget Webb's displeasure when

he'd shown up at the July Fourth dance to find her gone. And she would steel herself against the yearning to spend more time with Logan. Today she was a doctor. And her patients deserved the best care she could give them.

Through the closed door, she could hear Gerda talking to a woman with a crying baby. That would be the first appointment of the day—Mrs. Corcoran and Rupert, her colicky infant son.

Scheduling her busy practice had been a challenge. Kristin had finally resorted to posting a clipboard with a list on her front door, where patients could sign up for a time. The arrangement was helpful but far from perfect, especially in emergency cases. She could only hope the rumor was true that Blue Moon would soon have home telephone service. She would be first in line to sign up for it.

At least Gerda was doing a good job. The incident at the dance had upset her, but she'd recovered enough to be back at work the following Monday. Kristin was coming to depend on her more and more. When it came to record keeping, scheduling, and billing, she was a jewel. And she had a way of making the patients feel welcome and comfortable.

Now Gerda ushered the young mother and her squalling son into the surgery. The traditional remedy for colic was opium, but Kristin had reservations about the drug. After determining that nothing else was wrong with the baby, she prescribed warm baths, warm blankets, and back rubs. "If that doesn't calm him, let me know."

"I could use some calming myself." The mother managed a frayed smile.

"Then you might want to try the same thing." Kristin ushered her to the surgery door, closed it behind her, and waited for Gerda to show in the next patient.

No one came in.

After waiting a moment, Kristin opened the door and stepped into the front room. Her next patient, an elderly man with a history of heart problems, was waiting on the settee. There was no sign of Gerda.

"She ran back down the hall," the old man said. "Seemed in a bit of a hurry."

"Excuse me, I'll be right back." Kristin walked down the hall. Through the closed bathroom door, she could hear the sound of retching.

Her heart sank.

When her knock was ignored, she opened the door. Gerda was hunched over the toilet, her back and shoulders heaving. Kristin waited for the nausea to end. Then she sponged the girl's pale face with a wet washcloth. "Do you have something to tell me, Gerda?" she asked.

Tears welled in Gerda's pretty blue eyes. "I think I must be . . . pregnant."

"You think? When was your last menstrual period?"

"I . . . don't remember. A while ago, I guess."

Kristin sighed. "All right. I'll check you later today to make sure. But here's the big question. Assuming you're pregnant and you know how it happened, who's the baby's father?"

There was a long hesitation. Then the breath burst out of her in a single wracking sob. "It was Mason," she said. "Mason Dollarhide."

Kristin had never planned to visit the house where Mason lived with his mother. Growing up, she'd always imagined Amelia Hollister Dollarhide as a wicked witch like the one in fairy tales. She knew better now. Amelia was only a bitter, reclusive old woman, incapable of harming her.

And today, her business wasn't with Amelia. It was with Mason.

The sun was low in the late afternoon sky as she climbed out of her Model T and opened the front gate. She could hear dogs barking. Big dogs. But when no dogs appeared, she concluded that they must be chained or kenneled. No one was in sight. The door of the barn that stood south of the house was closed.

Resolute, she mounted the front steps to the porch and knocked on the door. After a moment she heard footsteps from the other side. The door opened to reveal an elderly man dressed in out-dated formal wear. He looked like a butler from an old British movie, she thought.

"How can I help you, madam?" he asked.

"I've come to speak to Mason Dollarhide. Please tell him his sister is here."

He shook his head. "I'm sorry, Mr. Dollarhide is—"

"I'll handle this." A silver-haired woman dressed in riding clothes strode into the room. She was small in stature with a stern, wrinkled face that commanded respect, if not fear. Peridot eyes inspected Kristin from head to toe. "I wasn't aware that Mason had a sister," she said.

"I'm his half-sister. If you'd kindly tell Mason I'm here—"

"Yes, now I see the resemblance to your father. I suppose I should invite you in." Her lips pursed, deepening the smoker's lines that framed her mouth. "Don't expect tea. Your family isn't welcome here. But it seems you have a nasty habit of showing up. First that bastard boy, and now you."

"I won't trouble you by coming in, thank you. But I need to speak privately to your son."

"Privately? Mason and I have no secrets. You can speak to him in my presence or not at all."

"I'm sorry, but that's not acceptable. If you'll tell him—"

"What is it, Mother?" Mason walked into the room. The dressing was gone from his nose, but the swelling had yet to go down. The bruise on his jaw had turned purple.

His mother shot Kristin a haughty look, then turned to her son. "This woman, who claims to be your sister, says she wants to talk to you."

"She *is* my sister," Mason said. "She also happens to be my doctor. Why are you standing out there, Kristin? Come on in and have a seat."

"This isn't a social call, Mason," Kristin said. "We need to talk privately. We can do it in my auto or wherever you like, but I'm not leaving until we come to some kind of understanding."

"All right." A worried look crossed his battered face. "Why

don't we talk on the porch. We can watch the sunset. Please excuse us, Mother."

Walking past the pouting Amelia, he stepped out the door, closed it behind him, and showed Kristin to a chintz-covered settee in the shade of the overhang. She took a seat at one end. He sat at the other. "Now, what is it, little sis?" he asked.

A memory flashed through Kristin's mind—how she'd adored Mason as a little girl. He'd been the fun brother, the charming brother. She'd tagged after him like a puppy. For an instant she wanted to spare them both the pain to come. But no, she had to see this through.

"What is it?" he asked again.

She sighed. "Remember what we talked about when I treated your nose? How you needed to stay away from Gerda?"

"Yes, and I told you I hadn't gone past a few kisses with her. I was telling the truth."

"Were you?" She shook her head. "I found out today that Gerda is pregnant. She named you as the father."

His swollen face paled. "No! She's lying, Kristin. I swear on my life! I never touched her, not that way."

"I wish I could believe you. But you've been seen with her. And knowing what you did before—same family, different sister—people will be talking."

"I know how it looks." Mason raked a hand through his hair. "But so help me God, I'm innocent this time. I knew from the start that she wanted me to get her pregnant, so I'd have to marry her. But I didn't fall for her scheme. I knew better. That baby isn't mine!"

He slumped forward, his arms resting on his knees, his hands clasped so hard that the knuckles had gone white. For a long silent moment, he stared out over the fields at the deepening sunset. At last, with a shudder, he spoke. "Good God, her father is going to kill me."

He was right—literally, Kristin thought. Lars had already threatened to kill him. When the big Swede learned that another daughter was pregnant, he wouldn't come after Mason with his fists. He would come with a shotgun.

"You could marry her," Kristin said. "It would quell the gossip and placate Lars. Besides, she's a beautiful girl. How bad could it be?"

"Tolerable for me, maybe. But I'm not good husband material. I'd only make her miserable. And I don't know if I'm up to raising another man's child."

"Your brother did it. And he loves Joseph like his own."

"That's a low blow, sis."

"Maybe it is. But in case you need a reminder, you abandoned Hanna's baby when you got on that train. And you have no right to him now—not even as a so-called uncle."

"I don't know why you're telling me this."

"I think you do. Whatever's going on here, Mason, leave Joseph alone. He knows about you and he's reaching out. If you let him get close to you, you'll only hurt him in the end."

He glanced away from her. "I don't know what you're talking about."

He was clearly lying. Maybe he'd lied about Gerda, too. Fighting anger, she stood. "Then maybe you should get back on that train. It would do us all a world of good. I've said what I came to say. Now I'll leave you to figure things out for yourself."

With that, she turned away, walked down the steps, and out through the gate to her auto. She didn't look back. She didn't want Mason to see her tears. She could only hope that someday he would learn his lesson. But how many hearts would he break along the way?

Cully had caught four nice-sized trout that were stranded by the low water in the creek. He had quick hands. He was able to grab each one and toss it, live and flopping, into the bucket he'd brought. The last one was still gasping when he mounted his horse and turned for home. He was in rare high spirits. His parents would praise him, and the fresh fish would make a tasty meal tonight.

He should have known that the happy feeling wouldn't last. It evaporated when he saw his father standing on the front stoop, a furious expression on his face.

As Cully dismounted with the bucket, Angus strode toward him. He shrank inside as he saw the bills clutched in his father's hand.

"This is what your mother found under your mattress! Where did you get this kind of money, Cully? Did you steal it? Can I expect the sheriff to show up here and arrest you?"

His free hand flashed out and slapped Cully on the side of the head. Cully saw stars as he lost his balance and went down. The bucket flew from his hand, spilling the fish in the dirt. He sat up. From the open doorway, he could hear his little sister crying.

"I didn't steal it, honest, Pa," he said. "I earned it." Cully could see his mother gathering up the fish and carrying the bucket to the pump to wash them.

"Earned it? How, in God's name? You're only a boy." Angus was still angry, but Cully detected a gleam of interest in his eyes.

Knowing he'd be found out and punished if he lied, Cully had no choice except to tell the truth. Little by little, with some prodding, the story spilled out of him. By the time he'd finished, his father was pacing with excitement.

"Why didn't you tell me sooner? If I'd gone with you, we could've made twice as much. Let me know when your boss has another shipment coming. I'll tag along. Since I'm older and stronger, he might pay me extra. Maybe he'll even give me a sample to take home."

Cully stifled a groan. His friends wouldn't like his dad showing up. The boss would like it even less. One more person in the mix, especially a talker like Angus, would only raise the chances of something going wrong.

There'd been no black ribbon on the fence for several weeks now. Maybe the shipments had stopped. Or maybe the boss had decided to stop hiring kids as helpers. Now that he wouldn't get to keep the money he'd earned, that was all right with Cully. Unloading cases of bootleg liquor and guiding the truck had been a fun adventure. But it wasn't worth getting arrested and sent to reform school.

Now that he'd finished the sixth grade, his school days were probably over. Joseph and Chase, and maybe Buck, too, would either travel to Miles City for more schooling or continue their studies by correspondence at home. The summer days spent riding, fishing, and swimming would soon be over. His friends would drift away, and Cully would have only his family. His father would expect his full-time help on the ranch. It wasn't much to look forward to. But then, nothing good ever happened to a boy like him.

With each passing July day, the drought deepened. The merciless sky beat down on sun-bleached grass so dry that it crumbled to dust underfoot. Webb Calder had thinned out his herd and driven the culls to the railhead in Miles City. Logan's small herd had gone with them. Better a disappointing profit than watching animals die of thirst. At least he hadn't tried to bring in horses this summer.

This afternoon Webb had stopped by for a visit on his way home from town. He'd brought a gift from home—a bottle of imported Scotch whiskey. The two men sat on the porch, in the shade of the overhanging roof, taking leisurely sips from porcelain mugs. The two large shepherd mix dogs that Logan had bought from a farmer sprawled in the shade of Lars's wagon.

From the far side of the barn came the sound of hammering. By now the exterior of the barn was finished, and the stable was almost framed. The three-man crew worked with wet cloths tied around their heads to ward off the heat. Logan had spent much of the day drawing up plans for sheds, corrals, and a round pen for horse training.

"When are you going to do something about the house?" Webb leaned back in the chair and stretched out his long legs, crossing them at the ankle. "You've been here four months and, except for hauling away the junk and scaring off the mice, the place hasn't changed. Hell, you've barely got furniture. And if you don't get the indoor bathroom finished by first snow, I guarantee you'll be sorry. It's not like you can't afford it. You could tear the place down and build yourself a damned palace with that oil money."

"And what would I do, rattling around by myself in a palace?" Logan chuckled. "I guess I got used to roughing it in the military.

It'll get done. But first things first. I need the ranch ready for horses in the spring. That means a lot of work has to be done."

"What you need is a wife," Webb said. "You've seen the Homestead. That house only got done because my mother was sick and tired of living in a shack. If it hadn't been for her, Dad would never have built it. Get yourself a good woman—like, say, that lady schoolteacher. She might not be much for looks, unless you like your women tall and skinny. But she's got a good, sensible head on her shoulders. She'd have this place looking shipshape in no time."

Logan bit back a curse. Webb didn't have a clue what was going on between him and Kristin. Maybe it was time somebody told him. But once the words were out, he wouldn't be able to take them back. It would mean the end of his budding friendship with Webb. Worse, Kristin would be furious with him for taking matters into his own hands.

"Speaking of women, did my advice work?" he dared to ask.

"You mean to back off and give Kristin some time?" Webb shrugged. "I don't know yet. She's been so busy with her medical practice, she barely seems to notice me. I showed up late at the July Fourth celebration hoping to get a dance with her, and she'd left to treat some fool with a broken nose. I waited, but she never came back. I can tell you I wasn't happy. What business does a woman have doing a man's job? She belongs at home, keeping house and looking beautiful. I wouldn't mind a few more babies, either. That would keep her busy enough."

"Then maybe you need to find a different woman. I don't think Kristin would give up her career for any man. She's worked too hard and sacrificed too much."

"That's what I keep trying to tell myself," Webb said. "But, damn it, I'm in love with her. There've been plenty of women I could've married if I'd chosen to. But she's the one—and when I want something as much as I want her, I don't give up. I keep after it until it's mine. It was like that with my Lilli. She was married to an old farmer. But that didn't stop me. Nothing did." Webb emptied his mug and set it on the porch. "So do you have any more advice for this lovelorn old man?"

Suddenly Logan had had enough. Webb might be the most powerful rancher in Montana, but that didn't entitle him to bend a woman to his will. It didn't give him the right to stand between two people who loved each other and insist on having things his way. Whatever calamity might follow, this maddening charade had to end—now.

"Maybe Kristin doesn't love you," he said. "Did you ever think of that?"

Webb looked startled. "I know how to win a woman's heart. That's not the problem."

"But what if Kristin's in love with someone else?"

"That doesn't make sense. If she's in love with another man, why would she be willing to spend time with me?"

"Because you've been kind to her," Logan said, "and she doesn't want to hurt you or to make you angry. She's hoping you'll lose patience and end things in a way that will save your pride. She cares about you. But she doesn't love you."

"Damn it, I don't believe you. How do you know that?"

"Because it's me she loves."

As the truth sank home, Webb's face went florid. Quivering, he rose to his feet. Logan rose with him, fully expecting what was about to happen.

He offered no resistance as Webb's powerful fist slammed into his jaw with a force that knocked him off his feet. Logan reeled backward, head spinning, as Webb stalked down the steps and mounted his horse. Without a backward look, he galloped away, a haze of dust trailing behind him.

CHAPTER FOURTEEN

AFTER THE LAST PATIENT HAD LEFT FOR THE DAY, KRISTIN MOTIONED Gerda to the couch and took a seat at the opposite end. "We need to talk about your plans for the baby," she said. "I want to be here for you any way I can, but it would help to know what you need."

Gerda stared down at her hands. "What's there to talk about? I'm going to have a baby. And when I tell Mason, he'll have to marry me."

Kristin sighed. The poor girl had some hard truths to face. "Gerda, you know that Mason's my half-brother."

Gerda managed a wan smile. "That would make you my baby's half-aunt wouldn't it?"

"Listen to me. A couple of days ago, I went to see Mason. I told him about your baby."

She gasped. "Oh, no! I wanted to tell him myself. Now you've spoiled it. Was he surprised? Was he happy?"

"Just listen. Mason swore that the baby wasn't his. He claimed that except for a few kisses, he'd never touched you."

Gerda's pretty face reflected shock. Then she laughed. "That Mason! You know how he's always joking. Of course the baby is his."

"In that case, only one of you is telling the truth. And I don't know who to believe. You know how people make babies, don't you?"

"Of course. The man puts his thing in, and . . . you know."

"Did Mason do that with you?"

"Yes. We did it a bunch of times—because we loved each other. That's what he said."

"And did you do it with any other man—like maybe Ezra?"

"No!" She was on her feet. "I can't believe you'd even ask me that. I don't want to talk about this. Can I leave?"

"Soon. I'm not trying to punish you, Gerda. You're family. You've done good work here and you're welcome to stay on as long as you like. But you need to think about your baby's future. What will you do if Mason won't marry you?"

"Mason loves me. He'll marry me. And if he won't, then my father will make him."

"Do your parents know about the baby? Do your sisters know?"

She shook her head. "Not yet. I'll tell them after Mason and I are married."

"My dear girl—" Kristin reached out to comfort her, but Gerda sprang to her feet.

"Please, I need to go." The girl was in tears. "Promise you won't tell my family—or anybody else."

"All right, for now. But if you wait much longer, you won't have to tell them. They'll guess."

"Why can't you just be happy for me?" Sobbing, Gerda rushed through the kitchen and out the back door. As she fled across the backyard in the direction of her home, Kristin stood in the doorway watching her go.

Maybe she shouldn't have spoken to the poor girl—or even to Mason. She'd meant to help, but it appeared that she'd only made things worse, even for herself. Had Mason lied to her? Had Gerda? Given Gerda's naivete and Mason's past history, it made sense to lay the blame on him. But a nagging instinct whispered that there was more to the story.

Pausing at the kitchen sink, she filled a glass with water and drank it all. She felt drained after the long, busy day, capped by the emotional exchange with Gerda. It was time for a break. She would get her surgery ready for tomorrow, make herself a sandwich and some tea, enjoy a leisurely bath, and curl up in bed with a good book, chosen from the pile on her nightstand.

After setting the glass on the counter, she walked back into the front room to lock the door—only to stop as if she'd run into a glass wall. A gasp caught in her throat.

Webb stood in the middle of the room, a thunderous scowl on his face.

Her laugh emerged as a nervous chuckle. "Goodness, you startled me, Webb. I didn't hear you knock. Is everything all right?"

His expression didn't change. "It would be all right, if I hadn't just been made a fool of by a woman I trusted—and thought I loved."

"What—?" She stared at him.

"Logan told me everything. How you strung me along because you didn't want to hurt me. Hurt me! Good Lord, woman, I'm not a child. I can take rejection. What I can't stand is deceit—not just from you, but from Logan, my own kin!"

Webb's voice was low and cold. His tirade would have been easier to take if he'd shouted at her.

"I can't believe I was asking Logan for advice on how to win you! And he was giving it to me—telling me to leave you alone and give you time. What a pair of liars. Damn you both to hell!"

Kristin found her voice. "We didn't plan for this to happen, Webb. I was already seeing you when we realized how we felt about each other. Logan would have told you right away. But it was my decision to save your pride by letting you be the one to break up with me."

"Save my pride?" he snapped. "You're making me sound like a child that needs coddling. It might've worked if I'd been paying attention to the signs. But I was too love-blind to see that you didn't care. And Logan—that bastard, pretending to be my friend, and all the while chasing after my woman! He'll pay for this."

"Don't blame him, Webb. He wasn't the one doing the chasing. I was. If anybody has to pay, it should be me."

"Since I've never punched a woman, I'll skip that part. But we're finished, Kristin. I wish you well with your new boyfriend, but I'll never trust you again. And if you ever need a favor, don't ask, because you won't get it from me."

He turned away and stalked across the room. Pausing in the open doorway, he looked back at her. "Damn it, woman, I would have given you the world—everything you could ever want and my heart along with it. But that wasn't enough, was it?"

Without waiting for an answer to his question, he stepped outside the door and slammed it shut behind him. Seconds later she heard his auto start up and roar away.

Kristin stood where he'd left her, emotions warring. She'd treated Webb shabbily. She deserved everything he'd said to her. True, the relationship was over, which was what she'd wanted. But she hadn't wanted it to end with Webb hurt and angry.

Blast Logan, why couldn't he have kept the truth to himself? He'd known that was what she wanted. So what had prompted him to break his silence? Had he and Webb quarreled? Or had Logan simply run out of patience?

Whatever the reason, he'd disregarded her wishes and taken matters into his own hands. Why couldn't he have waited—or at least warned her? As matters stood, they'd both made a dangerous enemy.

As she thought about how Logan had defied her, her anger grew from a spark to a blaze. The restful evening she'd planned was out of the question now. She couldn't rest until she'd faced Logan and given him a piece of her mind.

Horseback would be the fastest way to get to his ranch. Daylight was fading. If she wanted to get there before dark, she would need to leave soon.

Changing into her riding clothes took only a few minutes. Saddling the neighbors' roan gelding took just minutes more. After a word to the neighbors, she was on her way, taking the street at a trot to where the wagon road cut off, then opening the horse up to a ground-devouring lope, on a parallel course with the wagon track.

The lingering heat lay like a blanket over the landscape. The faint breeze from the west felt like a blast furnace. Kristin slowed to spare the horse. Looking back over her shoulder, she could see a faint brown dust devil dancing along the horizon. She could taste the grit in the air.

By the time she sighted the ranch, the sun was low above the western prairie. Its light, reflecting on dust motes in the air, streaked the sky with hues of flame and amber.

As she rode closer, she could hear dogs barking. Logan had

mentioned that he might get a pair. She could see them on the porch now—cattle dogs, a mixed breed common to these parts, big enough to take on coyotes. They were barking and wagging their plumed tails. As she stopped at the pump and dismounted to water the horse, they came prancing out to greet her.

Kristin scratched their ears and braced herself for what was bound to be a wrenching encounter with Logan. As angry as she was, anything could happen. But he had to understand the damage he'd done, to her and most of all to himself.

Logan had poured what remained of Webb's fine Scotch whiskey onto a hill of red ants outside the back door. If he'd kept it around, he'd have been tempted to drink himself into a stupor after Kristin finished venting her fury on him—and she would, he was sure of that. It was only a question of when.

His jaw ached from the crashing blow of Webb's fist. Logan had refused to defend himself. In going behind a friend's back for the woman he desired, he'd violated his own code of honor. Much as he loved Kristin, he deserved any punishment Webb chose to give him. But at least, whatever the consequences, the lies and secrets were over.

As he came back through the house, he heard the dogs barking out front. His workers were long gone. Was Kristin here already, or had Webb sent some of his cowhands to wreak more punishment? Winchester in hand, he opened the front door and stepped out onto the porch.

Kristin was walking toward him, with the sky ablaze behind her and the dogs frisking around her legs. The sight of her stopped his breath. He'd been prepared to speak up and defend himself. But all he could think of was how much he loved her.

Putting the gun aside, he battled the urge to stride across the yard and take her in his arms. She wouldn't want that now. "Would you like to come inside?" he asked. "It's dusty out here."

"I've been eating dust all the way from town," she said. "What I have to say won't take long. We can sit on the porch."

The chairs from his visit with Webb were still outside. He

brushed the dust off one of them and offered her the seat. She sat on the edge, tense, like a bird about to take wing.

"What were you thinking, Logan?" she demanded.

"That I'd had enough of lying—and enough of having to sneak around to be with you."

"Webb was furious at both of us."

"He'll get over it."

"Then you don't know Webb. I don't believe he'd hurt me, but he'll find a way to make you sorry."

"Whatever he does, I'll deal with it. I know this wasn't what you wanted. But it's for the best, and I'm not sorry."

In the stillness that followed, the wind picked up, swirling dust across the yard. Along the horizon, an ugly brown cloud blurred the fading sunset.

Kristin rose to her feet. A shudder seemed to pass through her body. "You ignored my wishes," she said. "You didn't even warn me what you were going to do. If you had, I'd have tried to talk sense into you. Now it's too late. You had no regard for my feelings No respect for me. And all you can say is that you're not sorry!"

She walked to the steps, then swung back to face him. "I'll be going now, Logan. Don't follow me or try to call on me. I need some time to myself—time to decide whether I ever want to see you again!"

He stood silent as she descended the steps and fled across the yard to her horse. He wished fervently that she would stop, turn, and look at him. But she mounted up without a backward glance and galloped off into the blowing wind.

Standing where she'd left him, Logan watched her vanish into the haze of dust. He'd deserved—even expected—most of what she'd said to him. But he'd never expected her to ride out of his life.

Now that it was too late, he understood her anger. Kristin had worked for years to earn her medical degree. During the war, and in the veterans' hospital, she'd performed the work of a man, supervising staff and doing everything a male doctor would do—

and she'd had to fight for every scrap of respect. In choosing to override her wishes and deal with Webb as he saw fit, he'd committed what Kristin would see as an unforgivable sin—he'd treated her as a foolish woman, incapable of making any decision without a man's help.

Such behavior would have been typical of Webb. She would have tolerated it because Webb didn't matter. But she'd expected better from the man she loved. And he'd let her down.

He could only hope he hadn't lost her for good.

The western sky was getting dark, not just the soft blue of twilight, but an angry swirl of black and brown. The streak of dust along the horizon that he'd noticed earlier was blotting out the last rays of the setting sun. Logan could see it moving closer by the minute, picking up more dust as it came. The cloud was becoming a monster dust storm.

And somewhere out there on the road was Kristin.

Surely she'd know enough to take shelter. Except there was no shelter between here and town, only open prairie. Given the time that had passed, she'd be less than halfway home. But even if she were to turn around and come back here, there'd be no way to escape the dust.

The wind was blowing harder, its texture like sandpaper against the skin. The dogs dived under the porch and crawled back against the rock foundation of the house. Mindless of the weakness in his leg, Logan raced toward the barn where his horse was stabled. Kristin had told him not to follow her, but that didn't matter anymore. She could die out there, alone against the brutal wind.

Logan had experienced dust storms in Texas and had even survived a bad one in the open. To get back to town, Kristin would have to ride into the storm, with the dust blasting her face and her horse's eyes. The safest plan would be to hunker down with her horse, stay low to the ground, and wait for the dust cloud to pass. But he couldn't count on her to do that. She could be pushing on, fighting against the wind. Whatever was happening, he had to find her.

Moving fast, he saddled the horse, filled a canteen, and grabbed a blanket and a couple of bandannas from the house. Minutes later he was mounted and flying toward the wagon road.

Kristin struggled to see the roadside through flying veils of dust. If she were to lose track of that road, even for a few minutes, the horse could wander off, and she would lose all sense of direction. The horse wasn't cooperating either. She remembered her father pointing out how horses would turn their backs to the wind in a storm. The gelding kept fighting the reins, trying to turn around and go back the other way. Maybe she should let it; but she'd lost track of how far she'd come, and home was where she wanted to go. Surely they would be there soon.

She breathed dust. She tasted dust. The blowing grit stung her eyes. Tears blurred her vision and made muddy streaks down her dirt-coated cheeks. She paused, relaxing the reins for an instant while she cleared them away.

Feeling the slack, the horse reared, wheeled, and bolted off at an angle, away from the wagon road. Kristin was thrown sideways, out of the saddle. For a terrifying moment, her boot caught in the stirrup. She was dragged, twisting and clawing, along the ground before her foot worked its way out of the boot and she fell free.

She sat up and tested her limbs. Aside from a turned ankle and some scrapes, she didn't appear to be badly hurt. But her boot was on the horse, and she had to get back to the wagon road. Staggering to her feet, with the wind and dust blowing from the right, she estimated the direction and set off limping.

She almost fell into the wagon ruts before she saw them. With a sob of pain and relief she sank onto the edge and hunkered down against the wind. She could go no farther.

Nobody was going to find her on this road. All she could do was wait here until the storm passed and limp her way back to town. With luck, the horse would find its way home. The neighbors would know she was missing and send out searchers. But she couldn't count on that.

Nor could she count on Logan. She'd made it clear that Logan wasn't to follow her. He was a proud man, and stubborn—not a man to come riding after her, begging her forgiveness.

She could be proud and stubborn, too. Her words had closed a door between them. Now it was her turn to pay the price.

Logan had ridden less than a mile before he was swallowed by the storm. He stopped long enough to tie a protective blindfold over the horse's eyes and cover his own nose and mouth with a bandanna. Kristin would have no such protection, he reminded himself as he urged the horse forward, guiding it with the reins. The well-trained animal responded to his touch, moving ahead with steadiness and trust.

With dust blocking the sky and filling the air, Logan could barely see ten feet in any direction. He had little choice except to follow the wagon road and hope for the best. If Kristin's borrowed horse had carried her off in some other direction, then Lord help them both. He would have no way to find her. Logan had never been a religious man, but he said a silent prayer as the storm howled around him. If he found her safe, he would never let her leave him in anger again.

By the time he saw her, almost hidden by blowing dust, he had all but given up hope. She was huddled in the hollow of the road, her body curled like a sleeping child's, her head protected by her hands. She was coated with dust.

He swung off the horse and knelt beside her. For one shattering moment he feared she might be dead. But when he touched her shoulder, she moaned and stirred. Breathing silent thanks, he pulled her up and gathered her into his arms.

She clung to him, her body shaking as he cradled her close. At first neither of them spoke. Some emotions were too strong for words. But at last Logan found his voice.

"I've got a blanket. We can wait out the storm here, or I can try to get you home."

She answered in a hoarse whisper. "Home."

By now the dust was thinning as the storm moved eastward. Overhead, the night sky was dark, with a few emerging stars. Logan gave her some water from the canteen, wrapped her in the blanket, and helped her into the saddle. After removing the horse's blindfold, he mounted behind the cantle and reached past her to take the reins. Now that he could see farther, he recognized where they were. Blue Moon was about three miles from here. With the horse weary from battling the wind, he would take the distance at an easy pace.

Leaning forward, he kissed the back of her neck. She responded with a soft murmur. Apologies, he knew, would be a waste of words. And there was no longer any need.

Blue Moon lay silent under a clear night sky, the streets, trees, and buildings coated with dust from the passing storm. Logan took the horse around to the back of the house. To Kristin's relief, the roan gelding, still wearing its saddle, was standing outside the gate to the neighbors' corral.

Logan helped her to the ground. "Go on inside," he said. "I'll take care of the horses—and I'll bring in your boot."

"I'll leave the back door unlocked," she said. Would he take it as an invitation?

The tightly closed house was free of dust inside. In the bathroom, Kristin stripped off her clothes, brushed out her hair, and ran a warm bath in the tub. Her sore muscles ached, and there were long, red scratches on her hands and arms from being dragged behind the horse. But the bath felt like heaven. She soaped her hair and lay back in the water to rinse it. When she sat up, Logan was standing in the open doorway with a mischievous smile on his face. "Too bad you don't have a bigger tub," he said. "I wouldn't mind joining you. And yes, I locked the back door when I came in."

"I can save you the water. But I've washed off a lot of dust in it. Or if you want, I could run you some more, but it might not be warm."

"It's probably better than the tin washtub with the dipper I use at home. But never mind, I need to get back to the ranch. I was planning to tuck you into bed and leave. But I might be talked into staying a little longer."

He was trying to keep things light, making it easy for her to send him away. But Kristin could see the raw hunger in his eyes. He needed her. They needed each other.

"I could use a good back scrub if you've got time," she said.

"I can make time." He rolled up his sleeves, walked to the tub, and stood looking down at her. Her nipples seemed to shrink under his gaze. She felt the stirrings of arousal.

"Lord, but you're beautiful." His voice was thick and husky. Heart pounding, she smiled and handed him the bar of lavender soap.

"It smells good, like you." He took a seat on the edge of the tub, lathered his hands, and slid them down her bare back. His masculine touch—the fingers strong, the palms big and rough and calloused—awakened whorls of need, setting off a pulsing in the depths of her body.

"Is that enough?" he muttered.

"Almost." Taking one hand, she guided it around to her breast. His other hand needed no urging. She lay back, eyes closed, lips parting in unspeakable pleasure as his soap-slicked hands cupped and caressed her tender flesh. When one hand slid down her belly, then lower to stroke between her parted legs, her womb clenched like a fist. She shuddered, whimpering as the climax rippled through her.

He gave her a knowing look. "I think we need to get you out of this tub." He offered a hand to help her up.

While she dried herself with a towel, he shed his clothes in the hall. Seen through the open doorway, he had a warrior's body, scarred with battle wounds. His left leg, below the knee, was mostly bone and scar tissue. Kristin gave silent thanks to the surgeon who'd had the skill and compassion to save it. Seeing her man naked and vulnerable, she experienced an overwhelming surge of love. She wanted to touch each scar, kiss it, hear its story and how it became part of him. But that could wait. Right now all she wanted was for Logan to make love to her.

Dropping her towel on the bedroom rug, she slipped into bed, turned down the covers on the near side, and held out her arms. He came to her, aroused and ready. Her body welcomed him, opened to him, and took him inside her, deep and hard. It was as if she'd wanted him there all her life. Him and only him.

"I feel like I've just come home," he whispered.

"You are home." She arched her hips, feeling him move inside her as she met each thrust. The stars seemed to spin as their climax mounted. They shattered together and lay still. Even then they held each other close, savoring the few precious moments before the world closed around them.

Logan stayed until she fell asleep in his arms. Then he eased away from her, dressed in the other room, and left by the back door. He'd watered his horse and left it to rest. Now it stood waiting, tethered inside the back gate.

It had taken all his strength of will to leave Kristin, but it wouldn't do for him to be seen at her house. And he needed to get back to the ranch. There could be damage from the storm; and with Webb on the warpath, anything could happen.

The sky was dark, the town still silent as he took the wagon road across the prairie. The air smelled and tasted of dust, but the storm, thank heaven, was over. It had probably blown itself out against the mountains. But if rain didn't come, there were bound to be more storms like it.

He thought about Kristin and how she'd reawakened the love that had died with his family. He wanted her in his life forever. But nothing was simple. Working out their differences was going to take time.

Webb had been right about one thing. He needed to improve conditions in his house. He had the money; he'd just been too busy to pay attention. Now, if Kristin was going to spend time there, he needed to do some painting, finish plumbing the bathroom, buy rugs, curtains, and furniture, and make sure the fireplace was working before winter set in. He was a wealthy man. It was time he stopped living like a dirt farmer.

As first light pinkened the sky above the mountains, he could see the house and barn in the distance. Everything appeared to be standing, thanks to Lars's quality work. The builders wouldn't be coming this morning, he reminded himself. Today was Sunday. But he'd be kept busy cleaning up the mess from the storm and fixing any damage.

As he neared the house, the dogs emerged from under the porch and came bounding out to meet them. Tongues lolling, tails wagging, they were happy, simple creatures, too friendly to be of much use as watchdogs. But Logan was already growing attached to them. Maybe it was time he came up with some names. Sam and Pal seemed to suit them.

He fed the dogs, then took the horse into the barn for water, oats, and a well-earned brushing. Its tan coat was thick with dust. Getting a second horse would be a good idea, he thought, maybe a gentle mare for Kristin to ride. He could let her choose one.

He was already planning for her in his future. He could only hope he wasn't wanting too much, too soon, or asking more than she was willing to give. Webb had already made that mistake.

Logan hadn't forgotten about his distant kinsman. Webb was not a good loser. There would be some kind of retribution—Logan could be sure of that. Webb was too smart to do anything that might land him in jail. But there were plenty of dirty tricks that weren't illegal. Without doubt, Webb had a few up his sleeve. For now, all Logan could do was watch and wait.

Dust had filtered into the house. While his coffee was brewing, he swept the floor and the porch and brushed off the table and bed. After a quick breakfast, he went outside to check for any damage to his property.

The barn was sound, without so much as a shingle out of place. The boards from the old, demolished outbuildings had been gathered and stacked, to be used on new sheds. Wind had scattered these around the yard. Several slabs of wood had blown against the pasture fence, loosening the wires. So far, there was nothing that couldn't be easily fixed.

Walking around to the back of the house, he found a half dozen tree limbs blown down. These could be gathered and cut up for firewood later. Everything else appeared fine, except that . . . Logan froze in his tracks. Something was different.

A moment passed before he realized what it was.

The creek that flowed in its bed, a few yards from where he stood, had run low over the rainless weeks. By now, it was so shallow that rocks thrust above the water, fish were trapped in the deeper holes, and the current flowed with a gurgling sound. That sound was gone.

Walking to the edge of the bank, Logan saw that the water level had risen at least eight inches. Most of the rocks were covered now, the current flowing smoothly around them—almost as if it had been dammed somewhere downstream.

Maybe a tree had blown over in the night, catching debris until it had formed a solid dam. Hopefully, he'd be able to move it out of the way by himself.

Minutes later he found it—not a tree at all but a rock barrier across the creek bed, covered with a canvas tarpaulin to keep any water from flowing past. Beyond the dam, the creek bed was almost bare. Someone had put this up after the storm—and as Logan looked ahead, he knew who, and why.

Coming toward him along the bank were four riders. Blake Dollarhide was in the lead, with three of his hands coming behind them. All of them were armed with rifles. One of them held a bundle of what looked like dynamite sticks.

Unarmed, Logan braced himself for a showdown.

Damn you, Webb Calder! he swore silently. *Damn you to hell!*

CHAPTER FIFTEEN

"*P*UT YOUR HANDS WHERE WE CAN SEE THEM, HUNTER," BLAKE barked. "If I ever doubted you were a loyal Calder, I know better now. We're going to blast this dam to kingdom come, and then we'll decide what to do with you."

Logan forced himself to speak calmly. "I'm not armed, Blake. And I swear on my life I didn't do this."

Blake sneered. "A likely story. I know Webb wants to put me out of business. You're his flesh and blood, and you follow his orders."

"I don't follow anybody's orders," Logan said. "You know I've always been fair with you, letting you use the wagon road and letting your share of the creek water flow on down to your property. I've even hired your father-in-law to build my barn, with lumber I'm buying from you. Why would I do this now?"

"Because you're a Calder, and the dam is on your property. If that dam stays, you can divert all the water onto your pasture. Then you and Webb can laugh and share a drink while my animals are dying of thirst."

Logan thought fast. Webb was devilishly clever. With this one act, he'd set his two enemies against each other. This, he realized, was how range wars started.

Kristin could prove that he hadn't been here long enough to build the dam. But Blake was her brother. Involving her would only add fuel to the fire. He would have to weigh every word he spoke.

Blake started forward on his horse, but Logan held up a hand to stop him. "Look at the ground where I'm standing," he said. "Look at the hoofprints and boot prints around me. I have one horse and no ranch hands. There had to be at least three men building that dam."

"So? Webb could have sent you all the help you needed."

"He could have, but I wasn't here. When did you first notice the empty creek?"

"This morning, when we got up to check the stock."

"Look, then. There's no dust on the top of the dam. And these tracks would've been covered or blown away. The dam was put up after the storm," Logan said. "And I just got home this morning. I hesitate to say this, but I spent the night in town with a very obliging lady. I could give you her name, but a gentleman never tells. And I'm sure that you, as a gentleman, would never ask."

Blake mouthed a curse. "Even if I believed you, why would Webb send his men to dam the creek on your property? None of this water is going to him."

"Webb and I had a falling-out. The reason doesn't matter. But if he can get the two of us fighting each other, he comes out the winner. Now, what do you say we get rid of this dam and get back to minding our own business?"

At a nod from Blake, the men dismounted and left their horses at a safe distance. One man, who appeared to know what he was doing, set the dynamite and detonator and strung out the fuse. Logan stayed back, letting them have the big-boy satisfaction of blowing the thing up. It was only then that he noticed what one of the horses was carrying.

A bundle of dry wooden stakes, of the size to be lit as torches, was slung from the saddle. From the other side hung two jugs of kerosene.

His flesh went cold as he realized what would have happened if he hadn't been here to speak for himself. Blake and his men wouldn't have been satisfied with blowing up the dam. Logan would have come home to find the house and barn in smoking ruins.

The men hunkered down and plugged their ears as the dam

exploded with an earth-shattering blast and a shower of dirt and pebbles. Water gushed downstream, slowing as it spread.

Blake's hired hands mounted up again. Their boss didn't speak as they turned around and headed toward the Dollarhide Ranch. Logan waited until he was sure they were out of sight. Then he walked slowly back along the creek to the house.

This time, at least, he'd averted an all-out act of war. But he'd learned three hard lessons this morning. First, even a minor misunderstanding could touch off an explosion of violence. Second, now that he'd lost Webb as an ally, he had no protection from either side. And third—something Kristin had warned him about—nobody who crossed Webb Calder could be allowed to go unpunished.

Joseph and his three friends had left their horses at the mouth of a narrow canyon and hiked up to a small, spring-fed waterfall at the top. There was no place to swim, but sitting on the rocks, with the spray misting the air around them, was just the thing on a hot summer day.

Although they didn't speak of it, a sense of growing apart hung over them all. The secret of the illegal shipments and ill-gotten pay had sown a separate and different darkness in each of them.

"I keep looking for that damned black ribbon on the fence." Buck finished the apple he'd been eating and tossed the core into the brush. "I've spent all the money I earned. I need to make more. When's it going to happen?"

"What the hell did you spend it on?" Cully asked. "You're too young for those whores that work at Jake's."

"I didn't throw it away on a good time," Buck said. "I bought a gun. A forty-four. The cowboy I bought it off even threw in a couple boxes of ammo."

"So what do you plan to do with it, rob a bank?" Joseph asked.

Buck shrugged. "For now, I'll just keep it—look at it, maybe practice a little. It feels good to know I'll have it when I need it."

"Just don't let your mother find it," Chase said, "or that gun will be gone before you can say 'Jack Robinson.'"

"You won't tell on me, will you, Chase?" Buck demanded. "You say one word, and I know enough other stuff to get you in trouble."

"You think I'd squeal on a friend?" Chase tossed a pebble into the water. "You'll never have to worry about me. None of you will."

"We are friends, aren't we?" Joseph had always admired Chase, despite the sense of entitlement that went with being the Calder heir. "So why do you think our fathers hate each other so much?"

"I don't think they really hate each other," Chase said. "They're like two stallions fighting over a herd. They do it because it's their nature, and because they both want to win. And sometimes, just like the stallions, they go too far and hurt each other."

"Do you think we'll be like that when we grow up?" Joseph had found himself thinking about that time, when he'd be the one in charge of the ranch, the mill, and maybe the Hollister Ranch as well. He didn't like to think about his father being gone. But otherwise, he found the idea exciting.

"I hope we won't be like them," Chase said. "But things happen. Maybe we'll change."

"I could use some change right now—in my pocket," Buck complained. "Do you think there'll be any more shipments coming?"

"I don't much care either way," Cully said. "Now that my dad wants to work, he'll be taking all the money we make."

"Maybe the boss won't take him on," Buck said. By now the boys all knew that the man they called the boss was Mason Dollarhide, Blake's half-brother. But they didn't know he was Joseph's father. That was a secret Joseph would never tell them.

"He'll have to take my dad on," Cully said. "Hiring him will be the only way to keep him quiet."

"That or shooting him," Buck said.

"Stop it, Buck." Joseph stood. "I've been saving something to tell you all. I met the boss in town yesterday. There's a new shipment coming soon. He didn't know when, but he's going to need us."

Joseph had been bursting to tell his friends the news. He'd been caught off guard when Mason had come up behind him in the store and whispered a few words in his ear.

Don't turn around, son. I'll need you sometime in the next few days. Tell your friends. I'll let you know when.

When Joseph had turned around, nobody was there. But the fact that his father had singled him out and even called him *son* made his heart swell—even though he knew that the word might not mean what he wanted it to.

"You don't have to do this," Chase said. "All it takes is one thing going wrong, and your life's ruined. Think about it."

"Your family's got money, Chase," Cully said. "We're poor. Even if my dad keeps all we earn, we need every cent."

"But is it worth going to jail?" Chase argued. "I've heard what happens in those places where they send boys. They come back changed. Some don't come back at all."

"That's enough, Chase," Buck said. "If you're not with us, we don't have to listen to what you say."

The afternoon sky had turned cloudy. The spray from the waterfall suddenly felt too cold. "Let's go. It'll be suppertime soon." Joseph started down the rocky canyon. One by one, the other boys followed. Truth be told, Chase's words had struck home. For his own reasons, which had little to do with money, he'd gotten Cully and Buck involved with Mason's illegal business. If something were to happen to them, he would be at least partly to blame.

Caution and common sense argued that it was time to put an end to this adventure. But the prospect of riding through the darkness with excitement coursing through his veins, completing the mission, and making his father proud was too powerful to resist. He would be watching every day for the black ribbon to appear on the fence.

Gerda had finished her work at the doctor's office and had chosen to take the long way home, down Main Street and around the third block. The worst of the heat was gone for the day. The sun hung low, a ball of fiery red above the parched yellow pastures.

This was her favorite time of day, with people hurrying home and the stores shooing their last customers out the door. From some nearby, unseen place came the sound of a piano—a simple piece, like a child practicing.

She dawdled a bit, taking time to study her faint reflection in the window of the hardware store. Her pregnancy wasn't really showing yet. She could still wear her pretty clothes, although the dress she'd chosen today was becoming tight over her swollen breasts. She'd done her best to hide her condition from her family, but her mother and Britta had already noticed the changes and guessed the reason. Even her father showed signs of being suspicious. She'd begun to dread going home in the evening when he was there. Once he discovered the truth, Gerda didn't even want to think about what he might do.

Only marriage could save her.

As if the thought of marriage had summoned him, she heard an auto coming down Main Street, approaching from behind. Mason's vehicle was a cut above the Model Ts that were a common sight in Blue Moon. The engine had a distinct sound, like a loud purr. Even without turning to look, Gerda recognized it.

She needed to talk to him, but he hadn't come around. It was almost as if he were avoiding her. This could be her only chance.

As the auto came closer, she turned, stepped off the boardwalk in front of him, and held up her hand. The brakes squealed as he stopped.

"Good Lord, Gerda, I could have hit you!" She could see his frustrated expression through the dusty windscreen.

She gave him her sweetest smile. "Hello, Mason. Fancy meeting you here. I hope you don't mind giving me a ride. We need to talk."

"Yes, I suppose we do." With the engine running, he went around the auto, opened the passenger door, and brushed the dust off the leather seat. "You know, it might not be good for either of us to be seen together."

"Then let's go someplace where we won't be seen."

"All right, for a few minutes. Then I'll be bringing you back."

He helped her into the auto, closed the door, and went around to the driver's seat. The dust that rose from under the wheels trailed behind them as they headed south, out of town, in the direction of his ranch.

At first Gerda thought he might be taking her to his home. But he turned west onto a narrow side road that ran along the top of a low earthen dike edging a patch of bogland. Fed by foul-smelling water that seeped from the ground, the bog covered three acres of willows, cattails, and sedges. Here and there, the skeleton of a dead tree rose above water where frogs laid strings of eggs that hatched into tadpoles. Red-winged blackbirds flitted and called among the cattails. Mosquitoes filled the air with their high-pitched buzzing. Gerda felt one bite her arm as Mason halted the auto on the road and turned off the engine that had drowned out any conversation. In the silence, Gerda could hear the chirr of insects and the croaking of frogs.

By now, the sun had set. The sky was deepening swiftly into dusk. Mason turned partway in the seat to face her. "All right, Gerda. You wanted to talk. I'm all yours."

Gerda fidgeted with her hands, wishing she'd prepared better. "Kristin told me she spoke to you."

"Yes, she did. And what did I say?"

"You said that my baby wasn't yours. But she didn't believe you. Nobody will believe you. So, you might as well marry me. That's what your brother did. He married my sister, even though the baby wasn't his. And now, look at them. They have a beautiful family."

Mason shook his head. "So you had this all figured out, didn't you? Get me between your legs, make me believe the baby's mine, and force me to do the right thing. Except it didn't work, did it?"

Hot-faced, she shook her head. "But it still could. You need a wife. I can cook and sew and keep house. And I'm pretty. Even you told me that."

"Then find a man who's looking for a wife, Gerda. What about the real father of your baby? What's the story? Is he already married?"

She shook her head. "I've been telling my family that the father is you."

"Well, tell them anything you want. It won't make any difference. I'm not cut out to be a husband or a father. I like my freedom, and I mean to keep it."

"Try saying that to my father."

Mason's expression darkened. "The last time your father tried to bully me, he ended up in jail. If he comes near me again, I'll have him arrested."

"I thought you loved me!" Gerda started to cry, deep, broken sobs and copious tears. "What am I going to do if you don't marry me? I'll be ruined. And when people find out, you'll be in trouble too. You can't arrest the whole town!"

For the first time, Mason sounded angry. "I don't give a damn what this one-horse town thinks of me—or you. If you can't stand the disgrace, find someplace to go, like a young mother's home. Leave the baby there and come back as pure and sweet as when you left."

"No." Gerda could be stubborn, too, when she chose. "I'm staying right here. And if I go down, Mason Dollarhide, I'm taking you with me."

"I don't like threats." His voice had dropped to a menacing growl. "Not even from pretty women."

Something in his tone and manner frightened her. She'd never believed Mason capable of hurting her physically. But he was a strong man, and she'd become an inconvenience. He was capable of killing her with his bare hands and dumping her body in the bog where nobody would find it.

Her fingers groped for the door handle. Finding it, she half tumbled out onto the edge of the road, righted herself, and took off running—not back the way they'd come, but following the road farther along the dike.

"Gerda! Come back here, you little fool!"

Gerda kept running. Even in a dress, she was fleet of foot. But her pregnancy had sapped her endurance. Her sides were already throbbing. She paused, losing precious seconds to catch her breath. Was he running after her? At first, she couldn't tell, but then she heard the pounding of rapid footfalls behind her. He was coming fast, gaining on her. Her only chance was to hide.

By now, it was dark, the moon still unrisen behind the mountains. She veered off the road, not to the left of the dike, into the bog, but to the right, into a neglected field where tangled weeds and grass grew to the level of the road.

As Gerda stepped off the dike, she realized too late that the weeds were tall, growing hip high from the solid ground beneath. She tumbled forward and plunged straight down. The distance wasn't far, and the weeds cushioned her fall. Still, she landed hard enough to hurt.

Stunned, she lay still as Mason called to her.

"Gerda! For God's sake, come back here. I don't know what you're thinking, but all I want is to see you safely home."

His voice sounded close, almost directly above her. But she had landed in the shadow of the dike. From where he stood, he couldn't see her. She lay still, hearing his voice grow faint as he hunted her down the road. Then as he came to the end and turned around, she could hear him clearly once more.

"Listen to me, Gerda. I didn't mean to scare you. If I don't see you by the time I get back to the auto, I'm going for help. Don't be afraid. I'll be back."

Gerda lay still until she heard the engine crank and start up. Only as the sound died away did she struggle to her feet. She felt vaguely sick. Her hands and the front of her dress were covered with burrs and stickers.

The moon had come up in the east. She could see her way now, but she had no good place to go. From this side, the dike was too steep for her to climb up. She would have to forge her way through the tall weeds to get back to the main road.

She took a moment to clear the stickers from her hands. Then she began pushing forward through the tangle. It was hard going—so hard that she began to rethink her reason for running away from Mason. Maybe he hadn't meant to hurt her. Maybe she should've answered when he came looking for her. But it was too late to change that now.

She'd scarcely covered a dozen yards when the pain struck, like a giant fist clutching her body below the waist, clawing and twisting. With a cry, she doubled over and felt a gush of fluid down her legs. She reached under her skirt. Her hand came away bloodied.

As another pain seized her, she dropped to her knees. *"No!"* she gasped. *"Please, God, no!"*

Kristin was eating a late supper of baked beans, ham, and a slice of the fresh bread a patient had brought her, when she heard a loud pounding on her front door. Another emergency, she surmised wearily. But this was what she'd gone to school for.

She answered the door to find Mason, looking frantic. His eyes were wild, and a lock of chestnut hair had fallen over his forehead. Outside the gate, his auto was still running.

"What is it, Mason?" she asked, genuinely concerned. "Is your mother—"

"It's not my mother. It's Gerda. We were talking out by the bog; she got scared and ran away from me. Now I can't find her. I think she's hiding from me. But she trusts you." He swallowed hard. "We can't just leave her out there, can we?"

"No, of course we can't. Let me grab a jacket and my bag. I'll be right out."

As an afterthought, along with the other things, she found an old pair of boots to take along. If Gerda had fallen into the bog, the boots would come in handy. She also found a flashlight.

What had the girl been thinking, running off in the night? Kristin could imagine what might have happened. But she would have to get the details from Mason. With luck they would find Gerda on the dike road or walking back to town. But given her pregnancy, anything could go wrong.

While Mason drove, Kristin slipped off her shoes and pulled on the boots she'd brought. It never hurt to be prepared. "Tell me one thing, Mason." She spoke over the noise of the engine. "Once and for all—could Gerda's baby be yours?"

"No." Mason answered without hesitation. "I swear it by all that's holy. I've done some despicable things in my life, but bedding that girl isn't one of them."

"All right. I believe you. But for her sake and for yours, you'd better hope we find her safe."

The drive from the house to the bog road took about twenty minutes. They'd kept watch all the way, but so far there was no sign of Gerda. At Kristin's suggestion, Mason parked the auto by the fence, next to the main road. If Gerda was afraid, the sound of the vehicle on the dike could keep her from coming out in the open.

Leaving her bag under the seat, Kristin climbed out of the car, turned on her flashlight, and started along the dike. Mason followed her with his own flashlight. "Keep quiet unless you see something," she cautioned him. "If she's really afraid of you, we don't want her to hear your voice."

"You know I'd never hurt her."

"I know. But maybe she doesn't."

As she walked forward, she played her light beam on both sides of the dike and called out every few minutes.

"Gerda! It's Kristin! I'm here to help you. Can you hear me?"

There was no answer and no visual sign of the girl.

They walked the length of the dike, turned around, and walked slowly back to the automobile. Nothing.

"We can't just give up and leave," Mason said. "What do you think could've happened to her?"

"I can think of several possibilities. She could have gone, and we somehow missed her on the way here. She could still be hiding. Or she could be in trouble." Kristin looked back down the moonlit dike. Her gaze roamed over the bog, catching glimpses of open water among the stands of cattails and sedge grass.

"A person could drown out there." Mason voiced her own fears. "But if she fell in the water, I never heard a splash or a voice."

"I think it's time to fetch the sheriff," Kristin said. "Take your car. He lives in that little house behind the office and jail. I'll stay here and keep watch."

Did he hesitate? She remembered the scene at the dance, when Lars had attacked him, and the new sheriff had arrested the big man and taken him to jail. That shouldn't give Mason any reason to fear the lawman.

But then again, if Gerda were to be found dead, Mason would be the most likely suspect.

"All right," he answered after a pause. "I'll be back as soon as I can."

As the auto started and pulled away, Kristin walked back along the dike. Maybe if she heard Mason's car leaving, Gerda would show herself.

But nothing happened. Forty-five minutes later, when Mason and Sheriff Jake Calhoun showed up in separate vehicles, Kristin was still watching and waiting.

"I sent my deputy to get more help," the sheriff said. "We won't stop looking until we find her. You may as well go home and get some rest, Doctor."

"I should stay. She could be hurt."

"If that's the case, we'll bring her to you, where you can treat her." The sheriff's lean face was unreadable, but the flat tone of his voice told Kristin what he expected to find.

"All right. But let me know as soon as she's found. Her family will be wondering why she hasn't come home. Somebody should tell them she's missing and wait with them. I'll do that myself as soon as I get back to town."

"That would be a kindness." Something flickered in his eyes and was gone. A memory flashed in Kirstin's mind—two elegant figures perfectly matched, whirling around the dance floor.

"Your brother can drive you to town," he said. "He offered to come back and help us search. But I ordered him away. He's too closely involved to be here."

"I understand," Kristin said. "If you don't find me at home, I'll be with the Anderson family. Do you know where they live?"

"Yes, I know."

Kristin joined Mason in his auto. He drove in silence at first, his lips pressed in a thin, tight line. Minutes passed before he spoke. "I didn't do anything bad, Kristin. I only flirted with her, and even that wasn't as much as she wanted. What if she's dead? What if I get blamed? I was seen with her leaving town—I could hang if her father doesn't kill me first."

"We don't know any of that," Kristin said. "Remember what our father always said."

"I can still hear him. 'Take care of today, and tomorrow will take care of itself.' I didn't believe it then, and I sure as hell don't believe it now. Tomorrow is a crapshoot."

"I'll be going to the Andersons' tonight. If you don't feel like driving back to your ranch, you're welcome to stay at my place."

"Thanks for the offer. But I don't want to miss the look on my mother's face when the sheriff comes to haul her darling son off to the calaboose. If you want to do me a favor, you can make sure she gets me a good lawyer."

"Stop it, Mason. We don't know anything yet."

They had reached her front gate. She caught his shoulder and gave him a quick hug. "Don't give up hope, brother. This isn't over."

She found the shoes and doctor's bag she'd left under the seat, climbed out of the auto, and watched him drive away. Mason was far from perfect. He'd made selfish mistakes and broken his share of hearts. But heaven help her, he was her brother; and she couldn't help loving him. If he was blameless in this likely tragedy, she would do everything to help him prove it.

After fishing the key out of her pocket, she unlocked the door and hurried into the house. As she changed her dirty boots and washed up in the bathroom, she thought about the Andersons. How could she best comfort them while they waited for news about their daughter? The family had already lost two sons, including her beloved Alvar. How much loss could these good people bear?

If only Logan were here. He knew the Andersons well. They liked and respected him. He was compassionate and skilled when it came to delivering the worst news. And his love would lend her the strength she needed.

The yearning she felt was so powerful that it brought tears to her eyes. But Logan was out of reach. She would have to support the Andersons as best she could, perhaps just by being there.

Mason drove the auto through the gate of the Hollister Ranch and parked it under an open shed. Shutting off the engine, he laid his forehead against the steering wheel as he struggled to collect his wits before he faced his mother.

Driving home, he'd passed the turnoff to the bog road. The deputies had arrived. He could see flashlights moving in the dark, searching every inch of land on both sides of the dike. If Gerda was there, alive or not, they would find her. He could imagine what Amelia Hollister Dollarhide would have to say about that.

Tell her nothing. For now, that would be the simplest way to handle things. Then he wouldn't have to listen to her rail on and on about the folly of getting mixed up with low-class immigrant girls.

The irony was that, for all the times he'd had his fun with women and gotten away clean, he should be tripped up when he was innocent. Even with Hanna, things had turned out all right. Joseph was a boy to be proud of, even though Mason knew he could have no claim on him.

But this time he'd been so careful. The business of shipping illegal liquor was so lucrative, and so risky, that he couldn't afford any kind of slip-up. But it had happened anyway—and with a big shipment expected by the end of the week. For all he knew, he could be in jail by then.

Even if Gerda were to turn up alive, she'd be clamoring for him to marry her. With her father and the whole town behind her, he might not have a choice. Either way, he was in serious trouble.

CHAPTER SIXTEEN

THE ANDERSON HOME WAS AN EASY DISTANCE FROM KRISTIN'S place. Walking under the stars, with a dry wind blowing her hair, she scoured her mind for a gentle way to tell a worried family that their precious youngest daughter was missing and possibly dead.

Should she tell them that the sheriff's team was searching the bog for her—would that be helpful or distressing? And what about her pregnancy? Her mother and sister were aware of it, but as far as Kristin knew, no one had told Lars. Better to leave it that way. And any mention of Mason was out of the question. But what should she say if they were to ask?

The Andersons tended to retire early, but tonight the lights in the house were on. They would be waiting for Gerda to come home, already fearing the worst.

She tapped on the front door. It was flung open by Britta, who returned her gaze with knowing eyes. After an instant's hesitation the two embraced.

"Something's happened to Gerda, hasn't it?" Britta whispered the words in Kristin's ear. "If you know anything, you can tell me. But I want to protect my parents for as long as I can."

"I'll tell you everything when we get a moment alone," Kristin said. "Then you can decide what to pass on." All the way here, Kristin had worried over what to say. But Britta had just taken the decision on herself.

Inga and Lars sat at the kitchen table. The mother of the family looked tiny next to her husband, as if grief and worry had shrunk her body. Kristin knew Inga Anderson to be a strong woman. But after the loss of her sons, how much more grief could she stand?

Lars was a caged lion—shifting, restless, as if it were all he could do to keep from bolting out of the house and tearing the town apart to find his daughter. "If she's run off with that Mason Dollarhide, I'm going to kill him," he said.

Ignoring her husband, Inga rose from her chair. "How kind of you to come, Kristin. Can I make you some tea?"

Kristin would have declined, but the poor woman probably needed something to do. "Thank you, that would be lovely," she said.

"We're probably worried for nothing," Inga chatted as she measured the tea and boiled the water. "You know Gerda. Any minute now, she'll come waltzing in the door saying she lost track of the time. We'll scold her, she'll toss her pretty head, and that will be the end of it."

Her words would almost have sounded convincing if it hadn't been for the break in her voice and the tear trickling down her cheek.

Britta touched Kristin's shoulder. "While the tea's brewing, let me show you the fabric for the dress I'm planning to make."

Kristin followed her down the hall to her room. Closing the door behind them, Britta turned to her. "Tell me everything," she said.

In as few words as possible, Kristin told her all she knew. "Mason swears he didn't touch her. He's my brother, and I want to believe him, but we won't know any more until she's found."

"So, there's still a chance they could find her alive?"

"That's why the sheriff refused to wait until morning. She could be hurt, trapped, or just scared and hiding. Time could make all the difference."

Britta shuddered. "Hope is such a cruel thing, isn't it?"

"Come on, let's go back and join your parents," Kristin said. "What you tell them will be up to you. I promise not to say a word."

Time crawled past, each tick of the wall clock weighted with despair. Kristin encouraged the others to get some sleep. But her words were wasted. No one could close an eye. Lars got up and went out to check the horses. The three women might have used the time to discuss what was happening. But they were drained of words, and there were too many secrets among them. All they could do was gaze at each other across the table or make feeble attempts at small talk. All of them were thinking of the beautiful, foolish young girl with the willful heart. Would they ever see her again or hear the sound of her careless laughter?

Lars returned. Britta looked at him and shook her head. He settled back onto his chair, muttering something in his native Swedish. It sounded like a prayer.

It was after two o'clock in the morning when the knock came. Kristin rushed to the door. Sheriff Calhoun, muddy and haggard, stood on the threshold. "We found her." His voice was hoarse with exhaustion. "I'm sorry."

The three Andersons rushed into the parlor. Lars was white with shock. Inga, half fainting, leaned on Britta for support.

"Where did you find her?" Kristin asked. "Can you tell us what happened? Was it an accident?"

The sheriff sighed. "No, not an accident. We found her lying in the field. Evidently, she'd had a miscarriage and couldn't stop the bleeding afterward. We'll need you to do an examination, Doctor, to determine whether there was any foul play involved. But it appears that she died from blood loss."

A sound like the cry of a wounded animal rose from Inga. Her legs sagged beneath her. Britta caught her and laid her on the couch before she could fall to the floor.

Lars had gone rigid with shock. "You say my girl had a miscarriage? She was with child?" he demanded.

"I'm afraid that much is true," the sheriff said.

"Then it was the baby that killed her!" Color flooded Lars's face as his emotions swung from shock to rage. "That devil, Mason Dollarhide! I'm going to kill him!"

"No, Papa!" Britta flew to his side, stroking his arm in an effort to calm him.

"Killing the man would be murder, Mr. Anderson," the sheriff said. "You'd probably hang for it. I suggest you get control of yourself and wait for the investigation."

"And how long will that take?" Lars stormed. "If you don't round up that devil now, he'll be on his way out of the country, just like last time."

"Mr. Dollarhide has been cautioned not to leave town," the sheriff said. "If he's responsible, the law will make him pay."

Kristin had been listening. When she'd set up her practice in Blue Moon, she'd been aware that serving as coroner might become part of the job. She certainly hadn't looked forward to it, but now, suddenly, she saw it as an urgent way to move forward.

Now she motioned the sheriff outside, onto the porch. "You've dealt with Mr. Anderson before," she said. "You know he can be difficult. But he's a father who loved his daughter. He deserves answers as soon as we can get them. So does his family. If you have Gerda's remains, I could do an exam now. Would that be possible?"

"My deputy's bringing in the body on a cart. There's a storage room with a gurney in the rear of the jail, but—"

"No, have him bring her to my surgery. I'll have everything I need there. What about her baby?" The question was vital for what she needed.

"It's with the body. She was holding it in her arms."

Emotion tore at Kristin's heart. But she was a doctor with a job to do. "Get your deputy to bring her to my place. I'll talk with the Anderson family and meet you there."

As the sheriff left, Kristin went back inside to face Gerda's family. Inga was sitting up on the sofa. Britta sat beside her, one arm around her mother's shoulders. Lars was pacing the floor. His fists were clenched, his face flushed with rage.

"Please sit down, Lars," Kristin said. "I have something important to say."

"I don't care what you say," Lars snapped. "If you're defending that no-good half-brother of yours, I don't want to hear it."

"I'm not defending anyone. But we all need to know the truth. The sheriff's men are bringing Gerda's body to my surgery. I'll be examining her in the hope of finding out how she died and whether anyone, including Mason, was responsible. I promise to tell you everything—no matter how painful it might be."

"Leave her alone!" Lars thundered. "We already know how she died. And we know who was responsible."

"Stop it, Lars." Inga was on her feet, shaky but defiant as she faced down her towering husband. "This must be done. We need to know the truth. Go ahead, Kristin. If you need permission, you have it from me."

"Thank you, Inga," Kristin said, although she already had permission from the sheriff. "As for you, Lars, I'll get back to you soon as I can—it shouldn't be more than an hour or two. Promise me you'll stay here with your family while I do my work. They'll be needing you."

"Just don't take too long," Lars growled. "That bastard got away once. He's not getting away again."

By the time Kristin arrived home, the horse-drawn cart, with Gerda's remains swaddled in a canvas sheet, was waiting outside the gate. The sheriff was there as well. The two men grasped the canvas by either end, lifted the body off the cart, and carried it through the door, across the front room, and into the surgery. Neither of them spoke. This was all that remained of a beautiful girl and a child who would never draw breath. Silence was all the respect they could pay.

With the wrapped body laid on Kristin's operating table, the young deputy was given leave to go outside and wait. The sheriff remained behind.

"I know you didn't invite me," he said as Kristin donned a protective coat and pulled on rubber gloves. "But since there might be an inquest, and especially since a relative of yours is involved, it could prove useful to have a witness."

"I understand," Kristin said. "In fact, I was expecting you to stay. Take that chair in the corner. You can sit as close as you like. I'll tell you what I'm finding."

In her hospital training, Kristin had assisted in autopsies. This examination would fall far short of those. In this room, with its limited resources, she wasn't equipped to run tests, bathe the body, or open it and remove the organs—nor did she see any need. This would be a simple inspection of what she could see and feel to determine, as best she could, what had led to Gerda's death. She could only hope it would be enough.

The sheriff had moved the plain wooden chair to a spot about ten feet away, at an angle that would give him a clear view. "Will you be all right?" Kristin asked him.

"I'll have to be."

"If you get queasy, just get up and leave. The bathroom's across the hall."

"I'll be fine."

"Then let's begin." She peeled back the canvas covering the head. There was Gerda, her face as white and still as Carrera marble. Only a long scratch down her cheek marred her beauty. Such a waste of a young life. Kristin fought back tears. She was a doctor, doing her job. She continued the examination, talking as her hands moved through the matted hair and down to the throat.

"Dry weed matter imbedded in the scratch. No other marks. No sign of swelling or bruising on her head. No bruises or contusion marks on her neck."

Now that the shock of seeing Gerda had passed, Kristin pulled back the rest of the bloodstained canvas. There she saw what she'd been most anxious to find. Cradled between Gerda's side and her arm was the unwashed body of her infant. The tiny girl was no bigger than a week-old kitten, but her fingers and toes had formed, as well as eyebrows, eyelashes, nails, and facial features— all typical of a fetus at four months. The sight was heartbreaking, but it proved one thing. Mason was telling the truth.

This little one couldn't have been his.

The baby would have been conceived sometime in March. Mason hadn't returned to Blue Moon and met Gerda until April.

The identity of the father was easy enough to guess. Gerda had been distraught when Ezra decided to move away with his parents. Although she might not have known it, she must have already been pregnant with Ezra's child.

If the sheriff hadn't been here, Kristin would have dropped everything and raced to the Andersons' to tell the family what she'd discovered. But she couldn't leave now. One more vital question had yet to be answered. What had triggered Gerda's miscarriage, and had that been the cause of her death?

After wrapping the infant in a flannel receiving blanket, she took a pair of sharp scissors and cut through the blood-stiffened layers of clothing to expose the body down the front. The sheriff's stoic expression didn't change. If the man felt any emotion, he kept it under control.

Gerda's corset was laced to excruciating tightness, probably to hide her pregnancy. Could that have caused her to miscarry? Not likely, but she wouldn't rule it out, Kristin mused as she cut through the stubborn busk.

Gerda's hands were skinned and embedded with weed matter, as if she'd fallen into the field and caught herself. But fallen how? Had she jumped? Maybe even been pushed? There were stems and stickers embedded in her skirt as well, including the bodice.

"What do you think?" she asked the sheriff. "Could Mason, or someone else, have shoved her off the dike?"

"Maybe they could have," the sheriff said. "But it doesn't make sense. If someone pushed her off the dike to kill her, why would they go off and leave her alive? She had to live long enough to miscarry and hemorrhage. That would have taken some time."

"So, you think Mason could be innocent?"

"You're the doctor."

Kristin continued her examination. "There's some bruising on her abdomen, as if she landed facedown. It's a fair drop off that dike. That kind of fall could have triggered a miscarriage. Or the pains could've started before she went off. Sadly, those things can happen.

"But look—her shoes are covered with stickers, even on the bottom. It looks like she got up and at least tried to walk before the pains started. If I'm right, you should be able to go back to the field in the morning and see the place where she landed and got up. That would confirm everything I've found."

Kristin rolled the body partway over to get a look at the back. "Nothing here. No bruises, no broken bones. Unless you have any questions, Sheriff, I think we're finished."

"No questions." The sheriff rose to his feet. "Unless we find evidence to the contrary in the morning, I'd say we can probably rule this tragedy an accident. I'll call my deputy in, and we'll take the body back to the jail. The family can claim it tomorrow. Thank you, Doctor."

Kristin tucked the canvas around Gerda's body, her legs unsteady beneath her. She'd managed to keep her professional demeanor during the examination. But now that it was over, she could barely stand. Tears welled in her eyes. She'd seen soldiers die in war. But this was different. This was personal.

At least it appeared that Mason wouldn't be blamed. As soon as the sheriff left, she would hurry to the Andersons to give them the results of the examination. Then she would drive to the Hollister Ranch and give Mason the good part of the news. Maybe this experience would teach him to be more cautious. But knowing Mason, she had her doubts.

As soon as she was able to close the house and leave, she raced around the corner and down the street to the Anderson home, where she rapped on the door. It opened to reveal a frantic Britta and Inga. There was no sign of Lars.

"Papa left a few minutes ago," Britta said. "He took the horse and the shotgun and rode off to settle the score with Mason."

"But he promised to wait for me!" Kristin exclaimed.

"I know. But he said he was tired of waiting. He was like a madman, Kristin. If he doesn't come to his senses, he could end up committing murder."

"But Mason's innocent. The baby couldn't have been his. Gerda was too far along—four months, at least. And the sheriff concluded that her death was likely an accident."

Britta shook her head, weeping. "I tried to stop him, but you know Papa. He's like a charging bull. I couldn't go after him because I had no way to catch up, and I couldn't leave Mama."

"I'll take my auto," Kristin said. "I only hope I can stop him—or that he'll stop himself."

Kristin kept her Model T gassed and in good running order. It started on the first try. She sprang into the driver's seat, opened the throttle, and shot down Main Street, headed south.

How far ahead of her was Lars? Did he mean to frighten Mason with the gun or shoot him? Even at a distance, a twelve-gauge shotgun was a deadly weapon. Up close, she didn't want to think about what it would do to her brother's body. Mason might have a gun, as well. If he were to fire first . . .

She gunned the engine to its top speed of forty-five miles an hour. On the rough dirt road, pocked with dried puddles, the Model T bucked over the uneven surface, airborne one second, crashing down the next with axle-breaking force. Fearing a wreck, Kristin forced herself to slow down. She had little hope of catching up with Lars as it was. With a disabled vehicle, she wouldn't get there at all. Too late, she realized that she should have taken time to saddle a horse. All she could do was keep driving and pray that nobody else would die tonight.

After a near-sleepless night, Mason had fallen into a doze.

A pounding on the front door jarred him awake. He sat up and took a moment to get his bearings. It was probably the sheriff, coming to tell him that Gerda had been found. The news was probably bad. Good news could wait till morning.

Hoping not to wake his mother, he swung out of bed and threw on his robe, which he'd flung over the bedpost. The pounding continued as he hurried downstairs. He kept a loaded pistol in the nightstand drawer but opening the door to the sheriff with a gun in his hand might not be such a good idea.

"Hold your horses—I'm coming," he muttered, sliding back the bolt, pressing the latch, and opening the door. "Sheriff, what's the—"

The words died in his throat. Framed in the doorway was the hulking form of Lars Anderson. His face was florid with rage. His big hands held a heavy-duty shotgun with the barrel almost touching Mason's chest.

"Say your prayers, Mason Dollarhide." He was breathing hard. "My girl's dead, and you killed her!"

"I don't understand," Mason stammered. "I didn't—"

"Shut up!" Lars rumbled. "She miscarried your baby and bled to death, alone in that field. It's all your fault. Ruining Hanna wasn't enough. You had to come back for Gerda. I'm here to see that you never ruin another innocent girl again."

He lowered the barrel a few inches, making it clear to Mason where he was aiming. Not that it made any difference. Anyplace the blast hit him, he'd be dead. Mason knew he couldn't dodge fast enough to get away. His best chance of living was to beg for his life.

"The baby wasn't mine," he insisted, pleading. "Gerda knew that. She lied to everybody. I never touched her. Please, for the love of God!"

"God doesn't love liars like you. You're going straight to hell!"

"You'll hang for this, Lars. Think of your family."

"God will forgive me. So will . . . they." Lars's face had gone beet red. His eyes bulged as he thumbed back the hammer. His index finger fumbled for the trigger—and froze.

As Mason stared, the big man's body went rigid, as if he'd received an electric shock. The gun fell from his hands as he toppled sideways and crashed onto the porch.

"Mason? What's happening?" Amelia emerged from the hallway. Her voice startled Mason to action. He shoved the shotgun to one side, making sure the hammer was released.

"Mason!" She came into the room wearing her frayed green silk robe. Her hair was frowsy, her eyes smeared with the kohl liner she wore by day. "I heard voices. It sounded like—oh!"

She caught sight of Lars's body through the open door. "Is he dead?" she asked in a tone she might've used to inquire about the weather.

"I was just about to check." Mason knelt beside the man's inert form. He could feel his own heart, still galloping, as he lifted one heavy hand to check the wrist for a pulse. He'd been certain he was going to die. Even now, it was hard to believe he was still alive.

He pressed a ropey vein, feeling for a pulse. Was he doing it right? He couldn't feel anything. Lars's eyes were open, staring at nothing. One side of his face drooped, the mouth sagging.

Mason was about to answer his mother's question when an automobile, its engine roaring, pulled up to the gate and stopped with a screech of brakes. Kristin sprang out and came racing up the walk.

"Mason, what happened?" Mounting the porch, she stared at the body in horror.

"I don't know. He was about to shoot me, and then he just fell. I think he's dead."

Kneeling beside him, Kristin checked the body for vital signs. She shook her head. "He's gone. From the look of his face, I'd say it was a stroke." Her breath emerged as a single broken sob. "His poor family! This will be too much for them! If only I could have stopped him!"

"He had the shotgun cocked and aimed," Mason said. "Another second and it would've been me lying here. He said I killed Gerda, and he was going to send me to hell for it."

Kristin laid a hand on his arm. "Gerda's dead. She miscarried and hemorrhaged in the field. But you didn't kill her, Mason. The baby couldn't have been yours. And there's no evidence that you hurt her in any way."

"You mean . . . I'm cleared?" His heart leaped.

"Except for a few formalities, yes. You were innocent. Foolish, but innocent."

"Lord, what a relief!" Mason flung his arms around his sister and hugged her to him. She returned his embrace, but with a measure of reserve.

"Listen to me, Mason," she said, releasing him. "You just escaped what would have been an awful outcome. But the slate isn't clean. A young woman and a good man are both dead because you got involved. If you hadn't flirted with Gerda, none of this would've happened."

"Hey, I thought you were my little sister," he said. "Why are you talking to me like my *big* sister?"

"Somebody needs to. It's time to grow up. And you can start by taking responsibility for what's happened here. Get some help to wrap this poor man's body. Then you can load it on a wagon, deliver it to the sheriff in town, and tell him everything that happened out here. Take the shotgun as evidence—oh, and the horse. I'll check with the sheriff tomorrow to make sure you've done your part."

"Shouldn't you come with me now, sis? I might need you to back up my story."

"Not this time. You'll be on your own because I've got a harder job to do. I'm the one who has to go back and tell Lars's family, starting with Hanna. Maybe she can help me break the news to her mother and sister. They're all going to be heartbroken."

"What's going on out there?" Amelia's shrill voice carried from the parlor.

"Everything's under control, Mother," Mason called back. "Go on back to bed. I'll tell you about it later."

"I'm leaving now," Kristin said. "Can I count on you to go to the sheriff?"

"You can. I'm not a complete scalawag, sis."

"Good. Prove it." She turned and walked back out the gate without another word. A moment later he heard her auto start up and drive away.

Mason sank onto the top step and pressed his hands to his face. His stomach was churning. His head was spinning. He didn't know whether to laugh or cry. He was alive. He was safe. As soon as he delivered the big man's body as promised, he'd be free to forge ahead, as if this nightmare had never happened.

Luck was with him. He could feel it coursing like liquid lightning through his veins. The upcoming product delivery would be the biggest yet. A few more like it and he'd be set. He could go wherever he wanted—New Orleans, maybe, or even Paris—and live like a king. When his mother died, he could sell this cursed ranch and have even more money—his to enjoy however he liked. To hell with cow shit and dust, miserable Montana winters, bland food, and boring people. He felt reborn. A new chapter in his life was about to begin.

Joseph was no stranger to sad funerals. Last year, when his Grandma and Grandpa Dollarhide had died of Spanish flu, he'd stood by their graves and cried his eyes out. But he was older now, almost a man. And although he'd loved his grandpa Lars, they'd never spent much time together. Truth be told, he'd been slightly afraid of the huge, gruff man who mostly talked about work. As for his aunt Gerda, Joseph had barely known her except that she'd been the prettiest of the Anderson sisters. He stood silent and dry-eyed as the graveside service continued under the guidance of a local minister.

The family had chosen a site on their old farm, where their oldest son, Alvar, was buried—three graves together now, instead of one. It struck Joseph as a desolate place to lie in the ground. But at least none of them would be alone.

The service was sparsely attended—maybe because the Andersons had kept mostly to themselves. The family was here, including Joseph's parents and sisters. The sheriff had come, too, and Lars's young apprentice, Pete. But there was no sign of Mason Dollarhide or his mother. There were no Calders here, either—unless you counted the distant Calder cousin who'd bought the old Tee Pee Ranch.

Major Logan Hunter had served overseas in the Great War. Grandpa Lars had done carpentry work for him, which was probably why he was here. Joseph had been curious about the man, who was rumored to be a war hero. But his father had insisted that nobody who shared Calder blood was worth knowing.

Now the major stood next to Aunt Kristin. As Joseph glanced at them, he saw her slip her hand into his. Now that was interesting. Did it mean that the major was going to be his uncle? Joseph would like that. But he knew that his father wouldn't.

Grandma Inga stood next to the graves, with Britta and Joseph's mother supporting her on either side. All three were crying, but Joseph could sense their strength. They would dry their tears and move on. Inga would be moving in with Joseph's family to be with her daughter and her grandchildren. Britta would be moving into the small house that adjoined the school. Their home in town would be sold for the money they needed.

Joseph's sisters were squirming and beginning to whine. "Take them to the buggy, Joseph," his father said. "Tell them they have to be quiet."

Joseph was happy to obey. He was getting tired, too. He could sit in the buggy, move around, and still hear most of what was being said.

He ushered his sisters to the buggy. Elsa curled into the corner of the seat and went to sleep. While the minister's prayer droned on and on, Joseph and Annie leaned back in the seat and watched the clouds that were drifting in from the west.

"I see an elephant," Annie whispered, "and there's a big fish with two tails. What do you see, Joseph?"

"I don't know. I'd like to see rain." Joseph was too distracted to focus on their old childhood game. He was thinking about what Mason had told him and wondering whether there would still be a shipment coming. Nobody had told him what had taken place between Mason and Gerda and Lars. But he'd overheard enough to piece the story together. If Mason was in trouble, maybe the shipment wouldn't happen.

The dull thud of dirt falling on coffin lids signaled the end of the funeral service. After a few moments of thanks and farewells, Joseph's parents came back to the buggy with Inga and Britta in tow. The family would be having dinner at the Dollarhide home on the bluff.

"Is Aunt Kristin coming?" Annie asked.

Joseph's father scowled. "I invited her to come—alone. But she said she had other plans. So, no. She's made her choice."

Crowded into the buggy, they drove back through town and south toward the road that cut off to the Dollarhide Ranch. Joseph's pulse quickened as they approached the fence on the right-hand side of the road. Would the ribbon be there?

He shaded his eyes. But there was nothing to see. There was no ribbon.

CHAPTER SEVENTEEN

*T*HREE DAYS AFTER THE FUNERAL, WHEN MORNING CHORES WERE done, Joseph rode down to meet his friends. That was when he saw it—the narrow black ribbon, tied to a fence wire, its loose ends fluttering in the wind.

Buck, Cully, and Chase were waiting for him behind the store. Joseph was bursting to tell them the news. As expected, each of them reacted differently.

"Hot dog!" Buck exclaimed. "I'd almost given up. Maybe the boss will let me guide the truck this time, instead of stacking boxes."

Cully sighed. "I'm in. But I guess I'll have to bring my dad along. He asks me every day when the next shipment is coming. I'd never get away without him."

"The boss won't like it," Buck said.

"I know. But there's not much I can do."

Chase, as always, was worried. "You know, you don't have to do this. What's ten dollars if you get caught and sent away? If you're that desperate for cash, I'll find a way to get you the damned money."

None of the other boys took him up on his offer. It wasn't just about the money—not for any of them, especially not for Joseph. But Chase, who had everything a boy could possibly want, couldn't be expected to understand that.

They rode their horses up to the mouth of the canyon and

hiked to the spring-fed waterfall. They arrived hot and sweaty, anxious to cool off in the spray. But the spring was down to a trickle now. The pool at the base was almost dry, the surrounding rocks hot enough to burn through their jeans when the boys tried to sit on them.

Joseph studied the blazing sky, finding only a useless wisp of cloud in the west. "I'd give ten dollars for rain right now," he mused aloud.

"My dad would give a thousand," Chase said. "But it wouldn't do any good. Rain isn't for sale."

"Let's go home," Buck said. "We'll need to rest up for tonight."

"Are you sure you can get out?" Cully asked.

"Pretty sure," Buck said. "At least, with your dad along, you won't have that problem."

They trooped down the canyon, mounted up, and rode back to town, where they would go their separate ways until late tonight, when they'd rendezvous at the black ribbon.

"It's not too late to change your mind," Chase said, as he and Buck prepared to ride back to the Triple C. "I don't have a good feeling about this."

"Stop fussing like an old biddy hen, Chase. We'll be fine," Joseph said. "The boss won't let anything happen to us."

"I wish I had your confidence." Chase turned his horse. Buck followed him as they headed out of town.

"Maybe Chase will talk Buck out of going with us tonight," Cully said.

"Maybe," Joseph answered. "If I know Buck, he'll show up no matter what Chase says. But even if he doesn't, we should have enough help with your dad along. I'll see you tonight."

Joseph arrived home early, hoping to hide out in his room and read. But his dad had other ideas. "We've got a fence down in the south pasture," he said. "You're just in time to come along and help me fix it."

Joseph suppressed a groan. "Can't one of the hands fix the fence?"

"They could. But it's time you started learning to be a man around here. Let's go, while your horse is still saddled."

Joseph was hot and tired from the hike up the canyon, but he knew better than to argue. On the ranch, at the sawmill, and with his family, Blake Dollarhide's word was law.

They mounted their horses and rode single file down the winding trail to the fenced pastureland. The afternoon was hot. Joseph was sweating beneath the band of his straw hat. From the trail, he could see the red and white cattle scattered in the pasture. Most of them were pregnant cows and spring calves. The steers had been sold off early, at a lower weight and price, because of the drought. Maybe that was why Blake had been so gruff and unsmiling lately. And of course, Joseph's mother was still mourning the loss of her father and sister. And there was Grandma Inga, too, who seemed to have aged ten years overnight. All in all, the Dollarhide household wasn't a happy place these days.

Lower down, where the trail widened out, Blake slowed his horse, allowing Joseph to catch up. "You know," he said, "when I was your age, your grandpa taught me every kind of work on the ranch, from mucking the stable to breaking horses and keeping accounts. I mean to do the same with you, so that when you take my place, you'll know everything about running a ranch. You're the future of this place, son. You and your children, and their children. And if I seem hard on you, that's why. My dad was the same with me."

Joseph nodded. Hearing this kind of talk made him squirm with guilt. He wasn't really Blake's son, and sometimes he wasn't even sure he wanted to run a ranch. It might be more fun to travel and have adventures—maybe even write books.

"I miss Grandpa Joe," he said, changing the subject.

"I miss him, too, son. And I miss my mother. They went before their time. But sometimes life takes a hard turn. Think about the two people we buried a few days ago. Neither of them deserved to die. And neither of them was ready."

Joseph was falling behind. Blake gave him a moment to catch

up. "I want to share something about your grandfather—something I've never told anyone, not even your mother."

Interest pricking, Joseph reined his horse closer to listen.

"You've heard the story about how he joined up with Benteen Calder's first cattle drive and got lost in a stampede. He got rescued by some outlaws, then ended up living with an old man who taught him how to break horses."

"I know all that," Joseph said.

"Here's something you don't know. Joe Dollarhide loved wild horses all his life. He told me once about a band of horses that he saw a few times from a distance—a band led by a powerful blue roan stallion. He could never get close before they disappeared. In fact, he was never sure whether they were even real. But every time he saw them, especially that blue roan stallion, he came to understand that something in his life was about to change."

"That's spooky," Joseph said.

"It gets spookier. I asked him when he'd last seen the horses, and he said not for years, not since he was young. But the night he died, I was sitting up, keeping watch. Everyone else had gone to bed. He was resting so I walked out onto the porch for a breath of fresh air.

"It was around midnight, with a full moon. The wind was blowing clouds across the sky, casting shadows on the ground. I stood at the rail, looking down, watching those shadows drift across the hillside when suddenly—so help me—the shadows seemed to become horses, shifting and milling in the dark. And in the middle of them was a big blue roan stallion. I glanced away, and when I looked back, they were gone. I could see nothing but shadows. I ran back to my father's room to find that he'd passed away, with a peaceful smile on his face. It was as if the horses had come for him and taken him away. Or maybe I'd just imagined it all. What do you think?"

"I don't know." Joseph frowned. "I never set much store by that kind of stuff. But why did you tell me this story today?"

"Maybe because I want you to understand what this land means to our family. My father said that the horses led him here, to this place, and to Sarah. Whether you believe the story or not, you are part of it. As Joe Dollarhide's grandson, this is your heritage. Think of that when you're tempted to be unworthy of what you've been given."

Blake halted his horse and reached for the tool bag that hung on the saddle. "Here's the broken fence. Now let's get to work."

Joseph said little while he helped right the fencepost and held the wire for splicing. But Blake's words played over and over in his mind. How much did his dad know?

As Joe Dollarhide's grandson . . . Blake had said. Was he aware that Joseph had discovered the secret of his birth? He might not be Blake's son, but there was no disputing that he was Joe's grandson. And then there was the part about unworthiness. Had Blake guessed, or even sensed, that Joseph was involved with Mason in a scheme that could get him arrested?

But never mind all that. He was already looking forward to tonight, when he would steal out of the house for another adventure with the man to whom he was bonded by blood.

Chase had almost finished his late dinner of roast prime rib, baked potatoes, hot rolls, and garden vegetables, with chocolate cake for dessert. At any other time, he might've asked to be excused. But tonight, he lingered at the table, dawdling with his food as he listened to the conversation between his father and Sheriff Calhoun, who'd been invited as a guest. As Webb always said, it never hurt to have the law on your side.

"Clearly you've had a lot of experience," Webb was saying. "The thing that puzzles me is what you're doing in a nowhere town like Blue Moon. I know we needed a sheriff, but why would a man who's practically a legend take a job here?"

Webb was flattering the sheriff. Chase had seen his father butter up dinner guests before. Most of the time it worked. He'd have them eating out of his hand by the end of the meal. But how well would it work with Jake Calhoun?

"Coming here wasn't my idea," the sheriff said. "It was the governor's. He sent a team of officers—two to Miles City and me

here. This part of Montana's been pinpointed as a funnel for
smuggling illegal liquor from Canada. Trucks, moving on back
roads, bring it to distribution sites where the customers can pick
it up. We have reason to believe that one of those sites is somewhere around Blue Moon, maybe on one of the ranches."

"Not the Triple C!" Webb sprang to defend his honor. "I have
eyes on every inch of my land. If anything was going on, I'd hear
about it. But you might want to check out some of the other
ranches—the Dollarhides', for instance. Or the Hunter place
south of here. The fellow who owns it claims to have been a major
in the army. But hell, he just built a big barn. Maybe that's where
the liquor's going."

Chase had questions, but he kept his mouth shut. To speak up
might get him dismissed from the table. He sipped from his water
glass and waited.

"We've already got a good lead," the sheriff said. "This morning, I put up a notice in the post office, offering a thousand-dollar
reward for information leading to the arrest of the smugglers. An
hour later, someone walked into my office."

"Who was it?" Webb asked.

"That's confidential, for the informant's safety. But evidently
there's a shipment coming through tonight. We know which
route it's supposed to take and where it's headed. My partners are
on their way from Miles City. We'll be waiting to apprehend the
truck and anybody who's meeting it."

Chase choked on his water. He covered his mouth until he'd
stopped coughing. "Excuse me," he mumbled.

"You don't have to stay, son," Webb said. "You're welcome to be
excused."

"Thanks," Chase said. "I need to finish my dessert first."

He toyed with the last few morsels of cake, his pulse racing. He
needed to warn his friends of the danger and make sure they
stayed clear of the illegal delivery.

Last year, Chase's father had hired a cowboy nicknamed Smoky
for extra help on the roundup. Smoky had been a good worker,
but he'd kept to himself and had a nervous way about him. If anybody touched him without warning, he'd jump and curse. And

sometimes, in his bedroll, he had nightmares that made him wake up screaming. Once, maybe because Chase was just a boy and didn't scare him, Smoky confided that he'd spent three years in a state reform school for stealing a watch to sell for food. Chase could still hear his voice.

"It was pure hell, that place. If you didn't toe the line, or just because they felt like it, they'd strip you naked and whip you till you bled. Then they'd lock you in a room with no heat and no food for a couple of days. But that wasn't the worst of it. The worst was when they'd haul you out of bed at night and give you to one of the guards. Lord help me, I was raised by a God-fearin' mother. But there weren't no God in that place. I'd pray that what the man was doin' would stop, but it never did. You see how I am. I wasn't like this before. But nobody came out of that hellhole the same as they went in. Some never came out at all."

The thought of his friends in a place like that made Chase feel sick. He had to warn them to keep away from what they were planning tonight.

Buck's house was on the ranch, less than a mile away. If he could get to his friend before he left for town, then Buck could warn Cully and Joseph. But Chase would have to get away without arousing the suspicion of his dad or the sheriff.

"May I be excused now, Dad?" he asked, trying not to sound nervous. "I thought maybe I'd go over to Buck's for a while. He wanted to show me his new comic book."

"You're going tonight? It's getting late."

"I won't be long." Before his father could question him further, Chase left the table and headed for the front door. Once it closed behind him, he broke into a dead run.

By the time he arrived at the modest Haskell house, he was out of breath. The place was as familiar to him as his own home. After his mother's tragic death, Ruth Haskell had taken in the motherless infant and raised him with her own son. She'd cared for him until Webb had brought him home to be brought up as the Calder heir.

It was Ruth who answered his knock. A slender, blond woman, she knew Chase well enough to sense his concern.

"Is everything all right, Chase?" she asked.

"Everything's fine," Chase lied. "I just stopped by to see Buck."

"I'm sorry, he went to visit a friend in town. He said he might stay there overnight. I'll be glad to tell him you came by. Would you like an oatmeal cookie? They're fresh out of the oven."

"Thanks, but I just finished dinner. I'll catch him later. Good night, Aunt Ruth."

Now what? Chase kicked a rock out of the path as he walked back toward the Homestead. He could go home and try to sneak out later after his father was asleep. He could also go to the stable now, saddle a horse, and leave straightaway for town. If Webb were to miss him, he'd catch hell when he got home.

But what did it matter how much hell he caught if he could save his friends?

Decision made, he set out for the stable. As he passed the main house, he saw that the dining room window was dark, and the light had come on in Webb's room upstairs. The sheriff would be on his way back to town by now. Chase hurried on. Time was passing. The sooner he could find his friends, the better.

Joseph, Buck, and Cully had talked freely about their plans for tonight. Chase knew the route the truck would take, what it was carrying, and where it would deliver the goods. What he didn't know was the timing. All he could do was make sure he found his friends and warned them off before the truck showed up.

There was no light in the stable, but Chase knew his way around. He chose a steady horse, saddled and bridled it, and led it outside. The sky was cloudy, the moon hidden—all to the good since he didn't want to be seen. Springing into the saddle, he dug his heels into the horse's flanks and shot out of the yard at a gallop.

Joseph and Buck met at the ribbon, where they waited for Cully and Angus to arrive. The night was dark, the air sticky with the day's lingering heat. Being outdoors was like wearing a too-warm black velvet overcoat. Crickets sang in the long, yellow grass at the roadside. Here and there, a star glimmered through the clouds.

Buck slapped a mosquito on his neck. "Dang, it's getting late. Maybe we should just go on to the ranch."

"Let's give them a few more minutes," Joseph said. "Then if they aren't here, we'll go on."

"I say we leave now," Buck argued. "If they get here late, Cully will know where to go. These skeeters are eating me alive. I can't stand much more."

"Fine, let's go." Joseph turned his horse and headed on down the road. Buck probably had the right idea. Mason would be cross if they showed up late. And, of course, they would need to be in place when the truck came.

Mason was waiting outside the barn. As Joseph had expected, he was in a bad mood. "You're late," he snapped. "And why are there only two of you? Where's your buddy?"

"Cully was going to bring his father," Buck said. "We waited, but they were late, so we came without them."

"He was going to bring his father?" Mason swore under his breath. "Good Lord, what next? Never mind, I'll send you two to guide the truck. The others, if they get here, can stack and un-load. Joseph, you know the drill. Buck can follow your lead. Now get going. That truck could show up anytime."

Joseph and Buck galloped their horses back the way they'd come. By now the sky was clearing. The moon gave enough light for them to see their way. As they passed the crossroads where the ribbon hung, Joseph remembered that they still hadn't seen Cully or his father. Maybe something had happened at home. But there was no time to worry about that now. He and Buck had a job to do.

They rode through Blue Moon and pulled up at the place where the wagon road turned off the main thoroughfare. They'd arrived just in time. Coming toward them, headlamps doused and engine growling, was the hulking canvas-covered truck.

Joseph stepped into sight and waved it off the road. This time there were two men in the cab, both strangers, each one meaner looking than the other. Joseph had no doubt that they were armed and well equipped to handle any trouble that might occur.

As he instructed them to stay between the riders and to avoid the wagon ruts, he felt a chill of premonition. This wasn't just an adventure. His father had sent him on a dangerous errand, with no regard for his safety or Buck's. Anything could go wrong tonight.

Logan lay sleepless in bed, his thoughts tumbling like water in a millrace. Since Lars's tragic death, he'd abandoned work on the stable and turned his energies into making his house more livable. His hoped-for marriage to Kristin still faced many hurdles. He would never ask her to give up her profession, but in order to continue her practice she would need to be in or near town. And he could hardly run his ranch from her house. For now, he'd settled for making his home a welcoming place to visit, where they could be alone, relax, and make love as often as they wished. Maybe when home phone service finally came to Blue Moon, she'd be able to spend more time with him.

But that wasn't the only problem. Logan knew that Kristin loved her family and had come home to be near them. But in their eyes, he was a Calder, and that had driven a wedge between her and Blake. The creek dam incident had driven that wedge even deeper. Until something changed, there was nothing he could do except be patient.

Pete was still working for him. But he'd paid Angus and sent him home. He didn't need two workers; and since the theft of the steer, he'd soured on the man. Logan still wanted to finish the stable, but Pete couldn't do it alone. Never mind that problem. It could wait.

He was making an effort to fall asleep when he heard the dogs barking outside. He sat up and reached for his clothes. It was probably just coyotes, but it could also be somebody making trouble—either the Dollarhides or Webb's men. Nothing had happened since the creek dam incident, but he'd stayed on the alert, knowing he could still be a target from either side.

The dogs continued to bark as he yanked on his clothes and thrust his feet into his boots. Opening the front door partway, he called them into the house—whatever was out there, the fool animals would only get in the way or could even be killed.

With the dogs safely inside, Logan lifted his rifle from its rack above the door and stepped out onto the porch. The wagon road was a good quarter mile away, but in the nighttime stillness he could hear the laboring engine of the truck—the same truck he'd heard a few weeks earlier. Logan cursed. The smugglers—if that's what they were—were back.

He would report them to the sheriff in the morning. Not that it would make much difference—unless he could get a description of the truck.

Leaving the porch, he set a course for a spot that would allow him to duck behind the brush and wait for the truck to pass. Given enough moonlight, he might even get a look at the driver.

Logan had gone only a few paces when a sound froze him in his tracks. It was the unmistakable pop and whine of gunfire, coming from the direction of the truck.

Gripping his rifle, he sprinted toward the sound.

Joseph and Buck had been riding a few yards ahead of the truck, on the right-hand side of the wagon road, when three mounted men, armed with rifles, had appeared out of the darkness. Two rifles were leveled at the open window on the passenger side of the truck; the third rifle was aimed at the boys.

"Sheriff," a voice barked. "Stop the truck and get out—now!"

The boys halted their mounts. "Oh, hell," Buck muttered. "Let's get out of here."

"No. If we run, they'll shoot us." Joseph swallowed the urge to throw up.

Suddenly the driver gunned the gas. The truck shot forward, the man on the passenger side firing shots from a heavy pistol. One lawman slumped in the saddle but righted himself. The other two kept exchanging fire with the moving truck.

"Come on, damn it!" Screened for a moment by the truck, Buck grabbed the bridle of Joseph's horse. Swinging to the right, he jumped the wagon track, pulling Joseph with him. As the boys headed away at a gallop, the wounded lawman fired his pistol. The first shot whined past Joseph's head. The second nicked his horse's haunch.

The startled animal jumped and bolted away, throwing Joseph into the long grass. Stunned for a moment, he raised his head. "Buck," he called. "I'm here! Pick me up!"

But there was no reply from Buck, only the sound of hoofbeats fading into the distance. Joseph's friend was gone.

He lay still a moment, hurting. Buck had gotten away clean. But here he was, sore, bleeding, and without a horse. Once the lawmen stopped the truck, they'd come after him for sure. And he'd be sent off to reform school, just as Chase had said he would. He had to get out of here.

Grunting with pain, he struggled to stand, but just as he got his legs under him, strong hands seized him from behind and pulled him back down.

"Stay low!" a voice growled. "They'll see you!"

Heart pounding, Joseph turned his head to see who had spoken. The man gripping his arms looked familiar in the moonlight. Then Joseph recognized him. He'd been with Aunt Kristin at the funeral. "You're the major," he said.

"And you're Blake Dollarhide's son."

"Yes, I'm Blake's son," Joseph said. And suddenly there was nothing more to say about that. He knew the truth of it, as he should have known all along.

Farther down along the road, the truck had run a wheel into the wagon rut and high-centered. It was tilted sharply to one side, but the motor was still running and the shooting continued. "Come on," the major said. "I'll get you somewhere safe. Then you can tell me what's going on and what you're doing here. Keep down and follow me."

Chase had planned to wait where the wagon road began, in the hope his friends would show up there. But after examining the fresh tracks in the dust, he'd realized that the truck had already arrived—and that his friends would have left with it.

His heart sank, but he couldn't give up and go home. If there was any chance to warn them of the danger, he would have to take it.

Following the wagon road, he kicked the horse to a gallop. Somewhere along the way, the sheriff and his partners would spring their trap.

His hopes had begun to fade when the sound of distant gunfire reached his ears. He paused for an instant, then urged the horse ahead. If there was gunplay, his friends could be trapped or hurt. He couldn't just turn his back and leave them.

Ahead now, in the moonlight, he could see the truck leaning to one side and hear the whang of bullets striking the thick metal chassis of the ex-military vehicle. The smugglers would be inside the cab, the sheriff's team hunkered down somewhere outside. But where were his friends? Had they already been arrested? Could they have been killed in the firefight?

He was moving closer when, with no warning, pain burst in his head and the world imploded into blackness.

CHAPTER EIGHTEEN

*L*OGAN SETTLED JOSEPH IN THE BEDROOM, WHERE HE'D BE SAFE and out of sight. Then he went outside and waited on the porch until he could be satisfied that there was no more activity on the wagon road. He needed to know what was happening, but he didn't want to be seen and questioned.

The story Joseph had told him was almost unbelievable. But the boy was too scared and shaken to be lying. Logan had never met Mason Dollarhide, but a man who'd manipulate young boys into doing dangerous, illegal work for him had to have a dark soul. Prison would be too good for him—even though he was Kristin's half-brother.

Logan sensed that the boy wasn't telling him everything. But maybe the rest of what he knew was best saved for his parents or the law.

After about twenty minutes without a sound, Logan walked down toward the road and made a cautious approach. If the truck had been carrying illegal liquor, the cargo could be worth hundreds of thousands of dollars. Even if the sheriff had left, someone might have stayed behind to guard it.

But for now, at least, no one was there. In the moonlight, he could see the truck, tilted partway into the hollow of the road, its cargo of wooden boxes spilling out the side. The canvas cover was riddled with bullet holes. Many of the boxes were shot through and their treasured contents dripping into the earth. The air was rank with the odors of alcohol and cordite. The ground was trampled and littered with brass casings from the rifle fire.

The outside of the cab was dented where the bullets had struck. There were a few holes where they'd penetrated. The inside of the cab was empty, the windows shattered. The driver's seat was splotched with blood.

How had the sheriff known the loaded truck would be coming this way? Had he known that the boys would be with it? But those questions could wait for a less urgent time.

A saddled horse, maybe Joseph's, was wandering loose. Logan was approaching the animal, hoping to catch it, when the two dogs came bounding through the grass with Joseph behind them. He must've let them out.

The horse shied and moved away as the dogs came close. Logan scowled at the boy. "I told you to stay in the house."

"I know. But everybody's gone now, and I'm feeling good enough to go home."

"You're sure?"

Joseph nodded. "I know the way. And that's my horse over there. I can catch him."

"Fine. Go ahead." Logan couldn't very well keep the boy against his will. And as long as he was safe, better to have him show up at home alone than to be delivered by an enemy.

"You'll need to check that little wound on your horse's hip," Logan said. "Looks like he might've been grazed by a bullet."

"Don't worry, I'll clean the wound when I get home."

"All right, then. But don't leave it too long. You don't want it getting infected."

"I won't." Joseph trotted off to catch his horse, then paused and turned around. "Thanks for saving me, Major. You aren't going to get me in trouble, are you?"

"Not unless I'm forced to. But I hope you've learned a lesson."

"Yes, sir."

Joseph had started after his horse again when one of the dogs, who'd gone off to explore, set up a frantic baying. Logan couldn't see the dog, but the sound came from about ninety yards back along the road, in the direction of town.

The fool dog had probably found a badger hole or scented a coyote. But Logan found himself running hard toward the sound, with Joseph passing him as they spotted the huddled figure in the moonlight.

It was Chase Calder.

"Was he with you tonight?" Logan demanded as they approached.

"No. I swear it." Joseph flung himself down beside Webb Calder's son. "Chase, are you okay?"

Chase was slumped next to the wagon road, with his feet in the rut. He raised his head; his face, pale in the moonlight, wore a dazed expression. "My horse," he muttered. "Can't find . . ." His voice trailed off as he recognized Joseph. "Are the others okay?" he asked.

"I think so," Joseph said. "Buck rode off, and the major here dragged me away from the fight. Cully and his dad never showed up."

"Let's have a look at you." Logan crouched beside the boy for a quick inspection. The only damage he could find was a red crease running from the top of his ear across his temple to the outer tip of his eyebrow, where he must have been grazed by a bullet. Logan had seen wounds like it in the war. This wasn't good.

"How do you feel, Chase?" he asked.

"Okay, I guess. Head hurts some. Can't walk too well. Where's my horse? Need to get home . . . Dad'll kill me."

Logan gripped the boy's shoulders. "Listen to me, Chase. I need to get you to the doctor, right now."

"No . . . just take me home. I'll be okay," he argued.

"Not this time." Logan turned to Joseph. "I've got to get him to town, and I'm going to need your help. Stay with him while I bring my auto. Then you'll have to be very brave. Catch your horse and ride to the Triple C. Find Webb—or have someone find him for you. Tell him Chase has been shot and is on his way to the doctor's. Have him meet us there. Understand?"

Joseph nodded. "Yes. But my folks—"

"They'll be worried. But there's no time and nobody else to do this. Stay with him. Keep him talking if you can. I'll be back in a few minutes."

Pushing his weakened leg to the limit, Logan raced back to the house, found some blankets, laid them in the auto's rear seat, and drove back to where he'd left the boys. He found Chase lying on his side and Joseph frantic.

"I tried to keep him talking, Major, but he just slumped over like that. Now I can't wake him up!" Joseph was on the verge of tears. "Is he dead?"

Logan checked for a pulse and found it. "No. But he needs the doctor. Now get your horse and go. Can I count on you to do this, Joseph?"

"Yes, sir."

Logan scooped Chase into his arms and carried him to the car. Laying him on the back seat, he arranged the blankets to cushion and support the boy's head. Then he climbed into the driver's seat. After making sure Joseph was on his horse, he headed out as fast as he dared drive without jarring his passenger.

If he'd guessed right, the passing bullet had fractured Chase's skull. A blood clot was forming beneath, putting pressure on his brain. Kristin would need to drill into the spot to relieve the pressure, which was increasing as the clot grew. She might have done the surgery during the war. But could she do it here? He had every confidence in her skill. But that was out of his hands. All he could do now was drive and pray.

The drive from the ranch to town seemed to take forever. By the time Logan pulled up to Kristin's gate, night was beginning to fade from the sky, and the birds were waking in the trees. He climbed out of the auto, opened a rear door, and lifted Chase in his arms. The boy mumbled and stirred as Logan carried him up the walk to the porch. He didn't open his eyes, but at least he was alive.

Balancing his burden with one arm, he rapped on the door with his free hand. Impatient, he tried the latch. The door was locked, but he heard a stirring from inside, and a familiar, muzzy voice.

"Hold on, I'm coming."

He heard the click of the bolt. The door swung open to reveal Kristin in her robe, still sleepy-eyed, her dark hair half falling over her face. She stared at him, stunned into silence, but only for a moment.

"That's Chase Calder! What's happened to him?"

Logan stepped inside. "He's been shot. A crease on the head, but I think—"

"Later. Get him back to my surgery."

Logan carried him through her office and back to the immaculate room where she did procedures. The long, adjustable table was covered with a clean sheet. He laid Chase on it. Again, the boy stirred and muttered something about a horse. But his eyes remained closed.

"Scrub your hands, Logan. I'll need your help," she said, sweeping her hair up under a surgical cap.

Logan did as he was asked, using the strong disinfectant soap she kept next to the basin. When he returned to the table, she'd lit a small candle and was lifting the lid of Chase's left eye to check the pupil. "Dilated with no response," she muttered. "And his limbs are flaccid on the left side. I'd say it's a fracture of the temporal bone and a subdural hemorrhage. We've got to get in there and remove that clot."

"How can I help?" Logan asked.

"The tools I need came in that medical kit I ordered. But we'll have to sterilize them first. There's a pan on the stove. Make a fire and get some water started while I get ready."

The water was starting to boil when she came back into the kitchen, dressed and wearing a white apron over her clothes. She carried several instruments—a scalpel and tongs, a razor, a device with a round blade called a trephine for cutting through the skull, and a pliers-like tool for lifting out bone. She laid them in the boiling water and handed him an apron like the one she wore, along with a surgical mask. "Wash up again and put these on. I'll mostly need you to keep him still and hand me things. But be prepared for whatever I ask you to do." Her manner was brusque, efficient, and impersonal. Logan wouldn't have expected anything less of her.

"I probably shouldn't ask," he said. "But what are his odds?"

Her breath caught in a brief display of emotion. "I've done similar procedures seven or eight times. For this kind of surgery, the survival rate is about fifty percent."

Chase lay on his side, his body draped with a clean sheet and his head cradled in position by folded towels. The area around his wound had been shaved and sterilized with carbolic acid. His breathing and pulse were stable, but he hadn't opened his eyes or spoken since those last labored words when Logan laid him on the table.

Tracking the boy's pulse, Logan watched as Kristin raised the scalpel to start the V-shaped cut through the skin that would be raised to expose the bone underneath. He felt the tension as she lowered the razor-sharp instrument with a downward stroke that left a clean red line. Working fast, she sponged away the blood and began the second cut of the V.

That was when the door crashed open, and Webb stalked into the room brandishing a pistol. "What the hell are you doing to my boy?" he demanded. "Nobody's touching him without my permission!"

Kristin gave him a calm glance. "This couldn't wait for you, Webb. Chase is unconscious from a blood clot on his brain. If I don't remove it now, he will die. Not *might—will.* Is that what you want?"

Webb strode to the table and stared down at his son. "*You're cutting into his brain?*"

"The blood clot's on the surface of the brain, under the membrane that covers his skull. Get back, Webb. You're not sterile. You could give him an infection. And put that blasted gun away. I'm going ahead with this operation. If you shoot me, you'll be killing your boy."

Webb backed away, then turned his anger on Logan. "Blake's kid told me the whole story—how the boys were helping Mason Dollarhide smuggle liquor. I know somebody betrayed them to the sheriff for the reward. Chase must have got winged when he went to warn his friends. The sheriff wouldn't tell me who blew the whistle. But I know it was you, Hunter. That shipment went right through your ranch. You were probably getting a payback to let them pass. But that wasn't enough. You had to have that thousand-dollar reward—even if it meant putting young boys in the line of fire!"

"You've got it wrong, Webb." Logan forced himself to speak calmly and keep his attention on Chase. "Somebody tipped off the sheriff, but it wasn't me. I didn't know anything until I heard the shooting start."

"You're lying, you Judas. This mess is all your fault. And if my son doesn't make it, I swear to God, I'm going to kill you."

"Sit down, Webb." Logan measured each word. "You don't want to distract the doctor who's saving your son."

Grumbling, Webb moved back and sat down on the edge of a wooden chair that stood against the far wall. But he hadn't put his gun away. Right now, everyone's first concern was for Chase. But if something went wrong and he didn't survive, Webb could go berserk. He could kill Kristin as well as Logan, and maybe himself.

Logan needed a plan in place in case of the worst outcome. Right now, only one thing came to mind—protecting Kristin at any cost.

He glanced at her. She was totally focused on her work, her eyes intense above the surgical mask she wore, her hands moving with precision and skill. She was so much more than beautiful, so much more than precious. He would gladly take a bullet to save her.

Webb was fidgeting with the pistol as if he'd forgotten that he had a deadly weapon in his hands. "How much longer?" he demanded.

"As long as it takes her to do it right," Logan said. "You can always leave and come back."

Webb's only answer was a derisive snort.

"Where's Joseph?" Logan asked. "Is he all right?"

"He's fine. After he found me, he headed home on his horse. He told me how you saved him. That should put you in solid with the Dollarhide bunch. Not that you aren't already. When I invited you to come to Montana, I was hoping for a friend and ally, not a man who would turn on his own blood."

"I never turned on you, Webb. Not even when your men dammed my creek, knowing the Dollarhides would come after me. They were ready to burn me out. I could've retaliated. But I didn't. All I want is to live in peace. Now be still and let me help Kristin save your boy."

Both men fell silent. Logan checked Chase's pulse. Was it getting weaker? Damn it, he didn't know enough to tell. Kristin had cut away a circular piece of bone and was using forceps to lift out the blood clot. It came away easily, but several tiny vessels were still bleeding. As time crawled past, she pinched them off. Logan could hear her breathing as she irrigated the spot with saline, checked it for fragments, and fitted the cut bone back into place. Drops of perspiration beaded her forehead as she eased the skin flap over it and reached for the sterilized needle, threaded with silk, that she'd prepared ahead of time. The stitches were as small and neat as a girl's prized embroidery.

After cutting the last of the thread, Kristin applied a dressing, checked Chase's pulse and respiration, and released a long, exhausted sigh. "Done," she said.

Webb sprang to his feet. "Is he all right? When will he wake up?"

She sighed. "His vital signs are stable. As to when he'll wake up, there's no way to tell. All we can do is wait and be patient." Truth be told, this was the most uncertain and fearful part of the procedure. Some patients woke up right away. Some, even after a flawless procedure, didn't wake up at all.

The pressure of the clot was gone, but Chase was still comatose—not the best of signs. But she wasn't ready to tell Webb that.

"Can we move him to the bed?" Webb asked. "He'd be more comfortable there."

"Let's give him a little time. When he starts to wake up, then we can put him on the cot. Meanwhile, I could use a few minutes to clean up. You too, Logan. Webb, could you keep an eye on Chase? If you notice any change at all, call me."

"You couldn't tear me away from him now," Webb said.

Kristin beckoned Logan out of the room and softly closed the door behind them. After what she'd heard from Webb, there was no way she was going to leave the two men alone together.

But now she had other concerns.

"What is it?" Logan asked as she came out of the bathroom after washing her hands and removing her apron and cap. "I can tell you're troubled. Is Chase's condition worse than you're telling us?"

"I've done all I can for Chase. The next few hours will be critical. And I'm worried about Webb, too. I don't know what he'll do if he loses that precious boy. But this is something else." Kristin felt as if her world was shifting. Part of her yearned to feel Logan's arms around her, but this wasn't the time.

"I was trying not to listen when you and Webb were talking," she said. "But I couldn't help overhearing my brother's name mentioned. That Mason should be involved in smuggling liquor, and that he had innocent boys like Joseph helping him—it's unthinkable. And I had no idea. Until now, I didn't even suspect what was going on."

"I didn't know about him either until Joseph told me," Logan said. "Otherwise, I'd have told you myself. I'm sorry, Kristin."

She shook her head, still processing what she'd learned. "Mason's always been something of a rascal—especially with women. I thought he'd learned his lesson. But he'll go to prison for this. And what it will do to Joseph, his own son, and to our family breaks my heart."

A knock at the door interrupted their talk. Kristin opened it to find the sheriff on the porch. The flash of gray morning light behind him made her blink. Where had the time gone?

"Good morning, Sheriff. Come in," she said, stepping aside for him to enter. "What can I do for you? Please sit down. Can I make you some coffee?"

"That's all right. I won't be long." He glanced down at his

boots, then, as if forcing himself, he met her gaze. "I'm afraid I have some news to deliver. I thought it best that you hear it from me, and not through the grapevine."

He took a breath—and in that brief interval, Kristin knew what he had to tell her.

"Your brother, Mason Dollarhide, was arrested last night on charges of illegal liquor trafficking," he said. "He's in jail now, awaiting transport to Miles City tomorrow, where his trial date will be set."

"I guessed as much." Kristin's legs were unsteady. She sank onto the sofa. "Does his mother know?"

"She knows, all right." The sheriff shook his head. "She was there when we came to take him in. The old woman put up more of a fight than her son did. First, she drove us back with a bull-whip. Then she set her dogs on us. I had to threaten to shoot them before she called them off. I wouldn't want to tangle with that lady again."

Logan spoke up. "I witnessed part of that gun battle with the truck. Did you know those men had a couple of young boys guiding them?"

"Not until it was too late to stop the shooting. I saw one boy ride away, and another one crawl into the grass. I hope they're all right. I'd have handled things differently if I'd realized."

"They're fine," Logan said. "But another boy, Webb Calder's son, Chase, knew about the plan. He rode out to warn his friends and was winged on the head by a stray bullet. He's still uncon-scious after surgery. His father is with him now."

"Oh Lord, I'm sorry for that!" The sheriff looked stricken. "I had dinner with the Calders last night. Chase heard me tell Webb about the plan. If there's anything I can do—"

"Only if you're a praying man," Kristin said.

The sheriff turned to take his leave, but Logan stopped him. "One more thing before you go. Webb accused me of being the one who told you about the shipment. I wasn't, of course. But it would help to know who really told you."

"That's confidential," the sheriff said. "But it's someone you know. If you think about it, you should be able to figure it out. He earned the reward and he'll get it."

Logan paused, then nodded. "I think I just did."

"I'll be leaving town once this case wraps up," the sheriff said. "I hope you'll let me know about Chase. I feel partly to blame for what happened."

"You couldn't have known about the boys," Kristin said. "Of course, I'll keep you informed."

After the sheriff left, Kristin slipped back to the surgery to check on Chase. She walked in to find Webb standing by the table, slumped over his son. Was he praying or weeping? Maybe both.

"Any change?" She spoke softly, not wanting to startle him.

"Not yet." He sounded broken.

Kristin moved beside him to check the boy's vitals. His pulse and breathing were stable. But it was his brain that had to wake him up.

"Are you all right, Webb?" She'd jilted him cruelly. But she still cared about him. She could only hope he understood that.

His only answer was a deep sigh. "My father, the great Benteen Calder, always told me that what mattered most was the land—winning it, holding it, living for it, dying for it. He lied, Kristin. The most important thing of all is right here. Chase is all I'll ever have of my Lilli. He's my past and my future. If he doesn't pull through, I'll have nothing to live for. I might as well die right here in this room."

"Don't talk like that, Webb. His vital signs are stable. Give him time." Kristin checked the dressing. "The sheriff was here. We asked him who claimed that thousand-dollar reward for alerting him about the shipment. He wouldn't tell us, but he confirmed that Logan had nothing to do with it."

"I know that now," Webb said. "It had to be that little weasel, Angus O'Rourke. I should've guessed it when Joseph told me that O'Rourke and his son hadn't shown up to help with the delivery. I wanted it to be Logan, damn it. I wanted a reason to hate him— a reason to kill him if my boy didn't make it. But it would've been for nothing."

"It was Logan who found Chase and brought him here," Kristin said. "He saved your boy's life."

"Providing my boy lives." Webb touched his son's face below the gauze bandage that wrapped his head. His breath sounded like a sob being drawn inward. "Can we move him off that table now? He'd be more comfortable on the cot."

"As long as we do it carefully," Kristin said. "We can use that sheet underneath him like a hammock and carry him by both ends, then put him down slowly."

"I'll help." Logan stepped in through the open doorway. "You take his head, Webb. I'll take his feet."

Working together, they lifted Chase in the sheet and carried him across the room to the cot Kristin kept for recovering patients. She went with them, supporting his head with her hands. "Slowly, now," she said. "Don't jar him."

As they lowered Chase onto the pillow, they heard a groan and felt a stirring. Kristin's lips moved in silent prayer. *Thank you.*

By the time they'd laid him down and pulled back the sheet, Chase's blue eyes were open. "Dad?" he asked in a clear voice. "What's going on?"

Tears were streaming down Webb's cheeks. "You're alive, son. That's all that matters."

Later that day

While his dad waited for him in the sheriff's office, Joseph walked down the hall and into the jail area. There were three barred cells. Two of them were empty.

It had taken some fast talking to get permission for this visit. Joseph was in big trouble. He wouldn't be going off to reform school, but he'd be confined to the ranch for the rest of the summer, forbidden to see anyone outside of his family. Still, he'd convinced Blake that he needed this one last visit with Mason. There were things he needed to say before he closed the book on this chapter of his life.

The man in the third cell was rumpled and unshaven, his chestnut hair falling over his bloodshot eyes. But he managed a smile as Joseph walked into sight. "Well, hello, son," he said. "Did you come to break your old man out of here?"

Joseph stood a little straighter. He'd thought a lot about the words he was going to say. "I didn't come to break you out. I'm not your son, and you're not my old man. A real father wouldn't teach his son to break the law or send him into danger, where he could get hurt, arrested, or even killed. I have a real father. His name is Blake Dollarhide."

Surprise flashed across Mason's face. "Then why are you here?"

"I came to say goodbye. When I first met you, I thought you were something special, like an adventurer or a movie hero. I would have done anything to please you, to have you call me your son. But I was wrong. You didn't care about me or my friends. You used us and put us in danger. I'm glad you're going to pay for it."

Mason smiled. "Those are tough words coming from a sprout like you. It'll be lonesome where I'm going. Will you at least write to me?"

"No. I don't want to write to you. I want to forget all about you."

His smile broadened. "You won't forget me, son. You'll remember me every time you look in the mirror and see those green eyes."

His laughter followed Joseph all the way back to the sheriff's office, where Blake was waiting for him. "I'm finished, Dad," he said. "Let's go home."

They walked outside to the family Model T. Clouds had been roiling in from the west all day. Blake put the top up before he cranked the engine and climbed into the driver's seat.

"Didn't you want to see your brother, Dad?" Joseph asked.

"Not after the harm he did to our family. Whatever I would have said, you said it for me. I'm proud of you, son."

As they drove out of town, the first clap of thunder echoed across the sky. The first drops spattered the dust on the windscreen. With another thunderclap, the clouds split open, spilling their life-giving rain over the Montana prairie.

* * *

Kristin finished tidying her office and sank onto the sofa. It had been a long day. Chase's recovery had gone so well that she'd allowed Webb to take the boy home on condition that he rest in bed. By then she'd had patients arriving. She'd cleaned up the blood in the surgery, ushered Logan out the door with orders to get some rest, and resumed her regular schedule.

She'd been so busy, and so tired from the long night, that she'd barely noticed the sound of thunder and the drumming on the roof. Even her windows were kept curtained for the privacy of her patients. Now she leaned back and let the sound wash over her. People would be celebrating all over the countryside. If Logan were here, she would celebrate with him. But she had sent him away.

Was this what she wanted? Her practice was fulfilling, but she needed more. She needed Logan in her life—his warm support, his passion, his love. She needed to fall asleep in his arms and wake up to his kisses, to give him a family to replace the loved ones he'd lost.

Her mother, Sarah, had managed it all. Could she?

If only Sarah were here. What would she say?

Her musings were interrupted by a knock on the front door. Blast, she should have hung out the CLOSED sign before settling down to relax. Probably some emergency. But no rest for the wicked.

Pushing to her feet, she hurried to open the door.

Logan stood on the porch, drenched in rain. His face wore a happy grin. He held out his hand. "Miss Kristin, come on out," he said. "I want to do something I've never done before, and I want to do it now."

"Have you gone mad? It's raining."

"I know. And I want to kiss you in the rain, for the whole world to see. And then I want to dance with you, as best I can manage." He tugged at her hand. "Come on. When will we get another time like this?"

Laughing, she ran with him, out into the rain.

EPILOGUE

Spring, nine months later

JOSEPH PERCHED ON THE LOG FENCE, WATCHING HIS UNCLE'S NEW two-year-old colts race around the pasture. Shipped from Texas by rail and driven in a herd from Miles City, they were wild and skittish. But as they galloped along the fence line, their manes and tails flying, they were so beautiful that they took Joseph's breath away.

He was already picking out his favorites. "Look at that palomino!" he exclaimed, pointing. "And that little chestnut filly! And that big black one—he looks like the boss!"

Standing beside him, Uncle Logan chuckled. Getting these horses here, to raise and break, had been his dream. Now, with the first twenty animals, that dream was coming true.

"Don't just look at their colors, Joseph," he said. "Look at how they're built—those powerful hindquarters for holding their weight against a roped steer. And their necks are strong and set forward, so they can work with their heads lowered. These horses are bred for working cattle. They're smart and they're fast."

"How fast?" Joseph asked.

"They're made for short, quick sprints. They can outrun any other kind of horse for a quarter of a mile. That's why they're called quarter horses."

"Those are right fine horses, Logan," Blake Dollarhide said. "But I'd say you've got your work cut out for you."

"I'm planning on it taking all summer," Logan said. "They'll have to be green broke, then saddle broke, then trained with cows. I'm hoping they'll be ready for fall roundup."

"But who's going to buy those fancy animals when our old horses do fine?" Blake asked.

"Word will get around. I've already promised Webb his pick. If he likes the first one, he'll likely want more."

"Well, the bastard can afford it." Blake and Webb would probably never be friends. But at least, with plenty of water this spring, no one was fighting.

"Can I help you with the horses this summer, Uncle Logan?" Joseph asked. "I know they're too wild to ride, but I could take care of them in other ways."

"We'll see. That will be up to your dad."

Joseph watched the horses, imagining how it would be working around them, making friends with them, maybe even getting to ride them by summer's end. Perhaps when he was older, he could learn to break and train them, like his grandfather. Joe Dollarhide had possessed a rare gift for working with horses. Maybe he'd passed that gift on to Joseph. It would be exciting to find out.

Last summer the fun times with his friends had turned dark and almost ended in tragedy. Joseph had drifted away from those friends since then—especially after Buck had ridden off and left him at the gunfight, and Cully had failed to warn them of his father's betrayal. Joseph could forgive, but he couldn't trust them anymore.

As for Chase, the close brush with death had changed him. His sunny nature had grown darker and wilder. He was no longer interested in the kind of boyish adventures he'd enjoyed with friends before. Joseph had barely seen him since that terrible night.

Mason was serving a five-year sentence in the state penitentiary. No one, as far as Joseph knew, had visited him or written to him. It was as if he no longer existed. But the Hollister Ranch was his home, and unless he sold the place after his mother's passing, he would be coming back to Blue Moon. By then, Joseph would be nearly grown.

The sound of an approaching automobile caught his attention. That would be Aunt Kristin coming home from a day at her office in town. Before they'd married last fall, Logan had cleared and graveled a new, direct road from the ranch so she could drive in all but the worst weather. The addition of home phone service made it possible for patients to contact her at the ranch. She'd also cut back on her days in town. Even so, finding time to be with her husband was a challenge.

The new addition to their house, which would be finished this summer, would include space to set up an office and surgery so that some patients could see her at home. It would also include quarters for a cook and housekeeper and a nursery which, she'd hinted, would be in use before long. "My mother managed to do it all," she was fond of saying. "So can I."

Now she drove into the yard and parked next to the house. The dogs came bounding off the porch to meet her. Seeing what was in the pasture, she flew out of the car and raced across the yard. "They're really here! I can't believe it!"

Celebrating with her, Logan caught her in his arms and swung her off her feet. Watching them kiss, Joseph found himself smiling. So many things had turned out badly last summer. It felt good to see a happy ending—and what he hoped was an even happier beginning.

BOOK GROUP DISCUSSION QUESTIONS

- Why would Kristin choose to come home to Blue Moon when she could have worked at a big, modern hospital?

- Why do you think Spanish flu killed so many people? How would you compare it to the modern-day Covid pandemic?

- How does Logan's idea of a good life compare to Webb's and to Mason's?

- How does Mason seem to feel toward Joseph?

- What changes Joseph's attitude toward Mason and Blake?

- What do you think would have happened if Mason had married Gerda?

- Do you think Mason should have been punished for what happened to Gerda and to her father? Why or why not?

- What if you had to choose between a career and a family, as Kristin did? What would you do?

- Who is the strongest character in this story? The weakest?

- Do you think prison will change Mason's character? Why or why not?

- Is Cully a good person? What is most important to him?

- If you were making a movie of this story, who would you cast in the major roles?

- Who is your favorite character in this story? Why?

Please read on for an excerpt from **Quicksand** *by Janet Dailey!*

Determined to keep their legacy bull-rearing operation strong, the Champion sisters go head-to-head—and heart to heart—with some of the toughest men on the rodeo circuit—and walk away victorious in love . . .

Tess Champion knows better than to trust Brock Tolman, the rancher who once swindled her late father in a land deal. But with the Alamo Canyon Ranch in foreclosure, Tess is forced to accept Brock's offer of a partnership. Brock claims he only wants to breed the Champion bloodline into his own herd. In exchange, he offers Tess one of his own young bulls. Soon enough, Quicksand is the rising star of the rodeo circuit, which only proves Tess is better at picking bulls than she is men. Because she's way too tempted to surrender to her attraction to Brock, despite her certainty he's only out to steal her family ranch . . .

It's not until the tycoon's private plane crashes in the wilderness, stranding him with Tess, that the truth of their relationship will come out. The Champion family's future is on the line, but it's Tess's heart that will take the hit if she's fallen for the wrong man . . .

CHAPTER ONE

Southern Arizona, March

AS THE SUN CLIMBED TOWARD MIDMORNING, A GOLDEN EAGLE ROSE from its perch atop a hundred-year-old saguaro. Its beating wings, wider than a man's reach, lifted the bird skyward, where it soared and circled on the updrafts, its golden eyes scanning the desert for prey.

Brock Tolman shaded his eyes to follow the eagle's flight. He felt a certain kinship with the great bird—both of them apex predators, both of them powerful. But the eagle's power came from its wings. Brock's came from his ambition.

As the eagle rose, its moving shadow passed over foothills painted with the bright gold of flowering brittlebush. Crimson-tipped spears of ocotillo and lemony clouds of blooming paloverde dotted the landscape with the colors of Sonoran spring.

In the weeks ahead, blossoming cactuses would blaze with hues of rusty yellow, pink, and magenta. Then white blooms would crown the giant saguaros that stood like guardians over the desert. Finally, the women of the Tohono O'odham who called the desert home would come with their long poles and harvest the seedy red fruit.

Brock had made enough money with his investments to live anywhere he wanted. But he had chosen this place, in the foothills of the Santa Catalina Mountains outside Tucson, to build his private kingdom. The Tolman Ranch was a patchwork of pristine desert and fenced pastureland where genetically bred bucking bulls—close to 100 of them not counting the cows and calves, along with a herd of Angus beef steers—grazed on native grass watered by mountain springs. The ranch's setting was beautiful, and Brock was not immune to beauty—whether admiring it, coveting it, or possessing it.

Today, as Brock sat astride his big sorrel gelding and watched Miss Tess Champion ride out across the pasture, Brock reflected that most men would be satisfied with what he had. But for him, it wasn't enough. To Brock's way of thinking, *enough* didn't exist. There was always more to want, always more to get.

And more to lose.

Brock shifted in the saddle, feeling the crackle of the folded envelope he'd stuffed into his hip pocket. It had arrived in yesterday's mail, but he hadn't opened it until this morning. What he'd found inside had jerked a noose around his heart. He'd recognized the yellowed newspaper clipping at once; but what did it mean? Was it some kind of warning? Maybe an attempt at blackmail? Was his whole perfectly ordered world about to come crashing down around him?

He'd been reading the text when Tess's truck had pulled up outside. There'd been no time to do anything but replace the clipping in the envelope, fold it, and stuff it into the deep hip pocket of his Wranglers, where it wouldn't be seen by any eyes but his. He would worry about it later. Right now, he had more pressing matters on his mind.

A few months earlier, he'd bailed Tess's family's ranch out of foreclosure and forced a reluctant Tess to take him on as a business partner. He might have had other ideas for Tess—like getting her into his bed. But if there was one thing he'd learned in life, it was that mixing business with pleasure was a recipe for disaster.

So, for as long as they were partners, the rule would be hands off. And that was a damned shame, Brock mused, admiring the way her slender body sat the horse and the way the wind played with the long dark hair that fell loose below her hat. Tess was well past girlhood, but she was a beautiful, smart, sexy woman. The fact that she was the most stubborn, muleheaded, prickly female he'd ever known only sweetened the challenge.

But Brock knew better than to cross that line. He was a man who made his own rules and played by them. With Tess, for now at least, the rule was strictly business.

This morning Tess was here to choose the bull he'd offered her in exchange for Whiplash, the rank bucker who'd been ruled too dangerous for the arena. Brock had long dreamed of breeding a world champion bull. It was his hope that Whiplash's fiery bloodline might make the magic happen.

In return, Tess had been given her choice from among Brock's three- and four-year-old bulls, who were just starting their careers in the rodeo arena. There were twenty-three of them in this pasture, all trained, tested, and ready for the big time.

Tess had a keen eye for bulls. She would no doubt pick one of his best. Brock was fine with that. As her partner, he would retain part ownership of any bull she chose. He had nothing to lose.

But curse the woman, why had she insisted on riding out alone to inspect the herd? Brock had saddled up, planning to go with her. However, after declaring that she wanted to view the bulls without the distraction of his company, she'd ridden off and left him fuming at the pasture gate.

Something told Brock that chasing after her would only add to his humiliation. He would let her go. But he couldn't help worrying. Tess was an expert rider, and she knew her way around bulls. But if anything were to go wrong, she'd be unprotected out there.

He would keep his distance, Brock resolved. But he wasn't about to let the woman get too far ahead of him.

Tess paused her mount to scan the pasture. The grassy expanse, scattered with creosote, ironwood trees, and clumps of sage, seemed to go on forever. But why should she let that surprise her? Everything Brock Tolman owned was too large, too grand, and too fine for ordinary folk. Even the horse he'd lent her, a registered Appaloosa, was probably the most superb animal she'd ever ridden.

Not that she was impressed. Brock was a show-off who lived for the power and possessions his money could buy. Tess couldn't abide the man. What was more, she didn't trust him.

True, he'd saved her family's Alamo Canyon Ranch from foreclosure, but he hadn't done it out of kindness. He wanted the ranch for himself. And now that he had a foot in the door as her partner, he wasn't about to back off.

Right now, she knew that Brock was watching her. If she were to look back—not that she'd give him the satisfaction—she would see him sitting his horse like John Wayne, just as big and rugged as the late actor—except that Brock was no movie hero. He was more like a scheming, avaricious villain.

But she wasn't here to judge him. She was here to pick out a promising bull—one that would dominate in the arena and strengthen her family's own small herd with his bloodline. The future of the Alamo Canyon Ranch could be riding on the choice she was about to make.

She could see the bulls now, loosely scattered at the far end of the pasture. Brock had shown her the stud book at the house, but looking through it had scarcely been worth her time. The young bulls appeared to have solid pedigrees and had been tested in the bucking pen. Any one of them could earn his keep in the PBR or PRCA rodeos. But would any of them have that fiery spark—the spark she'd witnessed in Whiplash before fate had led the big brindle to kill an intruder on the ranch?

Brock's intervention had saved the bull's life and given him a home. But Whiplash, so strong and full of promise, would never compete again.

The young bulls had caught her scent. They'd raised their heads and turned in her direction, watching her approach. Tess held the horse to a measured walk. She'd been dealing with cattle all her life, and she knew better than to alarm them, especially bulls.

She also knew better than to get off her horse for a closer look. Here, as on her own ranch, bulls in the pasture were handled on horseback or from sturdy vehicles. They were accustomed to mounted riders. But a human approaching on foot would be asking for trouble.

At a distance of about thirty yards, she paused again to study the bulls. They were splendid animals, sleek and muscular, their horn tips newly blunted for the arena. Green metal ID tags, inscribed with numbers, dangled like jewelry from their ears. Most of the bulls were a solid color, ranging from fawn to red to dark chocolate. Two of the bulls were pale cream speckled with black. One bull, the biggest of the herd, was as black as sin with a white slash, like a lightning bolt, running down his face. His left horn was missing—likely due to injury or infection. The other horn, even blunted, was long enough to do plenty of damage.

As Tess ventured closer, the bulls tightened their ranks, snorting and lowing in a way that clearly meant, *That's far enough, stranger.* The big black lowered his head and scraped at the grass with his single horn—a clear threat.

Tess backed off a few steps, keeping an eye on the bull who'd already captured her interest. It was too soon to make a decision. But her instincts were calling for a closer look at this tough brute.

"You're certainly no beauty." She spoke in a soothing voice. "But then, this isn't a beauty contest, is it, big boy?"

She should at least look at the others—and of course, she'd want to see some of them buck. It would be rash to make an on-the-spot decision. She needed time—days, even weeks, to choose the right animal.

The black bull tossed his head and pawed the ground. Tess didn't believe he'd charge, but just to be sure, she backed the horse farther away, onto the low, brushy rise where she'd stopped earlier. The Appaloosa responded to her lightest touch.

The bull stood his ground, eyeing her suspiciously. "It's all right, big boy," she said. "I'm not coming any—"

A sinister buzzing sound from the high grass chilled her blood. Her pulse lurched; but before she could act, the horse leaped straight up and twisted to one side, flinging her out of the saddle like a marble from a slingshot.

Tess hit the ground so hard that the wind whooshed out of her lungs. As she gasped for breath, struggling onto her side, she came almost eye to eye with the snake. The six-foot diamondback, its thick body coiling to strike, was only a few steps from her face. She could see its delicate forked tongue, testing the air. Testing her.

Terror fueled her reflexes. With no time to scramble to her feet or even get her breath, she tumbled backward and rolled like a log, letting her momentum carry her partway down the rough slope. Her back crushed something sharp. Pain shot through her ribs, but she didn't stop until she was out of striking distance.

Shaken, scratched, and sore, she forced herself to sit up. Glancing back, she could see no sign of the rattler. As she hugged her knees and took deep, gasping breaths, she recalled the words of Ruben Diego, an elder of the Tohono O'odham tribe and the longtime foreman of the Alamo Canyon Ranch.

"The rattlesnake doesn't want to kill you. He only wants to live. That is why he gives a warning. Let him go in peace."

After testing her limbs, Tess pushed to her feet. The horse had bolted and was gone. She was feeling some pain, but as long as her legs worked, she should be able to walk back to the gate, where she'd told Brock to wait for her.

Her hat lay nearby. She picked it up and jammed it onto her head. Only then, as she looked around, did she realize that she had another problem.

The bulls had moved in closer. They were staring in her direction, snorting, lowing, and tossing their horns. The black brute, standing in front like the lead tough in a street gang, scraped the ground with his horn, tossing up clumps of dirt and grass. If the bulls were to charge, she wouldn't have a chance.

Scarcely daring to breathe, Tess backed away a few steps. If she could duck out of sight behind a nearby sagebrush clump, the bulls might calm down—but the snake could be there, and there was nothing else close enough to serve as a hiding place.

"It's all right, boys. I'm not here to make trouble." As she inched backward, she spoke in a low tone—not so much to calm the bulls as to soothe her own nerves. Her heart was pounding. Bulls weren't stupid animals. They could sense fear.

The black bull bellowed and lunged, then stopped—another threat, nothing more. But there was no way she could outrun a real charge. For now, all she could do was retreat, step by step, making no sudden moves.

A memory flickered in her mind—tales of the old-time cattle drives and the cowboy songs that would calm the herd when it was time for them to bed down. Driven by desperation, she began to sing.

"'Down in the valley . . . the valley so low . . . Hang your head over . . . hear the wind blow . . .'"

Tess had never been a singer. Her untrained alto was off-key, her voice unsteady. The bulls didn't seem to like her song. They continued to snort, blow, and follow her as she tried to widen the distance between them. She wasn't making much progress. The pasture gate was still a long way off.

Coming out here alone had been a bad decision, made in a moment of pride—as if to show Brock she could manage without him. He'd probably been amused. He was probably laughing behind her back.

With her gaze fixed on the bulls, she started another stanza of the old song.

"'If you don't love me . . . love whom you please . . .'"

Step by step, her feet carried her backward over the uneven ground. A raven flapped out of the sky and perched on a stump, watching her with curious eyes. Even to the bird, she probably looked like a fool.

One more step, then another. Suddenly her boot heel caught in a tangled root. Stumbling backward, she lost her balance and went down hard on her rump.

That was when she heard a voice behind her—a deep voice, edged with amusement. Brock, on his big red horse, was perhaps a dozen yards behind her. "Don't stop," he said. "I was enjoying the entertainment."

Blazing with humiliation, she scrambled to her feet. "How long have you been there?"

"Not that long. When your horse came back, I figured you

might need some help. I was riding to your rescue, but when I saw the show you were putting on, I couldn't resist watching. I should've known you could take care of yourself."

The man was gloating. He didn't care that she could've been snake-bitten or trampled. If he'd been within reach, Tess would've punched him.

As he looked her up and down, taking in her scratched, dirt-smeared face and hands, his sardonic smile faded. "Are you all right, Tess?"

"I'm fine. How's the horse?"

"Just spooked. We need to put some salve on those scratches. Come on, I'll take you back to the house. You can tell me what happened on the way."

He leaned down from the saddle and offered a hand. Tess took it and let him swing her up behind the saddle. The bulls watched but made no more aggressive moves as Brock turned the big sorrel back toward the gate.

To keep from sliding off, Tess had to grip Brock's waist. He was rock solid beneath the denim shirt he wore. The aromas of man sweat and sagebrush teased her senses, stirring tugs and tingles in forbidden places. Not good. She cleared her throat.

"You wanted me to tell you what happened. The horse spooked at a rattler. By the time I came to my senses, the snake was gone and so was the horse. The bulls kept moving toward me—maybe just curious, but I couldn't be sure."

"So you decided to serenade them. Good thinking." He chuckled. Tess could feel the vibrations through her fingertips.

"I can't say much for my voice," she said. "I probably scared the poor things."

"So, did you see a bull you liked out there?"

"Maybe." Tess didn't want to sound too eager.

"If you want to see any of them buck, I'll have the boys set them up in the chutes."

"You know I don't want to make a hasty decision. But I wouldn't mind seeing that big black one."

He was silent for a moment, his gaze following the contrail of a military jet streaking across the sky. "The black one, eh? I had a feeling that son of a gun would catch your eye."

"Is something wrong with him—besides the missing horn?"

"There's nothing wrong with him. But if you were to take him, you'd have your hands full." Brock opened the steel-railed pasture gate with the remote control in his pocket. It closed behind the horse as they rode through. "When they say a bucking bull is rank, it's usually a compliment. But that black bastard—he's RANK, in capital letters—smart, unpredictable, and full of the devil. Just when you think you've got everything under control, he'll take you down—like stepping in quicksand when you don't know it's there."

"Quicksand." Tess rolled the word off her tongue, liking the sound of it and the way it fit the bull. "You like him, don't you?"

Brock's breath caught. Then the laughter exploded out of him, rumbling through his body. "Like him? You're damn right I do. He reminds me of me at my worst. But believe me, you don't want to choose that bull."

"I'll be the judge of that," Tess said. "At least I want to see him buck, along with a couple of others. You can decide which ones to show me."

"You've got it. I'll alert the boys to get them ready for the chutes. It'll take about thirty minutes to set up. Meanwhile we'll get those scratches doctored and maybe have something cold to drink." He spoke into the walkie-talkie he carried in a leather holster clipped to his belt. "There, it's taken care of. Now let's get you up to the house."

Brock's home was an imposing cube of glass, stone, and timber, with a broad, covered porch that offered a panorama of the ranch and the desert beyond. As far as Tess knew, he lived here alone with only a retired range cook to prepare meals and keep the house in order. If there was a woman in his life, Tess wasn't aware of it, but Brock was a private person. Apart from the side he chose to show her, she knew very little about the man.

All the more reason not to trust him, she reminded herself as he helped her dismount and turned the horse over to a waiting stable hand, a good-looking young man with blond curls and hazel eyes.

Sharing the yard with the house were two guest cottages, a bunk-house, barns, pens, and sheds, and a small arena equipped with bucking chutes. Somewhere beyond the pastures was an airstrip with a hangar where Brock stored the airplane he piloted himself.

Everything about the place was spare and simple, but constructed with the finest materials and workmanship money could buy. Knowing Brock, Tess wouldn't have expected anything less.

Walking beside him, she could feel the soreness from the fall she'd taken. As she took the first of the broad steps to the porch, her knee buckled.

"Take it easy." He caught her arm, saving her from a stumble. "You just got thrown from a horse. You're lucky to be walking. Let's get you to a chair."

In a move to steady her, he laid a hand at the small of her back. Tess yelped as the contact shot pain up her spine.

"What the devil—?" He moved behind her. "You must've tangled with a prickly pear. You've got a nasty spine stuck right through your shirt. You're bleeding. Come on in. We'll have you patched up in no time."

Inside, the house was sleek and immaculate, with tile floors and heavy wooden vigas supporting the ceiling. Plants in giant Talavera pots stood here and there. Massive leather furniture pieces were grouped on a thick alpaca rug. Touches of art enlivened the space—a genuine Charles Russell painting above the stone fireplace, a Frederic Remington bronze of stampeding buffalo on a sideboard.

"Impressive," she murmured, forgetting her pain for the moment.

"Thanks. I draw the line at mounted animal heads," he said. "Have a seat on the sofa."

"You said I was bleeding." She lowered herself carefully to the edge of the cushioned leather seat.

"You're fine. But it might help to drink something before we get started. We've got cold Coronas, or if you need something stronger, there's some good Kentucky bourbon in the cabinet."

"A Coke would be nice if you've got some," Tess said. "I wouldn't mind a beer, but with my sister a recovering alcoholic, I'm doing my best to support her. That includes following her rules—with no cheating, even when I'm away from home."

"Coke it is. Hang on. I'll be right back."

He returned a few moments later with two Coke cans and a large red cooler—some kind of medical kit. Opening the cooler, he took out a dispenser of antibacterial handwipes and handed one to her. Taking her cue from him, she cleansed her hands. The scrapes and cuts from the fall stung when the alcohol touched them. "We'll put some salve on those after I get that spine out of your back."

He popped one of the Coke cans and handed it to her. "Drink up. When you're ready, lean over the arm of the sofa. Getting the barb out is going to sting pretty bad. Can you handle that?"

"You'd be surprised what I can handle." Tess took a deep swig of Coke and put the can on the glass-topped coffee table. "As a kid, I was always getting stuck. My dad pulled the spines out with pliers. It hurt like hell, and he didn't hold with girls crying."

Brock would remember her late father, of course. Years ago, after Bert Champion had arranged to buy a desirable piece of land, Brock had bought it out from under him by offering the owner more money. The Champion family had needed that land for their cattle. They hated Brock to this day. Even in light of the new partnership, that hadn't changed.